THE VAMPIRE'S HELLION

THE ELITE: BOOK 1

STACY RUSH

Copyright © 2024 Stacy Rush.

All rights reserved. No part of this book may be reproduced, stored, or transmitted by any means—whether auditory, graphic, mechanical, or electronic—without written permission of both publisher and author, except in the case of brief excerpts used in critical articles and reviews. Unauthorized reproduction of any part of this work is illegal and is punishable by law.

ISBN: 979-8-89419-238-3 (sc)
ISBN: 979-8-89419-239-0 (hc)
ISBN: 979-8-89419-240-6 (e)

Because of the dynamic nature of the Internet, any web addresses or links contained in this book may have changed since publication and may no longer be valid. The views expressed in this work are solely those of the author and do not necessarily reflect the views of the publisher, and the publisher hereby disclaims any responsibility for them.

One Galleria Blvd., Suite 1900, Metairie, LA 70001
(504) 702-6708

PROLOGUE

JAX

As I stand here, from my temporary home on Cadillac Mountain, about 25 miles outside of Bar Harbor, I look out and enjoy the breathtaking view. I would never have thought that I would enjoy this solitude that I so desperately needed. One hundred and fifty years on this earth, twenty-four of them were my human years, I never once thought to take time for myself. Instead, I have spent the first seventy-six years of my vampire life roaming all over the world trying to find my purpose, using the first three years scouring for the one that left me for dead after consuming my blood, my life source, for his dinner.

Born Jackson Michael Whitley, now known as Jax, my birthplace was Sioux City, a town in the Midwest where no one ever believed in the stories of vampires or any other preternatural for that matter, but they were real; very real. I am living proof, or dead proof, however you want to look at it. Being turned two days after my twenty-fourth birthday destroyed all my future plans, replacing them with only one. To find the creature responsible for my immortality.

Three years later I found my maker in Augusta, Maine. He was feasting on one of the local ladies in an alley behind a gentleman's club. I got there too late to help the poor girl, but I took revenge on the one who made me what I am today, and for all the innocent lives he has ever taken. He did not put up much of a fight. Satiated after his meal consumption, the vamp was in, what I like to call, a blood coma. Drinking blood fuels our energy, but draining the whole body puts us in a state of incognizance for a while. It is like shooting up heroine, so I have heard. Never did care to try the stuff; I need to keep my head in the game always.

Once I obliterated the vile monstrosity, I decided to see where the road would take me. I traveled all over Europe, seeing the sights that I never thought I would see as a human. Being a vamp is not all that bad, once you get over the whole blood drinking issue. All my senses have magnified tenfold, I am stronger and faster, I can read minds when I touch someone, and my favorite…mind control, although I very seldom use that power. I do not like taking anything from anyone that they are not willing to give, but it does come in handy when fighting the enemy, not going to lie.

Tired of moving around with no thoughts of a future, I made my way back to the states and to Augusta. Aside for it being the location that I ended my first vamp, it was also a nice location to try and maybe settle down for a bit. The town was growing and with that, crime was also on the rise.

I was only a resident for about a month before I found my true calling. Restlessness sent me out to take a walk and get some air. Never had I thought I would run into a group of vamps, all in one place. They had a family of four trapped in a nearby parking lot. Shaking my head and thinking to myself on how stupid my next move was going to be, I cleared my throat, getting the attention of the fowl smelling creatures.

"Didn't your mothers ever teach you about cleanliness? I could smell you a block away!" I antagonize. A figure moved through the group trying to see who had the audacity to interrupt their dinner. Only standing about 5'8" to my 6'4", a male with dirty blonde hair, or maybe blonde covered in filth, and a slight pudge of a belly, he looked to be in his late forties. There is no telling with vampires since we stop aging when we are turned. I assumed he was the ringleader.

"This is no business of yours, vamp! Move along and find your own meal," The head vamp says with a raspy voice.

"Why don't you move along and leave this innocent family alone." I responded. A few chuckles from the group are heard as the ringleader turns his attention to the minions, his mid-section jiggling with his laughter. All laughter stops as he turns back towards me and without looking behind him, he says "Get him boys!"

All the while, I have this tingling on the back of my neck as if we are being watched and as half the men rush at me, a sound of pounding feet come from behind me. Thinking there were more of these vile creatures than I thought, I quickly jump to the side as I turn halfway to see what I was up against. Ten, maybe twelve more figures were descending on us, just what I need, but as I take my defensive stance, the newcomers blurred past me and advanced on the threat. I took a moment to comprehend what was happening. After blinking a few times, I jumped to action and followed suit, slamming my fist into the first vampire that I approached, sending him flying backwards and into a dumpster. Taking a second to look at the men who bulldozed their way in, some were using a form of weapon, whereas others just used their brutal strength. No matter what they used to fight with, it was clear to me that they were not human! I shook my head and got back into the game, maiming two more of the vamps before one of the other men decapitated each with his sword.

In the end, it was the newcomers and me left standing. The family that was being attacked took to running once the fighting began. All heads turn my way, no emotion showing on any of the faces as they stare.

"Uh, thanks, I guess." It was all I could manage. A huge brute of a guy steps forward, towering over me. He had to be almost 7 feet, with light brown hair that hung a little past his shoulders and ocean blue eyes. A good-looking guy if I may say so myself, but very intimidating!

"What's your name?" He asks me in a demanding tone.

"Jax, and you are?" I lift an eyebrow at him.

"I am Taven, and these men are my brothers-in-arms, also known as the Elite." He responds as he extends a hand out to me. I step forward and shake it.

Fifty years now I have been fighting side by side with the Elites, protecting the innocents and taking out the garbage. As much as I love what I do, I am worn out and in need of a little peace. Trying to avoid people as much as possible for the time being, I came here, to this mountain. As I am standing here though, I can't help but wonder; what now?

ONE

CASSIE

I'm sitting in the breakroom playing on Snapchat when Jill storms through the door and plops down in the seat next to me. I raise a brow, "Bad day?"

Ignoring my question, Jill looks over at me and then down at the phone in my hands. "Anything entertaining on Facebook today? I could use a good laugh."

"Not sure. Been on Snapchat for the last 10 minutes. They have some funny shit on here today. You should check out my Story if you want a good laugh." I giggle.

Jill rolls her eyes and smiles, "Oh, I can only imagine. Leave it to you to get me out of a pissy mood!"

"That is one of the reasons why you love me! You won't ever find a bestie like me!" I wink at her.

Watching my best friend since high school and coworker here at Wally World, I turn serious and ask, "What's up? Or should I ask, who pissed you off now?"

Jill lets out a sigh, "Just tired of people being lazy! They sit on their ass all day and then I get bitched at for the work not getting done! This day cannot end soon enough for me! Vacation, here I come!"

"What are your plans for the next week?" I ask.

"Not a damn thing! Just going to be a couch potato and catch up on Netflix. It's going to be heaven!"

I laugh and shake my head. Jill has always been like a sister to me, and I would rather cut off a limb than to be without my BFF! Jill is my rock and the levelheaded one in the relationship; we do everything together. So much, that people have asked us if we were an actual couple! There have been times where we acted like a couple while out on the town, but that was just to try and get some jerk to stop hitting on us. Most of those times it worked. Other times it fires back on us, and the guy thinks it's hot. Ugh, men are pigs!

As my break comes to an end, I stand. At the same time the door opens and in walks the new guy. Medium build, short brown hair and clean shaven; not too bad looking at all!

Not paying attention, he almost walks right into me. Luckily, the chair was in the way, so he stumbled into it and not me. I laugh as I grab his arm to steady him. "You may want to look up while walking through a door. You never know what's going to jump out at you! Although, I did see the chair stick its leg out and attack you! I'll be your witness if you want to press assault charges!" I muse.

Chocolate brown eyes stare back at her as a slight blush color his cheeks. "Uh, thanks, I think," he looks at my name tag, "Cassie."

I roll my eyes with a bored expression on my face. "My name is actually pronounced K.C." I correct him.

"Then why is it spelled C.A.S.S.I.E?" He asks puzzled.

"What can I say, my mom doesn't know how to spell. It's not her fault that she is illiterate!" I stare at the guy acting all serious. He shrinks back and starts stuttering apologies. I couldn't help but laugh as I punch his arm. "Just kidding, sheesh! She was actually pumped full of drugs and didn't know what she was writing. By the time she realized it, all the paperwork had been sent in, so she left it as is."

The poor guy didn't know what to think and he definitely was not going to open his mouth on the subject again. He looks up at me and extends his hand, "I'm Jason." I shake his hand and then turn towards

Jill who has been quiet during the whole exchange. "Will we be doing lunch today?" I ask.

Jill was staring at some imaginary spot on the wall and didn't hear the question. "Hello, earth to Jill!" I shout, startling her.

"Oh, I'm sorry! What did you say?" I give Jill a worried look, but then shake it off.

"I asked if we were still on for lunch?"

"Yes, of course! I will meet you out at your car at 11:30. Are we doing Mexican?"

"Doesn't matter to me; you pick."

"Honestly, I could go for a margarita!"

"You read my mind girl! Gotta go; see you later." I blow her a kiss as I leave, forgetting all about Jason, or whatever his name was.

Sitting in my Malibu, waiting on Jill to come out for break, I decide to check out Facebook. I swear, some days it just isn't worth logging on to the app, but then there are days like today where it seems like everyone wants to be a comedian and I find myself laughing at the most insane posts. After a few minutes I just shake my head and close out of the app. I begin to send Jill a text to tell her to get her ass out here when there is a loud knocking on my window. I jump, knocking my phone out of my hand, sending it down the crack between my seat and the middle console. My hand slaps my chest as a natural reflex, and I look up, and out my driver side window.

A guy that I do not know is staring at me with the most drop-dead-gorgeous smile that I have ever seen! Perfect, straight, bright white teeth shine down at me, with dimples on each side of his face. I work my way up to his eyes and all I can do is stare with my mouth gaped open. I am not one to swoon over a great looking guy, but let me just say, my ass would be on the ground from fainting right now if I wasn't already sitting in my car! Leaf green eyes surrounded by long thick, black lashes return my stare. I quickly snap out of it and fumble to crack my window.

"Jesus! Give a girl a heart attack, why don't you!"

"I am so sorry I startled you, it was not my intention. I walked from in front of your car and assumed you saw me approaching." The stranger replies. His voice sounding like the smoothest silk and so mesmerizing. Snapping out of the brief hypnosis his voice put me in, I clear my throat and smile out at him.

"It's okay. If I didn't have my face attached to my phone, then I would have seen you."

He graces me with another smile, "You wouldn't happen to have any jumper cables by chance?"

"Oh God, sorry. I don't. I'm usually the one that borrows that kind of stuff from everyone. Not sure why I don't buy my own, as much as I need them." I can't help but smile. Just then Jill walks up to the passenger side and slides in glancing at the gorgeous stranger and giving me a questioning look.

The stranger looks between me and Jill. Is that a look of irritation that crosses his face before smiling again? I probably just imagined it.

"Well, I won't hold you up any longer. I appreciate your time." He then turns and walks away.

"What was that all about?" Jill asks.

"Someone looking for jumper cables."

"You looked like you were about to jump something, and it wasn't his car!" She kids.

"Oh, you have no idea! I may need to run home quick and change my panties! Did you see that guy," I exclaim, "He was a God!"

Jill laughs and pretends to wipe slobber off my mouth. "Ha, ha, very funny!" I slap her hand away and then start the car. As we drive through the parking lot towards the exit, I notice a black Camaro sitting away from all the other cars. A figure with leaf green eyes watching as I pass.

"Watch out!" Jill screams as I hear a horn blare. I'm so engrossed with those eyes that I don't see the oncoming car. I quickly correct the steering wheel seconds before we collide.

"Jesus, Cassie! What was that all about?" Jill asks, her hands stretched out, gripping the top of the glove compartment.

"Oops, sorry! My bad," I respond as a giggle slips past my lips, forgetting about the Camaro.

"That was nothing to giggle about! No wonder you have so many accidents. You should not have your license."

I quickly turn to look at her, "But did you die?"

"Not yet but there is still a chance if you don't keep your eyes on the road!"

I roll my eyes as I turn back to the road. Jill has a point; I am a shitty driver. Not sure how I ever got my license. I swear I took that test at least 16 times, I shit you not! I think they just gave up and issued it to me. Pretty sure the instructor retired right afterwards.

Sitting at the Mexican restaurant waiting for the server to bring us our food, I look across the table and watch as Jill sips on her frozen Strawberry Margarita while scrolling through her phone. I have been waiting to announce the plans I made for us this weekend, knowing that she had made her own plans in doing absolutely nothing. In my defense, I made these plans days ago, not knowing she had made her own.

"So, the weekend starts in about 4 hours, and I made plans for us."

"Wait, what? I already told you what my plans are." She sighs.

"You have all week, starting Monday, to go into your Netflix coma! I want you for two days." I smile.

"Ugh, the last time you made weekend plans for us we ended up in a biker bar, in a town that we did not know, and you decided to run your smartass mouth to that scary biker bitch. What was her name again?"

"I don't even know. Everyone referred to her as Tiny's Bitch. Which is funny since there was nothing tiny about him!" I can't help the laugh that bursts out of me remembering that night.

Jill joins in adding, "That bar owner wasn't too happy about you busting his pool stick and starting the bar fight."

"Come on, she had it coming! I was minding my own business and she just walked up to me and told me that "my kind" wasn't welcomed there!" Shrugging my shoulders, "How was I to know that the Sherriff was her son and that we would be spending the rest of the time behind bars?"

Hesitating, Jill gives up knowing that I'm going to win this round, "So, what's your great plan?"

I give her my "I love you" smile. "Pack your bags girl because I rented us a cabin in Bar Harbor! We leave at 5 o'clock sharp!"

"You don't leave a girl much time to pack a bag; do you?"

"I'm giving you an hour to pack! How much time do you need?"

"Oh, never mind, I'll be ready." She puffs.

I smile and watch as the server delivers our food, "Thank God, I thought you had to make the tortillas by scratch; I'm wasting away over here!"

The server glares at me and then asks if we need anything else. Jill and I say "no thanks" in unison as we dive into our lunch. Another half hour and we are paying the check and heading back to work.

TWO

JAX

I wake early on the second morning up on the mountain. Catching a scent on the wind while stretching out last night's aches and pains, my stomach starts to tighten. Realizing that it has been three days since I last fed, I shut everything else out and concentrate on the scent of blood that wafts through the air. I jerk my head to the right and take off running in that direction. My speed cannot be detected on any human radar.

Within a half a minute I slow my speed to a slow jog as I near the area that reeks of blood. I stop all together as I listen to the forest around me. A branch snaps 20 yards from my location. As I close the distance, my hearing picks up a heartbeat. I crawl up behind a large boulder, not making a sound as I peer around it. A clearing of sorts opens up and there, in the middle, is a mountain lion, going to town on what looks to be a doe.

My canines ache at the smell of blood and my stomach tightens up even more. I inch my way up onto the boulder. With any luck, I will be able to pounce on the lion without it being aware of the danger. At that moment, my left foot slips and the lion jerks its head in my direction. "Shit!" is my only thought before I launch off the rock and fly through the air. The animal takes off running, but it is no match for this vampire.

I catch up with the cat within seconds and crash to the ground; my prey beneath me. I extend my fangs and latch on to the animal's neck; taking the sustenance needed. I don't kill my prey. I only take what is needed and then I let it go. With my stomach full and my energy refueled, I head back to my campsite.

Mid-morning comes around and I decide to make a trip into Bar Harbor for supplies. It is unusually warm for it only being late Spring and being up in the mountains; I sure as hell did not plan my wardrobe accordingly. Not knowing how long I would be gone, a nice dip in the cool river flowing by the quiet spot that I chose sounds awesome before heading out. Stripping out of my clothes, I walk over to the riverbank and step in. Being a vampire, the cold temperature doesn't bother me, but I'm sure a human would get hypothermia.

I wash quickly and then stretch out on my back to float for a bit. "So peaceful here." I think to myself as I stare up at the blue sky through the treetops. For the past fifty years, I haven't had any moments like this. I make a vow right now that I will make more time for myself. Hell, I have an eternity to fight the evil in this world, so a few moments here and there that I take for myself will be well deserved.

After about ten minutes, I slowly make my way back to camp to dry off and dress. Collecting my assortment of knives that I always carry on me, I start out down the mountain to my truck that is parked at the bottom and head out for Bar Harbor.

By the time I get to town, it's almost noon and the town's residents are out and about. It is still the off season for Bar Harbor, so the streets are not as crowded. I park my truck outside of a little clothing store and make my way to the door. One thing about small towns is that everybody is so friendly. Just getting out of my truck and walking the 15 feet to the shop I have four people smile and say "Hi" to me. Don't get me wrong, I can be just as friendly, but for the love of God, this is ridiculous!

The bell above the door chimes as I walk through and a woman in her late 20's looks up from behind the counter. Her eyes widen once they land on me, and I am welcomed with a seductive smile. I raise my hand as a greeting and turn towards the men's section, hoping she doesn't follow. No such luck! The woman is at my side sizing me up.

"Oh my, I'm not sure we carry your size! Even if we did carry clothing for your height, I'm not sure your muscles would fit!" She leers up at me as she slides her hand over my bicep. She is a pretty little thing with strawberry blonde hair and hazel eyes. Only coming up to the middle of my chest, she is petite, 5'3" at the most, and certainly not my type.

Feeling annoyed, I look down at her as I paste a smile on my face and step away, "I am only looking for some wife beaters."

She looks confused for a moment, not comprehending what I was asking for. Then I see the light bulb come on, metaphorically, and she snaps her fingers. Twirling around, she heads to the shelves by the wall and points me in the direction of the men's underwear section. I nod my head in appreciation and walk down the aisle.

I meet her back at the counter to check out and as she hands me back my change, she proceeds to inform me that a new shipment of breathable boxer briefs will be coming in the next few days. I think it was her way of finding out what I wear underneath my clothes. I thank her and before I turn away, I acknowledge her comment about the underwear, "I go commando, so I'm in no need for any, thanks." I show my pearly whites at her and turn to leave as her jaw drops and her eyes bulge. God, I love fucking with people!

Stepping out into the bright sun, I squint and shield my eyes with my hand. As I head back to my pickup, a light breeze blows by and on that breeze is a scent that stops me dead in my tracks. "What is that?" I think to myself. In a flash it is gone. I can't put a name to it. It's a mixture of chocolate and some kind of fruit; it smells amazing!

I throw my bag onto the passenger side seat and grab my shades. The sun doesn't do anything to us vamps like all the stories say, but just like with anybody else, it's annoying as hell when it's right in your eyes. I slide my shades on over my eyes and walk down a half a block before turning the corner.

I stop. All I see are store fronts lining both sides of the road and a café that is halfway down the block on my side of the road. I continue on down the side street and as I pass the café with patrons sitting outside enjoying the beautiful spring day, it slams into my senses again. I look around, but all I see are people sipping on coffee and snacking on pastries. There are only three tables being occupied. An elderly couple sitting together, three teenage girls gossiping and giggling at another table and then two women sitting in the corner having a private conversation.

I am drawn to that table for some odd reason. I can see the profile of one of the women, but the other has her back to me. I look back to the first one, but I feel nothing. Not knowing if I'm going insane, I turn and walk into the café. After ordering a large black coffee, I step out onto the patio and weave my way through the empty tables to the one table that will give me a full view of the other woman.

I pull out the chair and sit, then I look up. In this moment, for the life of me, I cannot take in a single breath! It is like staring at a porcelain doll. Her skin looks like silk, with a pert little nose & lips that look like they are made for kissing. Her eyes, oh those eyes, a perfect shade of aqua blue. All this perfection is surrounded by long dark brown locks with sun-kissed highlights. Thank God I have my shades on; I can't look away from her.

What the hell am I doing? This isn't me. I don't go gaga over anyone, but today I am. Not sure what is going on, but I am going to find out!

In a matter of seconds, the woman's head snaps up and she looks at her surroundings before her eyes land on me. The way I am positioned, she cannot tell that I'm looking straight at her, but we stare at each other for almost a full moment before her friend catches her attention. She turns back and continues her conversation only glancing my way once more.

"Shit!" What the fuck? I jump up, almost knocking my coffee over, and hop the little iron fence surrounding the patio. I never look back.

THREE

CASSIE

The cabin I rented is snuggled in a copse of evergreens on the outskirts of Bar Harbor. Just like the town itself, it is cozy and quaint. With a small kitchen, a living area, a bathroom with a jacuzzi tub and two bedrooms, because come on, two single, good-looking women? I am hoping at least one of us gets lucky this weekend!

We arrive a little after 8pm which is a half hour later than I wanted. Of course, I was the one running late. I can never accuse Jill of lateness. She always sets the time a half hour earlier than the actual arrival time is because she knows me too well.

"Oh wow! This is so cute Case!"

"It is definitely better than the last place we stayed where the hallways smelled of weed, the carpets belonged in the 70's, and I swore I saw bed bugs!" I cringe.

"No doubt. So, what is the occasion anyway?"

"No occasion, just thought we could both use a get-a-way." I smile, "Work has been so consuming lately, that I for one, am burned the fuck out!"

"Well, I am not going to say thank you just yet, but so far so good!"

"We just got here, Jill."

"And so far, you have done good," as she looks at our accommodations, "What's on the agenda for tonight anyway?"

"I thought we could have a late supper and then head over to one of the local bars and see what kind of trouble we can get into." Jill glares at me so, I hold up my hands, "Just kidding!"

By the time we settle ourselves in and freshen up, it is almost 9:30. We decide on trying a bar & grill; something Whale, I can't remember the full name, but they have late night food and food is what I need before putting a drop of alcohol in me.

I end up ordering the Chicken Pesto sandwich and Jill has the Chicken Fingers. Neither one of us care for seafood, which is totally weird since we have lived in Maine our whole lives. Sounds gross, but for me, it tastes like two lesbians going to town on each other, yuck! Not that I have anything against them, to each their own, but I will take a slab of meat over tuna any day!

The waitress brings us another round of Bud Light and then walks away. That's when I feel it…. tingles on the back of my neck, like we are being watched. I casually look around but don't see anything out of the ordinary.

Jill catches onto my agitation, "Hey, what's wrong? Is your food okay?"

"The food is great; I just had this uneasy feeling come over me, weird."

As Jill looks around, I pick up a fry and pop it into my mouth. The tingles have gone away, but the unease is still there. I munch on another fry.

"I don't see anything out of the ordinary, Case," she looks at me before turning her attention to her own food. I begin to relax a bit.

We order a few more rounds and then call for the check. It is almost midnight, and I'm exhausted. I turn to my bestie, "Are you ready to turn in or go check out one of the bars?"

"I think I'm ready to turn in. Get some good sleep and refresh for tomorrow, but first I need to empty this bladder." She throws some cash on the table and starts heading to the restroom.

"I'm going to wait outside; I need fresh air." I call out to her.

I step outside and breathe in the ocean air. As I'm standing here, the tingles come back. I jerk my head around looking for something, anything, there is nothing but darkness. Just as I turn to go back inside to wait for Jill, I feel something caress my hair. Again, I turn, but there is nothing, "Stop freaking yourself out." I mumble to myself. Taking one last look, I turn and walk back inside.

The walk back to the cabin is a short one, but it seems to take forever! My gut is telling me that something is just not right, and I hurry my steps.

"Are you practicing for a marathon or what?" Jill is trying to keep up, so I slow my pace.

"I just can't shake this feeling that I am being watched and it's freaking me out! It's resembling a horror movie, and you know how much I love those!"

I am a huge pussy when it comes to anything scary. Hell, I never get out of my bed between 3-4am because that is the "Devil's Hour". I have the movie "The Exorcism of Emily Rose" to thank for that, ugh!

Finally reaching the porch to the cabin, I take the keys out of my pocket and go to unlock the door. It's already unlocked, "What the hell," and look over at Jill.

"What the... I swear I made sure the door was locked when we left!" Her eyes showing her confusion.

I open the door, reach my hand in, and flip the light switch. I can see the living area and kitchen are empty. I walk over to the knives on the counter and grab the biggest one; the butcher knife, and hand it over to Jill. Come on, I'm not going to be the one to get my ass jumped first! We continue to walk through the house; I'm on Jill's heals with a death grip on the back of her shirt.

We reach the bathroom and Jill quickly hits the switch. Nothing. Continuing to the bedrooms, we first check Jill's room and then my own. Still nothing. We both let out the breath that we have been holding in since entering the cabin. I look at Jill and we burst out laughing, "Oh if people could see us now!"

We head back in the other direction. Jill plops herself on the couch and grabs the tv remote as I go to the kitchen and put the knife back where it belongs. I grab two Bud Lights from the fridge and go sit down with my bestie.

"This sure has been an interesting day, that is for sure!" Jill states as she opens her beer.

"No doubt! It's like we are on some kind of hidden camera show called, 'How to Scare Two Grown Ass Woman!'" I chug my beer.

"Well, since neither one of us are having sex with anyone tonight, we are sleeping together! I normally don't get spooked, but damn, I almost shit my pants tonight!" Jill says as she swigs her beer.

I wake up to the smell of bacon and eggs. Well, that and the fact that my bladder is about to explode. I flip the covers to the side and crawl out of bed. Making my way around the bed I stub my toe, "God damn... son of bitch!" Tears spring to my eyes, but I shake them and the pain in my baby toe, off. "Great way to start the day off, Klutz!"

I had tossed and turned all night, getting only a couple hours of sleep at most. When I did get sleep, eyes the color of green leaves in the summertime, haunted my dreams. "Get a grip, Cassie; they are only dreams!" I somewhat remember reading somewhere that all dreams have a meaning. "Yeah, in my case, my dreams last night were telling me that I need to get laid by a really hot guy!"

I grumble a "Hey" as I walk into the kitchen. Jill is at the stove, spatula in hand, scooping up the last of the eggs from the frying pan.

"Well good morning, Sunshine; how did you sleep?"

"Not worth a shit." I mumble, "You?"

"Obviously, better than you."

"I'll perk up once I get some of Jill's famous eggs into my belly and take a long hot soak in the jacuzzi." I give a slip of a smile.

Jill fills my plate full and heads to the bathroom, "Aren't you going to eat?"

"I already ate; been up since the ass crack of dawn," she says over her shoulder, "I'm going to jump in the shower while you eat."

I dig into my food as I grab for the newspaper laying on the table. Skimming through the pages of the paper while shoveling food into my mouth, I start to think about the night before. "What has gotten into me lately," I think to myself. A moment later, I shrug it off and give the town's paper my attention again. "Man, this town is boring!" The paper has no exciting news whatsoever, not even in the Police Log.

Scooping the last forkful of egg into my mouth, Jill comes into the kitchen wearing her blue silk robe tied at the waist and is towel drying her hair. I've always been envious of her hair. Once dried, it hangs almost to the middle of her back in thick, silky light brown waves and has its own natural highlights. Whereas mine is a dark chocolate color that frizzes out once it's dry. I spend a fortune on hair product to help keep the frizz out and give it shine. My hairdresser is the best around though. She gives my hair the natural sun kissed highlights that everyone comments on.

"Are you done in the bathroom?"

"Yeppers, I can finish my hair in the bedroom."

I shoot up out of the chair and hurry to collect my things before heading to the bathroom.

While waiting for the tub to fill, I stare at my reflection, grimacing at the dark circles under my eyes. Nothing a little make-up won't hide, but seriously! I continue staring at myself. No, I am not the conceited type. I'm the complete opposite. I don't find myself lacking by any means, but I'm no beauty queen either. My best feature, in my opinion, are my eyes. They are a bright aqua blue, an attribute from my mother's side of the family. Only the women in the family have the color, most have a duller shade, but a few have the brightness of my own.

Noticing the tub is full, I turn off the water and strip down to my birthday suit. Stepping in, I grab the sides of the tub and slide slowly down into the bubbling water. Steam is rising causing the mirror on the wall and the window to fog over. I close my eyes and lay there relaxing for a good 10 minutes. I faintly hear Jill moving around in the kitchen. She must be cleaning up the breakfast dishes. Only God and Jill know that I won't do it, I think to myself, which brings a smile to my face.

Realizing the water is cooling off, I prepare myself to get out. I open my eyes slowly trying to readjust them to the light filtering in through the window on the opposite wall. The window is still steamed over, but just then a shadow hovers just outside of it. I sit straight up and scream as I throw my hands up to cover my boobs!

The bathroom door flies open a few seconds later and Jill is standing there looking for any kind of danger. Not seeing any threat, she looks at me. "What the fuck Case," she yells, "You scared the shit out of me!" I turn back to the window, but the shadow is gone.

"I swear to God somebody was just at that window!"

"What!?" Jill runs over to the window and throws it open, looking to the left and then to the right. There is nothing and nobody there to find. She turns back to me, concern on her face.

"I'm not imagining it, Jill!"

"Okay, okay. So, what do you want to do? I can call the local police if you want."

"Ugh, no. It's probably some horny teenager trying to get his rocks off, damn perv!"

"Are you sure?"

"No, I'm not sure, but it's the best explanation." I look at her, "It's fine, really! You can go, I'm getting out now anyway."

Jill shuts the door behind her as I'm stepping out and quickly grabbing the towel to cover myself before the little pervert comes back.

FOUR

CASSIE

It is almost noon when we leave the cabin and head to town. The sun is bright, and it is extremely warm for this time of year. I immediately take off the hoodie I had thrown on while walking out the door and tie it around my waist. Jill was smart and didn't bring a jacket or anything, but then again, she never gets cold. I swear, it can be 70 degrees out, and I still need a hoodie or something.

As we enter town, we decide to try the little café that we passed by the night before. Neither one of us have had our caffeine today since we forgot to bring coffee with us. Besides, with having a big breakfast, it is best that we keep lunch on the lighter side.

We walk to the counter and order our usual. Jill, a large frozen Carmel Latte, and myself, a large White Chocolate Mocha Latte with whipped cream. We each grab a chocolate chip muffin, and then pay the cashier. Making our way to the back patio and a quiet table in the corner, we take our seats. I take the one, so my back is to almost everything and Jill takes the one beside me.

It is such a beautiful day to just sit, and people watch, but I'm not in the mood today, so Jill and I just sit peacefully while we fuel up and keep up light conversation. To anybody that sees us, it looks as if we are having a secret conversation, that's how close we are.

A short while later, I feel the tingles again, and I shoot my head up! Looking around, I see nothing. I think to myself that I am going crazy. There are three other occupied tables out on the patio. An elderly couple sit having a quiet conversation at one table, three teenage girls gossiping at another table and last, but not least, my eyes fall on the last table, which is occupied by a guy, a big guy! He is wearing sunglasses, but his head is turned a little to the side, so I highly doubt he is the culprit causing my tingles.

I keep my eyes on him for a moment longer, taking in the rugged perfection that is permeating off him. His hair is short but not so short that a woman couldn't grab hold of it while having wild, hot sex with him. It is a dark brown, maybe a tint or two lighter than my own, but it is the 5 o'clock shadow that he is sporting that really gets my attention. I love a man who keeps his beard just like his!

My eyes roam the rest of him. By the looks of it, he is a little over 6 foot and must work out, a lot! Before I can start drooling, Jill's voice interrupts my thoughts.

"Have you heard anything that I have said?"

"Uh, no. Sorry, but I was staring at the hot guy a few tables down." I quickly glance his way again,

Jill rolls her eyes at me and just then, we hear someone say "Shit!" and then movement and we turn in the man's direction. He is on his feet and in the process of catching his coffee before it crashes to the ground. The speed at which he catches it was amazing, almost as if he didn't move. He jumps the little black iron fence and then he is gone.

As I continued to stare at the empty sidewalk, I feel it again. I look down the road a little way, but all I see are some parked cars. Something in my memory causes me to look again. There, parked on the other side of the street, about a half block down, sits a black Camaro.

JAX

I am wound up tight by the time I got back to my truck. I don't know what is going on. I've had my share aplenty with beautiful women in my long life, so why is this slip of a girl getting to me? I shouldn't really call her a girl; she is more woman than anything! She looks like she may be in her early 30's, with a tight body of a 20 yr. old. Granted, I didn't get to see much with her sitting down and the angle wasn't right, but those breasts! Her t-shirt snugged those babies like a second skin! Perky and big, just the way I like them. Just thinking about them is making me uncomfortable in my jeans. If it grows anymore, my zipper will bust.

I sit in my pickup for a while longer trying to get my man parts under control. I still have to grab a few more items from the grocery store. Even though blood is my main sustenance, I still eat food and need some bottled water and maybe a bottle of Jack to help clear my head. I have also been craving Salt & Vinegar chips lately, so I figured I'd grab a bag or two of those. It's the little things that remind me of my humanity and keeps me from thinking I'm some kind of monster.

Pulling out of my parking spot, my thoughts go back to the woman. Without realizing what I'm doing, I turn the corner that leads to the café. Searching for some sign of her as I pass the little iron fence and look at the table where they sat; it was as if she never existed, "Oh well, I'm better off anyway. I don't need a woman, especially a normal woman." My gut tells me that this one would not be a fuck'em and leave'em kind of situation.

Pulling into the packed parking lot, I wonder on whether or not I should try even going in, I hate crowds.

"Ah, fuck it," I open my door.

I grab the last cart that is inside and proceed to read the signs above each aisle. The quicker I can find my items, the quicker I can get out of here, but of course the liquor aisle is on the other side of the store, and I have to walk through the throng of shoppers.

I am about to turn down the last aisle when I collide with another cart. I'm not paying too much attention, so I jump at the impact, as does the dark-haired beauty pushing the other cart. I have to blink a few times to makes sure I am really seeing her before me.

"Oh shit, I am so sorry!" She looks up and blurts "Sapphire!"

That's a weird thing to say, now I'm confused, "Uh, what about sapphires?"

Color rushes to her cheeks and she looks away as a giggle escapes her lips. Her acquaintance she was with earlier slips in beside her shaking her head back and forth.

"Please excuse my friend. She's always been a reckless driver and should be wearing a helmet at all times," she laughs. "Hey, you're the guy from the café!"

"Yes, I'm the guy from the café. Who obviously can't stand up without knocking shit over." I give her my best smile. She is a lovely woman, but nothing stirs when looking at her, unlike her friend. She also has a larger vocabulary than the woman beside her. Sapphire? "I think your friend is in shock." He nods in her direction.

"Who, Cassie?" She looks to her friend.

"I'm sorry, what?" Aqua eyes look up at me.

"Are you okay?" I ask her as she seems to finally come out of some kind of trance.

"Who me? Pfft, I'm fine. I was just startled. I am so sorry I crashed into you!"

"No harm, no fowl," I smile, "So, you are Cassie, and you are?" I turn to her friend.

"I'm Jill, Jill Earnhardt and this is Cassie Manson."

"Manson? As in Charles Manson?" I ask jokingly.

"Yep, sure is!"

"Well, it is a pleasure to meet you ladies! My name is Jackson Whitley, but I go by Jax." I lean forward and shake Jill's and then Cassie's hand, holding the last one a little longer than necessary, not wanting to lose contact. I swear I feel a little electricity when we connect.

"Well, we better let you get your shopping done. Maybe we will see each other around town again sometime." Jill utters.

"Yeah, maybe." Smiling, I turn the corner and head to the liquor. Maybe I'll buy two bottles of Jack instead.

Back on my mountain, with half a bottle of Jack in my hand, I sit in my folding chair and contemplate the events of the day. "What makes this woman, Cassie, so special?" I take a swig from the bottle. The smart thing to do would be to stay on this mountain until I am ready to head back to Augusta, but I never make the smart choices.

I pull out my cell phone and speed dial Taven. He answers on the second ring.

"Hey buddy, calling so soon? Must mean you miss me!" Taven's smartass comments make me smile.

"You wish Dickhead! Just wanted to check in with you to make sure I wasn't needed is all."

"You need to stop. Just relax and enjoy your vacation!" Taven chides me.

"I'm trying to, but it's harder than I thought. Can I ask you something without you repeating it or hassling me about it?"

"Sounds serious...shoot."

"I don't think it's too serious, more like just curiosity," I explain. "Why hasn't any of the Elite taken a wife or steady girlfriend?"

Holding my breath while waiting for his answer seems to last forever. Then after that lengthy pause, he bursts out laughing on the other end.

"You are such a dick, forget I asked." I'm fuming. I don't understand what he finds so comical about the question.

"Jax my man, you just made my night!"

"Goodbye Taven." I am about to hang up when I hear him yell "Wait!"

"What is it?" I'm not in the mood to conversate anymore.

"Are you seriously wanting to know?"

"I asked you, didn't I?" No need to be an asshole about it.

"Jax, we don't marry until we find our true mate and as for girlfriends, there is no point if they are not our mate," he explains.

Taken aback by this new information, I am speechless. True mate? How come in one hundred and twenty-six years I have never once heard of this?

"What is a true mate and more important, how do you know if they are your mate?" Confused and extremely astounded by this new revelation.

"Honestly, I don't know all the answers to this, because as you can see, none of the Elite have found theirs," the head Elite divulges, "I do know at least two signs. One being that there is some sort of scent that draws you to your mate, whether it be sweet, floral, or fruity, or more than one scented at the same time. The other, and this one is just hearsay, is "if" and "when" you touch, there is an actual spark or electric charge," Taven pauses for a few seconds before continuing, "What is this all about Jax?"

How can I answer that when I don't even know the answer myself? Taven is like a brother to me, and I have never kept anything from him, but if I do reveal the true reason, it will make it all the more real and I am not sure if I am ready for that, "Like I said earlier, just curious," then added for good measure, "Haven't you ever been alone for so long that your mind just starts thinking about stupid stuff?" I give a fake chuckle.

"Been there, done that! It kind of drives you crazy until you find the answer," he sighs loudly, "Is there anything else that brain of your is curious to know?"

"Uh, no, I guess not. At least not at this moment, but this is only my second day here on my own. I'm sure there will be more calls coming your way before I make it back." I respond back in a joking manner.

We say our goodbyes and end the call. I sit back and contemplate this new-found knowledge. Maybe I just imagined it all? The chocolate and fruit smell that lingered in the breeze could have come from the homemade pastries. That is a feasible explanation, but what about the charge that went through my hand when I shook hers earlier at the grocery store?

"ARGH!" This is driving me insane! "There is only one way to find out I guess," I mumble to myself as I stand up, "Head back to town and see if I can find out what Ms. Cassie Manson is doing on this lovely Saturday evening."

FIVE

CASSIE

It's just a coincidence that a black Camaro is sitting down the street from where I'm having my latte. It's not like there is only one Make of that car in the world…pfft! Why am I being so paranoid? Probably because strange things have been happening since I met the green-eyed hottie. I just need something to take my mind off that whole situation.

Turning my attention back to the present, I suggest that we head over to the grocery store and grab some food for supper. Jill nods her head in agreement and collects her garbage to throw away. I look back once more, and the car is gone. I shiver and then grabbing my own garbage, make my way to the trash can before exiting the café.

By the time we get to the grocery store, the parking lot is packed. Seems as if the whole town and their mothers all shop on Saturday afternoons. Luckily, there are still a handful of shopping carts left. I snatch one out of the corral and dive into the crowd of shoppers. Thankfully, we don't have too many items to get, so maybe we can get in and out quick.

"Damn, you would think they are giving out free cases of wine for as many people that are here!" I don't bother looking at Jill, I need to prevent myself from crashing into someone. "Speaking of wine, when was the last time we even did Wine Night?" This time I turn to look.

"It's been about two months now," licking her lips, Jill heads for the liquor aisle. I catch up to her as she is pulling two bottles of Stella off the shelf. She places them in the cart and then we are off to find the rest of the items and the shortest checkout line.

Not paying too much attention, I turn the corner and run right into another cart.

"Oh shit, I am so sorry!" I look up and into the deepest shade of blue eyes, sapphire. Crap, did I say that out loud?

I can feel color rush to my face, and I look away as a giggle escapes. Jill sprints to my side shaking her head back and forth.

"Please excuse my friend. She's always been a reckless driver and should be wearing a helmet at all times," she laughs. "Hey, you're the guy from the café!"

"Yes, I'm the guy from the café. Who obviously can't stand up without knocking shit over." He smiles from ear to ear. "I think your friend is in shock," I hear him say.

"Who, Cassie?" she looks at me.

"I'm sorry, what?" I glance at them both.

"Are you okay?" Mr. Hottie asks me.

"Who me? Pfft, I'm fine. I was just startled. I am so sorry I crashed into you!" I feel like a complete idiot. What is wrong with me?

"No harm, no fowl," he smiles. "So, you are Cassie, and you are?" He turns to my best friend.

"I'm Jill, Jill Earnhardt and this is Cassie Manson."

"Manson? As in Charles Manson?" He asks jokingly.

"Yep, sure is!"

"Well, it is a pleasure to meet you ladies! My name is Jackson Whitley, but I go by Jax." He leans forward and shakes Jill's and then my own hand, holding onto my hand a little longer than necessary. Sparks shoot through my hand as he does so.

"Well, we better let you get your shopping done. Maybe we will see each other around town again sometime." Jill utters.

"Yeah, maybe." Smiling, he turns the corner and heads to the liquor.

I was eager for a night on the town! After the last two days, all I want to do is relax with some adult beverages and dance the night away if there is anywhere to dance in this town. I always feel better after that combo. I am just touching up my make-up when Jill struts into my room. I give her a long whistle. She is usually a sweatshirt and jeans kind of girl, but tonight she is sporting a salmon-colored crop top, high waisted jean jeggings and stilettos! She looks smoking hot, and I couldn't be prouder! I love when my fashion sense rubs off on her every once in a while.

"Girl, if you don't take anyone home tonight, I'll take you home and do you!" I just might if I don't get laid soon!

"Seriously Cassie, I really worry about you sometimes."

"Shut it bitch, you know you want me too!" I jest.

"Well, let's just hope that it doesn't come down to that," she wiggles her brows at me playfully.

I take one last look in the mirror, satisfied that my red off-the-shoulder blouse and black pleather leggings still compliment my figure. I don't worry about putting on a couple extra pounds, but I do agonize about not fitting into my favorite clothing. I am a fashion addict, what can I say?

I grab my car keys on the way out the door. No way in hell I'm walking home in the dark again! We both double check the lock on the door, and then hop in the car. With our carefree attitudes, we head uptown with anticipation.

The bar isn't overly crowded, but we choose to sit out on the patio anyway since it is a beautiful evening out. Once we claim our table, I have Jill stay with our things while I go for drinks. The wait isn't too bad, before I have to give the gal my order and sit on the stool to wait. I smell him before he utters a word. Woods and spice.

"Fancy seeing you here, Ms. Manson." His seductive voice sending chills down my spine. I don't dare look. He finally slips in beside me and another stool, his arm grazing mine, sending little electrical charges through my body. Am I imagining that? Must be.

I decide to play his game and I slowly swivel on my stool, so he is standing between my open thighs, "Why we are old friends Mr. Whitley, surely we can be on a first name basis." I bite my lower lip as I slowly look up at him.

The bartender brings my drinks and Jax quickly pulls a twenty out and orders himself a beer, telling the gal to keep the change. "May I join you ladies? I am assuming that Jill is with you."

"Yes, she's holding down the fort until I get back. Thank you for the drinks and as for joining us, I would be very disappointed if you didn't." As we turn to make our way to the patio, his hand goes to my lower back to help guide me through the crowd, his pinky caressing the top of my ass.

Once Jill sees us coming, her eyes widen and her "someone is getting lucky tonight" smile appears. I roll my eyes at her but can't help and smile anyway.

"Hey Jax! Are you stalking us?" Jill jokes.

"Would you ladies run away if I say yes?"

"Hell no! You are too hot to run away from!"

If I didn't see it for myself, I wouldn't have believed it. Mr. Whitley is blushing! I choke a little on my drink at that moment and Jax starts rubbing my back asking if I am alright. It is now my turn to blush.

We make easy conversation with each other, joke, and laugh, then laugh some more. After about an hour, Jill excuses herself to go to the restroom, "Hey Hooker, grab a round on your way back please."

She lifts her hand as she is walking away, "Will do Whoreface." I just shake my head.

"You two sure are a strange pair!" Jax beams.

"Why thank you. I always love a compliment!"

"Not quite sure on if it is meant as one or not." He teases.

"Oh, it is a compliment in my eyes! Jill and I do strange very well. It makes life more enjoyable."

"May I ask what else you do very well?" A sparkle lights up his amazing eyes.

"Hm, now that would be something that you would have to find out for yourself some time I think."

He stares at me for a bit, almost like he wants to say something, but isn't sure if he should. I bite down on my bottom lip. He stands up and stretches a little bit before leaning in over the table and closer to me.

"I have been wondering something ever since the café today." His voice almost a whisper.

"And what would that be?" I coax.

He leans in a little closer and before I can comprehend what he was doing, his lips are on mine. A slow caress at first and once I start to respond, he dips his tongue into my mouth, but keeps the kiss innocent. I close my eyes.

All too soon it is over, and he is pulling away. He licks his lips and smiles, "Mm, chocolate and strawberries."

"Huh?" I am so dazed; I can't understand what he is saying.

"Your taste. It tastes of Chocolate and strawberries," he explains.

"Ahh, and you are woodsy and spice."

My Lord! With just a small kiss from those lips I can feel wetness pooling down under and to make it worse, there is just a hint of flare to his nose that makes me believe that he can smell it! It excites me even more.

I jump up out of my seat, "I'm going to run to the restroom and see what's taking Jill so long with those drinks."

Jax stands up straight, and gently grabs my upper arm as he does so, "I didn't overstep with that kiss, did I?"

Surprised that he is concerned enough to even ask, I grin, reach up and bring his lips back to mine for a brief kiss. "Not at all," and I walk away smiling.

I pass Jill on my way to the lady's room. I give her a thumbs up and continue on. Just as I reach the door, it opens, and a pretty college aged girl walks out.

She greets me with a smile, and I return it as I reach for the door, thinking about how friendly people are in this town.

Out of nowhere, someone grabs me from behind and hurries me the rest of the way in. I hear the lock on the door go into place and then I'm spun around.

Sapphire eyes burning with desire gaze down at me and then his mouth is on mine, begging me to let him in. I oblige and open up for his tongue to fuse with my own. He crushes me to him, one hand wraps around my waist and the other at my nape. I wrap my arms around his neck and kiss him back just as fiercely.

Next thing I know, he has both hands on my ass, lifting me up as he slams us against the wall. My legs automatically locking behind his back. He breaks the kiss to look into my eyes, "God, you are fucking sexy!" My heart skips a beat and then he is at it again, tracing kisses down my neck and across my collar bone. My body has a mind of its own as my pelvis starts to move against him. He moans, and so I continue.

His mouth reaches the top of my blouse, and he stops yet again to look at me. As if he is asking for permission, I answer by arching my back and pushing my tits up. Grunting, he uses his teeth to shove my shirt down and then continues to lick and suck my boob through my thin lacey bra. My nipples are so hard, they could cut glass. His mouth feels like heaven!

I'm so wet, I'm sure he can feel it through our clothing. That just makes me gyrate my hips more. His hardness rubbing against my clit makes the pressure build inside me. Then he bites my nipple and takes me over the edge! Continuing to nip and suck, I ride out the storm, not caring if anybody hears me. He comes back to my lips and slowly brings me back down to earth. I slide down the length of him and he holds me close until my legs are able to hold me up on their own. I rest my forehead against his chest while I catch my breath as he moves his lips in my hair, we stand here for just a bit longer, until there is a knock on the door.

My head shoots up to look at his face, afraid of seeing what reaction he is having to what just took place. He is grinning from ear to ear. It puts me at ease knowing that he enjoyed it just as much as I did. Although, looking at the huge bulge trying to pop out of his zipper, he probably could have enjoyed it more had he gotten his own release. I lick my lips, ravenous for more. He chuckles and backs away, holding me at arms-length.

"Oh no you don't my little sex kitten, we can continue this later. Unless, of course, you want them to break the door down and catch us in the act?"

I sidle up to him and run my hand over his chest, making my way down his abs, ending right above his jeans, "If you insist." I turn around and head for the door, but not until I catch the hunger in his eyes.

I return to find Jill talking to some guy. His back is to me and as I get closer, I feel a tingling. I slow my steps but continue around him to find my seat. I quickly glance his way… and then freeze.

SIX

JAX

I take a few moments to myself hoping to get this massive hard-on under control. I should have taken Cassie up on her offer, but things had already gone too far. I had only planned on stealing another kiss from her, but when her passion ignited, I lost myself. Never have I lost control like that. All I wanted to do was rip her clothes off and shove my cock in her warmth. I am looking forward to getting her into a bed and letting that sex kitten run wild!

Now that my dick is no longer throbbing, I head back to the table. As I reach it, I sense the tension between Cassie and some dude that is conversating with Jill. I can also sense that he is a vampire. I go and stand by her side, putting my arm around her shoulders, and squeezing. She turns to look at me and I can see the unease in her eyes. I lift my own, questioning her. She shakes her head back and forth conveying that now isn't the time. I wonder if she knows that he isn't a normal person.

For about a half hour Jill and the stranger keep up with their conversation, while Cassie and I make our own small talk. My arm never leaving her shoulder, letting her know that I'm here for her. I notice the slight glances that the guy keeps stealing of Cassie and it makes me hug her to me a little more. I am getting a bad vibe from him and I'm anxious to know why Cassie was uncomfortable with him nearby; I press a kiss to her forehead for reassurance.

Excusing himself, the guy heads back in for a round of drinks. I begin to ask Cassie what that was all about when her cellphone started ringing. "Oh, it's my mom, I better take this. Be right back." I nod my head.

I whirl on Jill, "What the hell was that all about?"

"What was what about," she looks confused.

"Did you not see her reaction to that guy you are talking to? She is wound up tight!"

"I don't know why, she met him Friday afternoon. He had asked her if she had a set of jumper cables he could borrow."

"Really? I wonder what has her all antsy then."

Jill shrugs her shoulders, "Who knows. She has been skittish since we arrived in town. She normally isn't like this."

"Wait, what do you mean, arrived in town? You guys don't live here?"

"God no, we live in Augusta and just came for the weekend to relax a little."

"Then when did you meet what's his name?" I inquire.

"His name is Zayne and we met him when we were headed to lunch during our break, why?"

"Hold on. If you met him in Augusta, then why is he here now? In the same town you ladies are vacationing in. Isn't that a little weird?" My senses are on alert at this point. Something just isn't adding up. "Did he give you a last name?"

"I believe he said it was Elliot." She seems to start realizing that something may not be right.

A quietness comes over the table as we wait for Cassie to return. I immediately send a text to Taven asking him to do a background check on a vampire named Zayne Elliot and to let me know A.S.A.P. He texts me back informing me that our IT guy, Kole is on top of it.

I whip my head around as my hearing senses pick up on a muffled scream.

"What is it?" Jill questions.

I shake my head and stand, "I am not sure, but I'm going to go check on Cassie."

"I'll come with you," she says.

"No, stay here in case she comes back. I won't be gone long."

As I'm walking through the bar, I see no sign of Cassie or Zayne. A bad feeling creeps in. I look towards the restrooms, but there are lines for both, so I highly doubt they are in either one.

My gut is telling me to go outside. I hastily make my way through the people that are lingering in my path. A woman, scantily dressed, walks in my path and smiles. Without missing a step, I gently push her out of my way and make for the front door. Using a little too much strength as I'm pulling the door open, it slams into the wall, bringing attention to myself. "Damn gust of wind," I mumble. The few that had looked my way, go back to their conversations.

Standing outside, I'm surveying the surroundings for any sign of Cassie when I hear a faint scuffle off to my left. Not seeing anything immediately, even with my vamp senses, I take off in that direction.

CASSIE

Reaching the door to go outside, I answer my cellphone before it goes to voicemail. "Hey Mom, what's up?"

"Hi honey, I am sorry to bother you. How's your weekend going?"

Hmm, how do I answer that? I couldn't possibly tell her that it's going great because I just almost had sex with a stranger in the restroom at a bar! I go the easier route, "It's going pretty well. It's so peaceful here and everyone is so nice."

"That's good to hear. What is all that background noise?"

"Jill and I went out for drinks. I had to step outside because it was too loud inside."

"Well then, I won't take up your time chit chatting. I just wanted to let you know that I swung over to your place and borrowed your roaster. Ours took a crap and your father wants roast for Sunday dinner. Will you be home by then, dear?"

"I am not sure yet, but I'll call you once I know. Hey Mom, I better get back inside with Jill. I love you and will talk to you tomorrow."

"Okay honey, have fun and be safe. I love you too!"

"Oh, how sweet!" A voice speaks from behind me.

Startled, I whip myself around and come face to face with "Green Eyes".

"You need to stop sneaking up on me like that! It's also impolite to listen in on other people's conversations!" I inform him. He doesn't seem to care as he gradually makes his way over to me. Feeling uncomfortable in his presence, I take a step back to put more space between us; he seems amused that I do so.

"Why are you here? Are you stalking us?" I ask.

"I'm here, because I require something that belongs to me," he replies, "Something that someone else believes belongs to them."

"What is this thing that belongs to you?" I question.

"It's not a thing that belongs to me, Dear, it's WHO belongs to me." He informs me as he leers.

I am not liking how this is going or how he is staring at me, as if he is about to pounce. "Hate to break it to you, but slavery was abolished over a hundred and fifty years ago. You can't just OWN somebody." I can't help the sarcasm, "But I'll play along for now. Who is this person that you possess?"

"Why it's you, of course!" He chuckles at my shocked expression.

His words slam into me like a fist to a punching bag. I lose the ability to speak; I'm too stunned by what he is saying. Finally, I snap out of it and start to laugh hysterically, "Oh, my God, you had me going for a moment there! I'm heading back to Jill and Jax, you coming?"

Pivoting on my heel, I go to leave, but my path is blocked, by him. "How did you…" I gawk.

"Let's just say there is a lot that you don't know about me or the abilities I have." As he smiles, I gaze in horror as his canines grow in length.

"What the fuck are you?"

"I'm the one who will take you as his own and kill anybody that tries to stop me!" He grabs hold of both my arms and smashes his mouth against mine, his fangs drawing blood as they pierce my lip.

I try to push him away, but he is strong. I do the only thing that I can think of, I slam my knee into his balls. He lifts his mouth from mine and grunts at the impact. I draw in as much air as I can and scream! His grip loosens and I take advantage of the freedom and try to run, but he must have dived at me, because his arms wrap around both my legs, sending me crashing to the ground with him on top.

Horrified of what is happening to me, I just start thrashing out at him with my hands and feet, not knowing if I was even hitting anything. He lifts me up off the ground and starts dragging me, kicking, and screaming. He whirls around so fast that I'm not prepared for his fist that makes contact with the side of my head. I see stars and then everything goes black.

JAX

I come around the corner just as Zayne knocks Cassie out cold. I see red at the moment! Nobody puts their hands on my mate! I roar, alerting Zayne that I am present. He becomes alarmed as he glances upon my maddening features. Letting go of Cassie, she drops to the ground in a heap. Zayne spins around and flees into the surrounding woods, but then slows enough to inform me that he will be back for her.

I am too concerned for Cassie to give chase, but I vow that I will find him, and he will die.

I fall to my knees by Cassie and lift her head to lay it on my lap. Even though it's dark, my vampire senses allow me to see clearly. I examine the side of her face where she was struck and see that it's already starting to bruise. I continue to look her over for any other bruising or marks. I check her neck for his bite, but there is nothing there. Sending up a prayer to the big guy, I scoop her into my arms and stand.

Not caring what people were going to think, I walk around to the patio and spot Jill still sitting at the table. Gaining looks from other patrons, I walk over to get as close as I can to Jill and holler up to her. She looks down over the railing and gasps at the sight before her.

"What happened to her?"

Knowing that others were listening in, I lied. "Someone had a little too much to drink tonight. Let's get her back home, shall we?"

Jill questions his excuse with a lift of her eyebrow, knowing as much as I do, that Cassie did not consume that much tonight. She grabs their things and disappears into the bar, reappearing a moment later from the front door.

"Did you walk or drive here?" I ask.

"We drove. Cassie got a little freaked out walking back last night, so she wanted to drive tonight," she explains. "Her car is right there, pointing to a Malibu.

Jill unlocks the doors and I gently lay Cassie in the backseat. I hold out my hands for the keys, but Jill holds them tight. Ugh, I don't have time for this!

"Please give me the keys, Jill."

"I can drive and get my best friend home. I have done it plenty of times," She informs me.

"You and I both know that she isn't passed out drunk. I will explain in the car, but we have to go now, she is in danger!"

"What? What kind of danger? From whom?"

"I don't know what kind yet, but Zayne attacked her outside and was trying to take her." I couldn't keep the anger out of my voice.

"What the fuck! Why would he do that? He seemed so nice." Tears forms in her eyes.

"I will find out the reasoning behind it and take care of him!" I reply, softening my tone, "Can I please have the keys now?"

Jill hands over the keys and quietly slides into the passenger seat. Starting up the car, I look over at her. She is on the brink of opening the flood gates, so I place my hand on her shoulder, causing her to look at me. "Everything will be fine; I am not going to let anything bad happen to either one of you!" She nods at me then turns to stare out the window.

Jill gives me directions to the cabin, which is only 5 minutes away, thank God. We get Cassie into the house and lay her on the couch.

"Why don't we lay her in her bed?" Jill questions.

"The two of you are not staying here tonight, that's why. I need you to go pack yours and Cassie's things up and I will help get them in the car."

"What do you mean we are not staying here? Where are you taking us?" She sounds a little frantic.

"We don't know if he knows where you are staying. Apparently, he has been stalking the two of you since Friday. If he followed you from two and a half hours away, I am sure he knows where you are staying, and it isn't safe anymore." I try explaining to her, "It's best that we get you ladies back home tonight, but we need to stop back at the bar so I can grab my truck. If it's okay with you, I'll have you drive it back, so I can drive Cassie."

"I can drive Cassie back on my own. We don't even know you!" She exclaims.

"I understand, but what if Zayne knows we are leaving and follows us? You are no match for him. Trust me, this plan is better." I know she is struggling with the decision, but in the end, she agrees.

SEVEN

CASSIE

I wake up to a throbbing on the side of my head. Instinctively, my hand flies up to the area with the pain, but I feel only tenderness. Unaware of my surroundings, I feel movement beneath me. My eyelids flutter before I am able to open them completely. Panic seeps in as I gain full consciousness, recognizing the movement beneath me. I am in the backseat of a car!

Not wanting to make it known that I am awake, I lay as still as I can while trying to remember what all had taken place. Slowly, it is all beginning to come back to me. A phone call from my mother, a strange conversation with a guy that I had only just met the day before, fangs, a struggle…wait…fangs! I distinctly remember seeing fangs lengthen before my very eyes! There is only one creature that I know of that would have those sharp canines, but it is impossible, because vampires don't exist!

I remember trying to run from him and then crashing to the ground. I struggled, hoping to free myself and that is when he hit me. I don't remember anything more. Does this mean that he was able to take me away? Am I being kidnapped? My heart begins to race with the realization that I'm in the hands of a monster that is so much stronger than I am!

"You're awake," comes a voice from the front seat. A voice that I know all too well!

"Jax?" Relief floods me. "What's going on? Where are we going?"

"What all do you remember?"

Revealing all that had transpired, starting with the phone call, and ending with "Green Eyes" hitting me, I can't help but wonder about my state of mind, "Am I going crazy Jax?"

I can hear his long sigh from the backseat. "No, unfortunately you are not going crazy. It would be so much simpler if you were, though."

"So, you are saying that vampires are real?"

"Yes. Vampires are very much real."

"Oh, my God, how is it possible? How come nobody has ever heard of them being real? I mean, they are blood sucking monsters that kill people! Surely the deaths of all the victims cannot go unexplained, especially if their throats are ripped out!" I'm in complete shock.

"Okay, let's not go overboard," he laughs, "The stories of what vampires are and what they actually are in real life are completely different."

"Oh, so you're saying that they do not drink human blood then?" Sarcasm drips off my words.

"Why don't you crawl up front here. We have a bit of a drive back to Augusta and I will try to explain everything."

As I climb between the seats, I realize that we are in my car and then thoughts of Jill appear as my ass hits the passenger seat, "Shit, where is Jill?"

His hand goes to my thigh and rubs it, "Don't worry, she is in my pickup right in front of us." He goes on telling me how they went back to the cabin to grab our things and that it would be safer for me to head back home.

Feeling relieved, I sigh and cover his hand with mine. It feels so natural being with him, I'm not sure why, "How did I come to be here, back with you and Jill? I thought for sure that he was trying to drag me away with him."

"I believe you are right. I messed those plans up when I interrupted his escape with you." He continues on, "I had a bad feeling come over me and went looking for you. As I came around the corner of the building, I watched him strike you and I took off running to get to you. He ran off into the woods, but I couldn't go after him. Tending to you was more urgent. I will get him, though, my people are working on it as we speak."

"Your people?"

"I work with a group of men, called the Elite. We go after people like Zayne."

"Who is Zayne?"

Jax glances at me like I had grown a second head, "He's the guy that attacked you! You mean to tell me that you didn't even know his name?"

"No, he never officially introduced himself to me."

"He told Jill that his name was Zayne Elliot. It could be a lie, but I'm hoping not. It will be harder to track him down if it is a fake name."

"So, you go after bad guys, huh? That's fucking hot!" Smiling, I wiggle my brows at him.

Choking on his laugh, he squeezes my thigh, "You think so, huh?"

"Mm hm, but we can get into that later. I want to hear about these vampires."

"Okay, so first off, vampires are basically just like regular people except there are some differences in their DNA. They can eat, drink, and sleep just like you. Sunlight, garlic, crosses, and Holy water doesn't do jack shit to them. A stake through the heart, decapitation, and fire are the only things that can kill them, but if you think about it, all three of those things will also kill a regular person. Vampires do need blood to sustain life, but that does not make them killers. Their hearing, eyesight, and sense of smell are all magnified also. Vamps can move so fast that you don't even see their movement and they have incredible strength. There are a few with special abilities like being able to read minds and mind control. Otherwise, vampires are pretty much human, it's just what they have in their DNA."

I contemplate everything that he just said, soaking it all in. "You said that vampires are not killers, but how can they drink someone's blood and not kill them?"

"They don't have to drink straight from a person. They can drink from animals or bags from a blood bank. If they do drink from a person, they only need to take a little, but there are some that will drain a person. Those are the ones that are vile and the ones that the Elite take down."

"Is Zayne one of those monsters then?" I question.

"I can't tell for certain until we have more information on him, but just by him attacking you, I would put him in that category." He confirms my rising fear.

"I think I'm going to try and get some rest. This is all too much to take in right now." I close my eyes hoping I can sleep after all this new information. I feel his hand start to pull away and I strengthen my grip on it, relaying to him that I want it to stay there as I slowly drift off to sleep.

JAX

As we pull into her driveway, I let out a sigh of relief. I had kept watch the whole drive back making sure that we weren't being followed. With my hand still resting on her high, I gently squeeze, "Cassie, we are here." What I wouldn't give to be able to wake her in a more pleasurable way.

A hint of a smile appears on her lips as she opens her eyes and looks at me. The muscles around my heart tighten when she smiles over at me the way she is doing right now. "Good morning sleepy head, rise and shine!"

"Ugh, I plan on going right back to sleep once I find my bed," She mumbles, and I smile.

Jill is already making her way over to Cassie's side of the car as I'm getting out, "I am so glad you are okay! Don't ever scare me like that again Bitch!" She squeals while embracing Cassie in a bear hug.

"My bad, I'll try not to, but I'm not making any promises," Cassie giggles.

I grab her things and follow them into the house. It's a nice little ranch style home, not too big, not too small. It fits her just right, along with the décor inside, "Where would you like me to put your things, Cassie?"

"Oh, thanks for bringing them in. You can just leave them by the door."

"How long were you planning on staying in Bar Harbor? It looks like a month's worth of luggage," I joke.

"We were only there for the weekend, but a girl needs to have options at all times."

I shake my head and chuckle as I turn back towards the door, "I'll go grab Jill's luggage."

"You don't have to. I'm planning on heading home in a few and will grab it when I leave." Jill calls out.

"I think it would be safer if you just stay here for a few days. At least until me and my men find Zayne. I can keep watch over you both if you are together."

"But I'm not the one he wants, Cassie is." She stammers.

"Yes, and he won't hesitate to use you to get to her if need be." I nod towards Cassie. I see understanding light her eyes.

"I'll stay for one night, but then I need to get back to my own place."

"Fine, I will just have one of the Elites watch your house then." I sigh and turn to go retrieve her bags.

Before going back inside, I pull out my cell phone and speed dial Kole. My call goes to his voicemail, so I hang up and try Taven. He answers on the first ring, "Talk to me buddy." he answers.

"Just wondering if Kole has found anything on Zayne yet," I'm getting impatient, "He tried to kidnap a woman late last night, outside of a bar. We need to find the son of a bitch!"

"Calm down there, buddy," Taven soothes, "Kole is following up on a lead as we speak."

"Thank fuck!"

"What else is going on with you?" He questions.

I know I can't keep it from him any longer. I am one hundred percent sure that Cassie is my mate and the Elite need to know, so we can keep her safe. "I found my mate." I blurt out.

There was silence on the other end. Finally, "Are you sure?"

"Yes."

"This woman that Zayne attacked last night... it was her, wasn't it?" He guesses.

"Yes, and he warned me that he was coming back for her, so she isn't safe, and neither is her best friend. He will go after her friend just to get to her! Do we have any extra bodies that can help with watch detail?" I wanted the best and was hoping that Xavier or even Taven himself were available.

"I'll send Xavier, he just finished a job. When do you need him?"

"She is going to stay with Cassie until tomorrow morning, so I will be here to watch them both. I'll text Xavier later with all the info he will need."

"Sounds like a plan. So, this Cassie, she is your mate you say?" I hear the humor in his voice.

"Don't start dickhead, I'm still getting used to it myself."

"Hey, I'm not starting anything! I just find it funny that YOU are the first to find a mate, that's all." He is laughing now.

I can't blame him really. Out of all the Elite, I am the one that should have been last in finding a mate. I'm all about work and finding the next bad guy; I live for it!

"Yeah, I guess it is. I'll tell you what, this one is going to keep me on my toes, she's a feisty one!" A smile plays across my face at the memory of last night.

"Oh really? I can't wait to meet our soon-to-be sister-in-law then!"

"Slow down there buddy, she doesn't know everything yet. I don't even know if she will have me." I chuckle, "But hey, I got to get back inside. Inform Xavier that I will be in touch."

"Will do, take care out there."

"Always." I end the call and head back inside with Jill's things.

Cassie has changed into, what I'm assuming is, sleepwear, and is coming down the hallway as I'm walking through the door. I can't help but notice her tight-fitting tank top and very snug spandex shorts. My eyes shoot back up to her chest as something registers. The little minx isn't wearing a bra and her nipples are straining against the fabric. Our eyes meet and she has a shit-eating grin on her face. She knows exactly what she is doing! All I can do is smile and shake my head.

I clear my throat, "If you don't mind, I would like to stay a while just to make sure it's safe. I can crash on the couch if I need to catch a few winks."

"Oh, I have a spare bedroom you can use. Jill can sleep with me." Cassie offers.

"I'll be better off on the couch; in case anybody tries coming through the front door, but thanks for offering."

She shrugs, "Suit yourself."

Jill picks up her bags and starts heading down the hallway, "I'm heading to bed, I'm exhausted."

"Okay, goodnight hon, I love you." Cassie responds.

"Love you too, bitch. See you in the afternoon," Jill calls out.

Cassie then turns my way, "I'll go grab you a pillow and blanket."

She is back a moment later and lays the items on the couch, "I'm gonna go hit the hay myself. Thank you Jax, for everything. I'm sorry that we ruined your night."

"No need to thank me. I would do it again if it means keeping you safe." My comment makes color flood her face, "Goodnight Cassie, sleep well."

EIGHT

CASSIE

I've been tossing and turning for the past hour, sleep eluding me, not because of Zayne and the attack or the fact that vampires are real, but due to the man in the other room. Tall, muscular, and rugged, Jax Whitley is God's gift to women. I keep reliving the night before in the women's restroom at the bar. No one has ever taken me like that before. Unrestrained, raw, and passionate is the best way to describe it.

I don't know what it is about him, but it's like he fits. I have always been an independent woman, never needing a man as a permanent fixture, but with Jax, I can't seem to think of what it will be like once he is gone. I won't think about it. God, I barely know the guy and here I am acting like a lovesick fool! I think it's just been way too long since I last had sex and last night's tease just has my senses all whacked out.

The look on his face earlier as I walked down the hallway was pure lust. He wants me just as much as I want him. I hear him moving around the house and thinking about the things I want him to do to me, my hand slowly makes its way to the waistband of my shorts and dips below. I'm already wet from just my thoughts of him. My finger slides into my pussy, my juices lubricate the digit and I pull it back out to rub my clit in slow, gentle circles. My mind wanders back to Jax's mouth when he licked and nibbled my nipples. A moan slips past my lips and I close my mouth tightly, not wanting anybody to hear me.

As I continue to pleasure myself, I hear Jill's door creak open only to be quickly closed. Suddenly, I hear my doorknob turning. My back is to the door, so I can't see who is entering, but I can smell his woodsy and spice scent. Only opening my door a crack, I can sense his eyes on me. He goes to close it and I speak up, not wanting him to leave just yet. "I'm awake," I say softly, "can't sleep."

"Are you okay? Can I get you anything?" he asks.

I lean up on my elbows, shaking my head no and pat the bed beside me, "Let's chat."

He hesitates but closes the door softly anyway and makes his way over to my bed. Kicking off his boots, he climbs in and leans his back against the headboard, stretching his legs out and crossing them.

"So, tell me all about yourself Jackson Whitley."

"What do you want to know?"

"Anything and everything you feel comfortable sharing with me."

"With you, I feel comfortable sharing everything." He whispers.

I sigh. The meaning behind those words go straight to my heart. "Let's start with where you are from."

"Well, I was born in Sioux City, Iowa where I lived until I was twenty-four years old. That's when I decided to travel and left for Europe for a few years, roaming the Continent. When I was ready, I came back to the states, I settled here in Augusta."

"You don't live in Bar Harbor?"

"No, like you, I was on vacation."

"Now I really feel awful! You cut your time there short, because of us." I frown.

"Don't feel bad. My work is my life, and I am always prepared to do a job." He explains, "Actually, Taven made me take the time off. I chose that place because it was far enough away to call it a vacation, but close enough in case I was needed back here. I didn't really know what to do with myself anyway." He chuckles.

"So how did you end up working for the Elite anyway?"

"Ah, yes. That happened by sheer stupidity on my part." He laughs, "I had only moved here a month prior when I came upon a group of vamps preying on a family of four. I was hoping to just scare them away by letting my presence be known, but my smartass mouth wouldn't shut up. They all charged me at once and that is when the Elite arrived and helped me fight them. I started my training with them and have been an Elite ever since."

"Wow, I can barely comprehend everything that I have been told and here you are, living it every day. Helping innocents and not asking for anything in return. You are truly a hero."

"I wouldn't go that far; I just love my job. Now, why don't you tell me a little about Cassie Manson."

"Ha! I'm not nearly as interesting as you are."

"Oh, you are interesting alright!" I see the outline of a grin on his face.

I'm not sure what to say to that, so I begin with my boring life story. "I was born and raised here in Augusta. My parents are Patricia and Gary Manson, and I am an only child. I have only traveled within the states but traveling overseas is on my Bucket List. I met Jill in high school, and we have been inseparable ever since. We do everything together. We both got jobs at Walmart while we were still in school and are now Assistant Managers in different departments. It's not a dream job, but the pay is great, and we are good at our jobs. There are only three people who understand me, my parents and Jill. Everyone else assumes I'm angry or a sarcastic bitch. That about sums it up... see, boring!"

"I hardly find you boring, Cassie."

"Oh, I never said I was boring, just my life story. I'm hell on wheels baby!"

"I can definitely work with that!" He grins.

We stare at each other for a few heartbeats. He brings his hand up and caresses my cheek, and I lean into it. He slides down beside me and whispers into my ear, "Tell me Cassie, who were you thinking of when you were pleasuring yourself just a bit ago?"

JAX

Her body stiffens at my question, but I can smell her arousal begin to flow. She is turned on from being caught, interesting, "It's nothing to be ashamed of, in fact, just hearing that soft moan escape your lips, turned me on so fucking much!" I grab her hand and bring it the hardness throbbing to come out. I hear her whimper as she tightens her hold around my cock. "Now tell me, who were you thinking of?"

She swallows, "You. I was thinking of you."

Hearing her admit that she was thinking of me while fingering herself pushes me over the edge, I can't hold back any longer. Slowly, I bring my lips to hers, demanding that she let me in as I move over her, trapping her beneath me. Grabbing both of her arms, I pin them to the bed above her head. I spread her legs apart with my thigh and move in between them. Already smelling her arousal, I gyrate my hips against her, earning another moan from her.

I break away from her mouth and travel slowly down to her neck, placing soft kisses as I go. Holding both her hands in one of mine, I bring the other one down, yanking her tank top down, revealing her glorious tits. My mouth latches on to her nipple, sucking, licking, and nipping, only letting up on the assault to move to the other, and repeat. When she arches her back to get closer, I release her hands and they instantly go to my head; her fingers tangle in my hair as she pulls my head closer, demanding I give her more.

I grab the bottom of her tank top and pull it up over her head, leaving her tits long enough to get her top over them and then my mouth is back on her. Gradually, I move down over her middle, kissing and licking my way down. My fingers slide into her waistband, and I pull down her shorts. If I had my way, I'd rip her clothes off using my vampire strength, but I don't want to scare her away just yet. I sit up, so I can pull them all the way off, and then refocusing on her body, I move to her pussy, spreading her legs nice and wide, and swipe it with my tongue. She jerks at the sensation. Licking her folds, I can taste her sweetness. Never have I tasted anything so heavenly! My tongue finds her clit as I slide a finger into her warmth. Oh God, she is so tight! Sliding in and out of her steadily, I insert another one and repeat. A third enters in next to the other two. I need to stretch and prepare her to take my vampire cock. I remove my fingers just to pump them back into her at the same time I nip her clit, causing her to release the pressure. Her orgasm is music to my ears as I lap up the sweet nectar, savoring the taste.

NINE

JAX

Moving away so I can undress, I leave her but for a moment. I strip my t-shirt up over my head and move to the button of my jeans. "Stop, let me." Cassie is crawling seductively towards me. I stop what I'm doing and wait, enjoying her movement towards me. With her back arching and that fine ass up in the air, she is on the prowl, my body being her prey. She stands before me, admiring my physique. Her hands are on my chest tracing the contours until she reaches the bottom. Sucking in a breath, I'm mesmerized by what her hands are doing to me. She unbuttons my jeans and tugs them down, startled as my cock springs forward. I kick my jeans off the rest of the way as she wraps a hand around my engorged shaft. She looks up at me and I see a play of a smile on her lips right before they find their way around my tip, then taking me in as much as she can.

My breath hitches, "Fuck, I love your mouth!" With only half of my dick fitting in her mouth, she wraps one hand at the base and her other hand goes to my balls to gently massage them. When her mouth picks up speed, I lace my fingers through her hair, restraining myself from putting pressure on her head and gagging her, so I let her keep the lead.

It doesn't take long and I'm getting ready to spill, so regrettably, I pull out of her mouth, "If you keep that up darlin I'm going to cum and I want to save that for when I'm buried deep inside of you!"

She shrieks as I grab her up and throw her on the bed, following in her wake. I crawl over and settle myself between her sweet thighs. Taking hold of both her legs, I spread them wider, admiring the view of her pussy before placing the tip of my cock at her opening. I slowly press forward, "Ah, you are so fucking tight Cassie! I'm going to love ramming into this pussy!" I close my eyes and savor the feeling as she takes me inch by inch. I stop halfway in and demand that she looks at me. Her eyes are glazed over, she's panting heavily. I dare not move.

"Are you okay Cassie? Do you need me to stop?"

"If you stop now, I will stab you. I need you to fuck me right now!"

Without another word, I growl as I pull out to the tip, and then slam back into her with such force, her eyes rolled to the back of her head. I continue ramming her over and over and she meets each of my thrusts with her own. She wraps her legs around my waist, opening herself up further for me. I lean down and take her mouth, my tongue and dick moving at the same tempo. Reaching in between us, I find her clit, and that's all it takes to send her over the edge. Once that orgasm is over, I pull out, grab her waist, and spin her around so she's laying on her stomach. I yank her hips up until she is in the doggy-style position, and then spending another moment to take in the breathtaking view of her tight ass, I run a finger through her folds. After sucking her juice off my finger, I plunge my cock back into her.

"Oh... My... God, your cock is a fucking monster, Jax! It feels so damn good, don't stop!" Cassie pants as she slams her ass into me, keeping up the rhythm.

She is dripping in wetness; I collect some on my thumb and bring it up to her ass, inserting the tip. She moans and so I do it again, this time going further in. I continue the pace until her ass takes all of my thumb. I feel her pressure building again, so I keep slamming my cock into her tight pussy, while my thumb continues its assault in her ass. I take her over the edge, which in turn, causes my own release to tear through me. I remove my thumb and slam her back onto my cock and hold her there as my cum fills her. Pumping into her slowly a few more times, I make sure every last drop is out.

When I pull out, I crawl in beside her, pulling her close to me, and wrapping her in my arms. I lean in and press a kiss to her temple, "Get some sleep, love", but she doesn't hear me because she is already fast asleep.

CASSIE

I gradually open my eyes and look at the clock. It's only 9:30 in the morning. I feel warmth cocooning my body and look down. Jax's chest is to my back, his arms wrapped tightly around me and one of his legs are draped over mine. I snuggle in a little deeper and close my eyes again.

"I suggest that you don't move like that again unless you want me to ravish you and have a repeat of earlier." His husky voice sounding so sexy in the morning.

I don't know, I may like that." I smiled to myself.

Next thing I know, he is lifting his leg off of mine and lifting my own. I feel his cock at my entrance a mere second before he slides it in to the hilt, and then I hear him sigh. I'm a little tender, but God does it feel good! He slowly makes love to me from behind, kissing my neck tenderly. I turn my head towards him so he can take possession of my mouth. Using his free hand, he also possesses my clit.

Keeping it at a slow pace, the passion still burns hot and in no time, we are finding our release together. With him still imbedded in me, I once again find sleep.

There's a knock at my door and Jill's voice floods my senses, "Hey Case, have you seen Ja...." She opens my door and stops short, "Dammit, I'm sorry!" She spins around.

I snicker and look at Jax. We are in the same position that we fell asleep in, and I mean the same... his cock still inside me. He is grinning, but his eyes remain closed. I notice his ass is hanging out of the covers and realize what the grin was for. Jill got an awesome view!

Shaking my head and chuckling, I move away from him, causing his cock to lose its shelter and gaining a grunt from Jax. I cover his ass up, doing the same for myself.

"It's safe, Jill."

She turns back towards us, "So much for watch detail, but I guess you did a mighty fine job watching Cassie." She laughs.

"He is very good at his job." I wink at her.

"I saw that minx!" Jax grumbles, causing both Jill and I to laugh.

"Give us a few minutes and we will be out."

"No problem. I just thought it was odd that he was nowhere around, but his truck was still here. Oh, by the way, I ordered pizza for lunch just a little bit ago."

"Great, thanks a bunch."

As the door closes, Jax looks at me, "How are you doing? I didn't hurt you, did I?" He pulls me back into his arms.

"Actually, I feel great. A little sore maybe, but I'll live. Stop worrying so much, vaginas are made to take a pounding." I joke.

"You are amazing, darlin. I plan on pounding that vagina of yours quite a bit if you will let me." A shitty ass grin appearing on his face.

"I'll have to think on it for a while." Trying to sound as serious as I can but failing horribly.

Without warning, he starts tickling me. "You will have to think on it for a while?"

"Okay, okay… stop! You can pound my vagina whenever you want!" I'm hysterical with laughter, "But first we have to get dressed and get back to the living." I crawl out of bed and dress in my discarded pajamas. Looking back at Jax, he is still lying in bed watching my every move with those sapphire eyes. I wink at him and walk out the door.

TEN

JAX

After having a nice hot shower, I had forgotten that I left all of my belongings back on the mountain in our haste to get back to Augusta. Remembering that I keep a clean set of clothes in my pickup, I wrap the bath towel around my waist and exit Cassie's room. I hear their chatter and know they were in the kitchen, so I head in that direction.

I find them at the table devouring pizza and breadsticks from Domino's, "You girl's aren't hungry, or anything are you?"

"Ravenous," Jill answers with her mouth full and glances up, a look of shock on her face when she sees my state of undress.

"It's rude to comment on a woman's eating habits, ass!" Cassie scolds me without even turning around in her chair.

I walk over to her just as she lifts a slice of pizza to take a bite and I swoop down, demolishing half the slice with one bite.

"Hey get your own! Next time I'll stab you with my fork!" She picks up her utensil to prove she means business. I lean over and plant a kiss on the top of her head and then turn and move towards the front door.

"Where are you going?" she asks.

"I have clean clothes in my truck, be right back."

"You're going outside like that?"

"Yeah, why not? All my best parts are covered."

"Who says those are your best parts?" She raises a brow.

"You know, you're right! No one has ever told me that they are my best parts. Guess I don't need this after all." I toss my towel at her chest and walk out the door bare ass naked. All I hear is "Oh My Fucking Word, he did not just do that," then lots of laughter. It makes me chuckle and shake my head.

I'm back in the house in less than a minute and the women are still laughing. Jill spins around when she notices my junk is still out and hanging free, "Will you please put that thing away for God's sake!"

"You act as if you have never seen a dick before."

"Not one that needs its own concealed weapons permit!"

"Stop making Jill uncomfortable." Cassie reprimands me while grinning.

"Anything for you darlin!" I steal a kiss from her before heading back to her room.

I join them a few minutes later and grab a slice of pizza. "Has anyone seen my phone?"

Jill points to the counter by the fridge, "Is that it?"

"Yes, thank you!" I slap a wet kiss on her forehead as I walk past and grab it. She rolls her eyes at me and smiles.

"Shit!"

"What's wrong?" Cassie looks at with concern.

"I've missed three calls from Taven and two from Xavier. I better call them back."

"Who is Xavier?" she questions.

"He is an Elite and will be on Jill's watch detail once she leaves here. He is one of the best."

"Oh goodie, my very own Elite Warrior!" Jill claps her hands and wiggles her eyebrows.

"Xavier takes his job very serious, and he is a hell of a good man. Don't give him any of your shit, Jill." I taunt.

"Hey, I'm not making any promises," as she holds up her hands.

I walk to the living room so I can make my calls, Taven being first on the list. He picks up on the first ring, "Where the fuck are you? I've called you three damn times!"

"Calm down, I was busy and then I misplaced my phone. I'm calling you now, aren't I?" It wasn't really a lie. I was busy, fucking the best piece of ass ever, and I did kind of misplace my phone.

"Dammit, Jax, you had me worried! It's not like you not to call me back like that. Aren't you on a watch detail?"

"Yes, I'm at Cassie's place."

"Ah, well, that explains it then." Taven chuckles, "Well, I wanted to give you a heads up on this Zayne Elliot."

My body tenses, "What did you find out?"

"That's the thing, we haven't found anything on him yet. We found a Zayne Elliot born in 1902, but no death record. We are searching other avenues to see if it's the same guy."

"So, what are you wanting to give me a heads up on?"

"One of the avenues that we are looking at are banks and we received a notification that a Zayne J. Elliot used a Mastercard at a Kenoco station on Western at 9:22am this morning."

"Fuck!"

"You think this is our guy then?"

"It's got to be. Send whatever backup we have to patrol the area."

"I have Cooper and Duncan available. Text me Cassie's address and I'll send them over within the hour."

"Will do, thanks." I end the call and speed dialed Xavier.

"Jax my man, you're alive!"

"Funny man today, are we?" I'm getting irritated.

"Well, when you drop off the face of the earth for hours, you're going to get shit."

"Can't a guy have a little fun anymore without people blowing up his phone, sheesh!"

"Whoa, just messing with you dude! I just wanted to check in and see if you had the info for the watch detail you want me on."

"Swing by Cassie's as soon as you can, and I will fill you in. We may have company sooner than I thought; I'll text you the address."

"No problem, I'll leave in five." He hangs up before I can even thank him.

Cassie is still in the kitchen when I walk in. I glance at the phone in her hand then to the Bud Light in front of her, "You have another one of those? I could use a drink."

"Yep, there is a case in the fridge," as she continues to make kissy faces at her phone, "There is a bottle of Jack in the cupboard if you want something stronger."

"Thanks, I better not, though. I need to stay alert."

That gets her full attention, "Why is that? Did you get news on the douche bag?"

I have to smile at her colorful vocabulary, a girl after my own heart! She doesn't take any shit... Hell on wheels is right. "We don't know for certain, but a credit card belonging to a Zayne J. Elliott was used this morning at the Kenoco station on Western. I'd rather be prepared than not."

"How the fuck does that piece of shit keep finding me?"

"That's a good question. You said that you had just met him Friday afternoon?"

"Yeah, sort of. I mean, I was sitting in my car waiting for Jill so we could go to lunch, and he snuck up on me. He asked to borrow a set of jumper cables, but I didn't have any. He seemed nice enough and I thought he was pretty hot."

I grunt at her last statement, and she looks up, "Oh, is someone jealous?" she asks in a sweet voice.

"In your dreams Hellion!" I grin.

She gets up out of her chair and strolls over, stopping in front of me. Her hand massages my dick, "No worries, he has nothing on you." She bites her lower lip.

I can't help the bulge that grows within her grip and notice the rapturous look in her eyes. I place my beer on the counter, haul her into my body with one arm wrapped around her waist and entangle my fingers in her hair while I pull her head back, "Remember that the next time a "hot" guy asks you to jump him." I slam my lips into hers. She opens up for me and my tongue dips in to taste the sweetness of her essence.

Just as I'm about to carry her back to her room, the doorbell chimes. Damn! Now is not a good time, especially with my dick all hard! I slowly ease up on her mouth, before pulling completely away, "We will continue this later, minx!" I head for the door.

Expecting it to be an Elite, I'm surprised when I open the door to find a long gift box with a bow on it. The tag says it's for Cassie, so I walk back in with the box in hand, "You have a delivery." I hand her the package. I don't smell any danger within the box, so I assume it is safe for her to open.

I watch as she opens it and then frowns, "What the fuck is this?"

Coming to her side, I peek into the box. There, sitting on white tissue is a single black rose. I spy the slip of paper underneath the creepy flower and picked it up to read it. Anger like I have never felt before spreads through my entire being; I crumble the note within my grip.

"What did it say Jax?"

"It's not important."

"Obviously, it is. You should see yourself!"

Shit, I need to calm down before my fangs erupt and Cassie sees it. I haven't quite figured out how I'm going to tell her yet, but I definitely don't want her finding out by me losing control.

"Jax, it came for me, and I am a grown ass woman! You do not need to protect me from a little note, now hand it over!" She holds her hand out, palm up.

Reluctantly, I relinquish it over to her. She flattens out the creases, so she can read it.

My Beloved Cassie,

Please except this rose. It signifies death to those who take what is mine! Leave your lover and I will let him live. The next warning will be your last. Blood will spill.... HIS blood!

YOU BELONG TO ME!

I watch as she reads the note and then rereads it. If it scares her at all, she doesn't show it. If anything, I would say that she is pissed, royally pissed!

"How dare he!?" she yells, "I don't even know who this ass wipe is, and he has the audacity to not only tell me who I can fuck, but that he owns me! Fuck that! Let him come, we will see whose blood will spill!" She is seething.

All I can do is stand here and grin. Hell on wheels baby!

CASSIE

It takes all I have not to go out and look for that mother fucker myself! He is certifiably bat shit crazy and needs to be taken out! I don't understand why he thinks I belong to him. Have we met before, and I don't remember? Definitely not, I'd remember those eyes. FUCK! This shit is not happening to me! Why do I always attract the losers? Well, except for Jax, although I haven't known him very long, so I can't count him out just yet.

I feel strong arms wrap around me from behind, "Hey Tiger, are you going to be okay?" Jax kisses the top of my head.

"Yeah, I'm just really super pissed!"

"Well, I for one, am very proud of you! You surprise me at every turn."

"If this is too much for you, I'll understand. I wouldn't want to get messed up with someone who has a lunatic as a stalker."

He laughs, "Are you kidding me? I have a front row seat baby and the fun has only just begun! I'm not going anywhere."

"Hm, maybe you are just as crazy as he is." I remark.

"Nah, the difference is, I'm not letting you go because I know you want me just as much as I want you!"

"You think so, huh?"

"How about I go show you just how much you want me?" He wiggles his brows.

Jill walks in, "Oh, come on you two, get a room!"

"See, even Jill is saying that we need to go fuck." He jokes.

The sad thing is that is exactly what I want to go do! He starts to pull me towards my room, and I let him, no restraint I tell ya! Just as we get to my door, the doorbell chimes again. I look at Jax, "I sure hope you have brushed up on your handyman capabilities, because that doorbell needs to come out!" He gives a hearty laugh and heads for the door.

I follow Jill into the kitchen, "Where have you been hiding?"

I started getting a headache, so I went and laid down, why?"

"You missed all the excitement!" I hand her the box and the note.

She pulls a disgusted face when she sees the black rose, but when she reads the note, her eyes get wide, and I can see the concern on her face, "Case, what the fuck? Why does this lunatic want you so bad?"

"That is the Million Dollar question!"

ELEVEN

JAX

I meet Jill coming out of her room as I'm about to knock. The bedrooms are the last two on my list to check. So far, I haven't found any bugs and with any luck the rest of the house will be clear of them as well. "Do you mind if I check your room now for any bugs?"

"Oh, I didn't know you were looking. Go right ahead. Actually, I was hoping to run to my house to grab my work clothes for tomorrow.?"

"That's fine, just take Xavier with you. It will be safer for you."

"No problem… thanks."

"No need to thank me, Jill."

"Yes, I do. I always hated babysitters, but then again, I never had a smoking hot guy as a sitter. So, thank you for changing my view on sitters!" She wiggles her eyebrows at me and saunters off to go find Xavier, leaving me laughing in her wake.

I finish searching the spare bedroom, not finding anything. I walk across the hall and knock on Cassie's door but there is no answer. Peeking in to find an empty room, I notice the bathroom door is cracked open and I hear the shower going. I enter the room and start my search, until I realize that we have the house to ourselves for a little while. My thoughts wander to her, under the shower's spray, naked and wet. My cock swells. Why am I still standing here?

I undress quickly and sneak into the bathroom. I can see her through the sheer curtain; her back is to me. Silently, I step into the shower behind her and wrap her in my arms. She gives a startled yip and then slaps me on the arm.

"Don't ever sneak up on me again if you want to live! I will ninja cut your ass and feed you to the werewolves!" She really tries giving me her serious face, but it doesn't work.

I nibble her earlobe and the whisper, "What crazy talk is this? There is no such thing as werewolves."

"Are you sure, because I may prefer to be a destined mate to a werewolf over a douche bag that checks himself out of the psych ward!"

I tense up at just the thought of her being with him. Spinning her around, I grip her arms gently and staring into those aqua eyes, I remind her, "You are not His mate, Cassie! Even if you were, I don't plan on giving you up, so you can stop worrying." I watch relief flood her eyes and then she slams her mouth to mine, taking what breath I have. I reciprocate as I lift her up against the tiled wall. I waste no time. I bring my hand between our bodies and find her sensitive nub, she moans and starts to move her hips, rubbing her pussy up and down my shaft.

"Tell me what you want, baby! All you have to do is ask." She stays silent. "Say it!" I demand of her.

"My pussy wants your fucking cock now!"

"And what do you want, Cassie?"

She stares at me, "You. All I want is you!"

Her words undo me. I lift her up enough for my tip to find her entrance and slowly, inch by inch, I lower her onto my cock, savoring the feel of her tight walls around me. Once I am completely seeded in her, I bring her back up at the same pace and then slam her down and continue slamming into her while my mouth goes to her tits, sucking hard! God, what I wouldn't do to be able to bite her right now. To taste her, to feel her very essence course through me! My canines ache to be released, but I hold them back.

Her muscles tighten around my cock as I reach a finger up and rim her before sinking my finger into her lovely ass. Her orgasm rips through her hard. She is left panting in my arms. As I start cherishing her with my lips, her body comes back to life.

I reach over and turn the water off and then reposition her, so she is now cradled in my arms. Carrying her through the bathroom, I snatch the tie to her bathrobe that is hanging on the door and take her to the bed, tossing her into the center. She shrieks and before she can move, I am on top straddling her and capturing her hands in mine. I bind her wrists together with one end of the robe tie and, leaving enough slack, I tie the other end to the headboard.

I look down at her, but her eyes are glued to my dick that is laying nestled between her spectacular breasts. Grasping them, I smash them together, securing my shaft and start pumping, sliding through the silkiness of her skin.

"Do you like that?" she asks while watching her tits get fucked.

"You don't even know how good this feels, Baby."

"Let me suck you. I want to taste you in my mouth."

I release her tits and still straddling her, I inch up until my cock reaches her mouth. I get on all fours and lower myself until I feel her mouth around me. I start slow and then increase my speed till I'm pumping in and out of her, my balls slapping at her chin with each thrust. When I'm on the brink of explosion, I pull out.

"What are you doing? Why did you pull out?"

"I was about to explode in that pretty little mouth of yours if I didn't stop." Her lips swollen from being stretched and used. She is a sight to behold.

"I want you to cum in my mouth, I want to know what you taste like." She is actually pouting, and I don't have it in me to deny her.

"Well, when you put it like that, open up for me."

She does my bidding and I'm now snuggled back inside. She moans and vibrates my cock in doing so. I start thrusting into her faster and as she moans again, I explode, shooting my hot liquid down her throat. I thrust once more into her, holding it so the tip of my cock is touching the back of her throat. She continues to swallow, taking it all in.

I finally pull out, looking down at her, I smile, "Did you like that?"

She licked her lips, "Very much so!"

"My turn."

Licking my way down her body, causing goosebumps on her flesh, I reach her glistening channel. I lick her folds once and then shove my tongue into her, plunging in and out of her. Finding her clit with my thumb, I start rubbing it causing her hips to move faster, and then I grab her thighs and lift them higher. I cease fucking her with my tongue but continue to lap up her arousal.

Lifting her a little more, I have a better view of her ass. Moving down further, I swirl my tongue around her tight hole. I continue to assault her ass, lubricating it. Letting go of one of her thighs so I can finger her and get her juices flowing again, I get her all nice and wet and use some of her juices for more lubrication on her ass.

Cassie moans at the sudden invasion as my finger enters her ass. I love her sounds in the throes of ecstasy. My cock wants to be inside her, but I hold off. I keep finger fucking her tight hole, adding another finger as I go. "One of these times you will be ready for my cock in your ass, and you are going to love it, Cassie!"

"Yes!" She whimpers.

Hearing her confirmation, I can't hold back anymore. "As much as I love watching your tits bounce while I'm fucking you, I need you on all fours for me Baby!"

"Untie me then."

"No need."

Leaving a big enough gap between her and the headboard, I'm able to flip her over and she squeals.

With her head on the pillow, I pull her ass up, spreading her legs wide, I plunge my fingers back into her hole adding the third one. I ram my cock into her wet pussy and grind inside of her. She is so fucking wet. I pull my fingers out of her ass and using my dick, soaked in her juices, I enter her ass with my tip.

Cassie tries to push back on it, but I hold her in place. "Slow down, baby, I don't want to hurt you."

"But I need to feel you in me. I'm dying over here!"

Chuckling, I pull out and slide back in another inch. I continue to do this until I'm buried to the hilt, all the while, she's killing me with her moaning and mewing sounds, "Your fucking ass is so unbelievably tight, Cassie!" I pull out and go to slide back in, but she pushes her own ass back on my cock, impaling herself. I slap her ass and she stops.

"Oh my God Jax, do that again!" she begs.

"So, my little sex kitten likes to be spanked, huh?"

"There is a lot that I like that you don't know about yet."

I begin to fuck her ass again, gradually increasing my speed until I'm slamming into her over and over again, spanking her every few thrusts. I feel my balls tighten up as they slap against her pussy, so I reach around and squeeze her clit, ripping her orgasm out of her at the same time I explode, pumping her ass full with my cum.

Both of us sated, I watch as I pull my cock out of her ass; a sight to behold. I reach up and untie her, rubbing the kinks out of her shoulders. Dropping a kiss on her still swollen lips, I stand up. "Wait right here baby, I'll be right back."

I return with a wet washcloth, and I clean her up. Throwing it on the floor when I'm done, I slip in bed beside her and snuggle her to my chest, "Was that to your liking?" I joke.

"Are you kidding? That was the best sex ever! Sorry, but I am kidnapping you and using you as my sex slave!"

"Like I said before, I'm not going anywhere, so use away."

Before long, we were both sound asleep.

CASSIE

I wake up alone in my bed. Looking at the clock, it is already 5:30 in the evening. I grind the sleep out of my eyes and crawl out of bed. I go straight for my bathroom and another shower, hoping I can get through this one without getting molested. Not that I didn't enjoy it. I smile to myself. I only met him a little over 24 hours ago and I already know he is going to be the death of me. 'Death by Continuous Sex with a Monster Cock'. Hey, there are way worse ways to die!

After drying off, I walk out to my room to grab some clothes. Jax is sitting on my bed watching me, "Hey gorgeous, a guy can get use to this kind of treatment! Seeing a hot chick walking around naked is a huge turn on!" He winks at me.

"And having you see me walking around naked all day is a huge turn on!" I plop myself on his lap totally naked.

He wraps me in his arms and kisses me. Not a chaste one either. I think he may have a wet spot on his jeans now. He sniffs me and then raises his brows, "Again already?"

"Hey, I can't help it when a guy mauls me while I'm sitting naked in his lap!" I laugh.

"Why don't you get dressed. I want to talk to you about something." He sets me on my feet and slaps my ass to get me moving.

Once I'm dressed, I sit in the rocker by my window while Jax is still sitting on my bed.

"So, is this where you tell me that this isn't working for you and that it's not me, it's you?" I ask him, being completely serious. That is how I took his tone when he said we needed to talk. I've been dumped a few times; I know how it works.

He chuckles, "Is that what you think? We have mind-blowing sex, and you think I want to dump you?"

"Well, you should never start a conversation with "I want to talk to you about something", because that's what it usually means."

Laughing now, "Actually no, I started it with "why don't you get dressed".

"Smartass! So, what's up, if you're not dumping me?"

He hesitates before going on, "I had Xavier search both Jill's car and your car for any tracking devices. Jill's car was clean, but yours wasn't. That's how Zayne has been tracking you."

"That fucking piece of shit! If you don't kill him, I will!"

"I'm afraid that's not all."

"There's more?"

He acts as if he really doesn't want to tell me, so it has to be bad, Fuck!

"I did a search of the house for any bugs and what not. Well, I got through all but one room before I was sidetracked. All those rooms were clean. The last one I checked while you were sleeping, I found something."

"Well, what did you find?"

"A hidden camera."

"What!? What room was it in?"

He remains silent as he stares at me, and I can see rage forming in his eyes and a tick in his jaw. I know right away what room it is.

My hand flies to my mouth as I become horrified, "It was in here, wasn't it?"

"Yes."

Rage that I have never felt before consumes me!

"I am so sorry Cassie."

"It's not your fault Jax, you're not the perv!"

"I know, but if I didn't let my dick get in the way, I would have finished searching your room earlier."

"Oh my God, you mean all that was on camera?"

"Yes, and I'm assuming this morning as well since he called me your lover in the note that he sent you."

"Is it something you can delete before he watches it?"

"I'm afraid not. That is all on his end."

I put my head in my hands, just wanting to crawl under a rock and die. I can't believe he saw me having sex, ugh! Well, there isn't anything to do about it now. At least maybe now he will see that I am happy with Jax, and he will leave me alone. Hey, it could happen! Yeah, and monkeys can fly out of my ass! I'm not going to let this get to me. I have complete faith that the Elite will catch him!

"Well, good; I hope he likes the show we put on! It will piss him off that you please me in ways that he never will! Maybe we should leave the camera up and keep going at it until he gets so pissed that he comes out in the open and we can kill the son of a bitch!"

"As much as I like your idea, it's not happening!" He pulls me up into his arms, "I'm not letting him or anybody else watch me make love to my woman anymore!" He smashes his mouth to mine and gives me one of his long passionate kisses.

Whoa, did he just say, "make love to his woman"? How do I take that? We barely know each other, but on the other hand, I'm kind of feeling the same way. Too bad Jax can't be the one that I'm destined to be mated to. Just my luck, I find a guy that I can be happy with and have a future with, but we are only on borrowed time, until my true mate shows his face.

TWELVE

CASSIE

It's been a whole two weeks since I met Jax and aside from the whole stalker issue, it's been the best couple of weeks of my life. Living with him wasn't as bad as I thought it would be living with a guy. Then again, Jax isn't your ordinary guy, at least not like any I have met. The attraction we have for each other is insane and the daily sex, usually two to three times a day, is out of this world! We fit together perfectly. Does it scare me? Hell yes, but I am determined to battle this fear, for a chance of happiness for once in my life.

Aside from work, I've pretty much adopted the hermit life. Not really having to go anywhere, because Jax will just send one of the Elites to run the errand needed. He isn't taking any unnecessary risks when it comes to keeping me safe. Zayne is still out there and even though there have been no incidents since Jax and Xavier found the tracking device on my car and the camera in my room, we know it is just a matter of time, like the calm before the storm.

My mother has been calling daily, begging me to come visit, but I keep putting her off. It's not that I don't want to see my parents, I'm just trying to protect them from Zayne. If he is still watching me, I don't want him using my mom or dad to get to me. Xavier and Duncan rotate shifts, continuing to protect Jill, and I am extremely grateful for that. I don't want to ask them to protect my parents as well.

My mother never texts, so when I receive one from her this morning, I know I'm in deep shit. Sure enough, she informs me that if I do not show up to their annual Beginning of Summer BBQ Bash this evening, both her and my dad will be at my doorstep first thing tomorrow morning. I can't have them coming here, not with all the Elites coming and going all day long. Hell, I haven't even told her about Jax, yet. I am surprised that they haven't come sooner, knowing how much of a worrier my mother is.

I might as well just get this over with. Grabbing my phone, I speed dial my mom. I'm about to hang up when she finally answers, all out of breath, "Hello, honey."

"Oh man, please don't say I called while you and dad were doing the nasty!" I enjoy fucking with my mom. Most people don't even want to think about their parents having sex, but it doesn't bother me. More power to them. I plan on having lots of sex well into old age!

"Don't be a smartass, Cassie."

"You made me who I am today, Mother." I laugh into the phone.

"Did you call for a reason or just to talk about my sex life?"

"Well, you did text me, so I thought I had better call and tell you to keep your panties on, I'll be there for your Bash."

"If a text is all it takes to get you to come visit, then I will start texting you instead of calling!"

"Whatever Mom! Don't be so dramatic. Also, put me down as a plus one."

"Oh honey, you know Jill doesn't count as a plus one, she is family."

"She isn't my plus one." I try leaving it at that, but you know mothers.

"Oh? So, who is it?"

"Mom, I don't have time to get into all that right now. You will meet him this evening. Oh, and Jill will have a plus one as well."

"Wow. I don't see you for weeks and all of a sudden you both have dates! No wonder I haven't seen you." She giggles into the phone.

"Goodbye, Mother!"

"See you tonight, I love you!"

"Love you too."

Leaving my bedroom, I run into just the man I am looking for. Sapphire eyes smile down at me as he places a tender kiss on my lips, his 5 o'clock shadow scratching me as he does so.

"There you are, I was about to send a search party for you." He taunts.

"I was on the phone with my mom. Thought I had better call her back before she shows up on my doorstep."

"Is everything okay?"

"Yeah, she's just being a mom."

"Well, that just goes to show that she loves you very much." He pulls me into his embrace.

Looking up at him, "I have a mission for you this evening, it could turn ugly."

"What is it?" He asks as he raises a brow.

"You are meeting my parents." Holding my breath, I worry that it may be too soon for him.

"Will I need back up?" he jokes.

I let out that breath and smile, "You will already have back up. Jill needs to bring a plus one as well."

"Well then, this should be fun. I don't' think Duncan has ever done the whole meeting the parents thing; it should be comical."

"And you have?" I ask quizzically.

"Not since I was a teenager." He laughs.

"Are you sure this isn't too soon for you?"

"How many times do I have to tell you that I'm not going anywhere? So, whether it's now or later, makes no difference."

"How did I get so lucky?"

"Luck has nothing to do with it, Baby! It is what's meant to be." His lips find mine.

I pull slightly away and slide my hands across his chest, "You know what else is meant to be?"

"Hmm?"

"You taking me into this room, bending me over, and pounding my vagina." Sliding a hand lower, I feel his arousal pulsating in my hand. Without another word, he shoves me into my room and slams the door behind him.

He pulls away from me, "Undress now!"

I do as he says and start with my shirt. I turn and throw it on the chair, but I don't turn back around. Instead, I unbutton my jean shorts and bend over as I pull them down slowly, like a stripper does when teasing her audience.

He growls and then he is behind me, taking hold of my thong and pulling it. I hear a tear and then it's gone, he does the same to my bra. The whole ripping my underwear makes me so hot! His fingers slide through my wetness and find my opening. While fingering me from behind, he walks me over to the foot of the bed and demands me to bend over; I oblige.

"Grab hold of the footboard and do not remove your hands until I say so!" His voice is tight and full of lust.

I put my arms out to the sides, gripping the board as I shiver with anticipation. Not all of our love making is like this, but it gets me so hot when he gets demanding in the bedroom.

He removes his hand, replacing it with his cock. Without showing any mercy, he shoves it in with one hard thrust and continues pounding me, never letting up. I feel the fire building with each hard thrust, and I whimper for my release. He brings his hand around and attacks my clit, rubbing and pinching it as he is slamming into me. My body explodes, and I scream. The pleasure is too much, but still, he never lets up. Grabbing my hair, he pulls my head back and smashes his mouth to mine, muffling my sounds.

I feel his own release as he rips his lips away from mine and roars. Grabbing my hips with both hands, he slams into me even harder, causing me to orgasm yet again. Finally, he starts to slow his thrusts until they stop completely. His body falls over mine and I feel his ragged breath against my neck.

"Holy fuck! What was that?" I ask him in amazement.

"I don't know what you do to me, woman, but you bring the animal out in me! Why? Why do you do and say things like that when you know what it does to me?"

"Because I love it when you take me like this."

He grunts.

Still hard with arousal, he starts to slide in and out of me, slowly. It feels so good, "Round two?"

"Technically, I never pulled out, so it's still the first round." He says as he reaches around and grabs my tits.

The doorbell chimes.

"Ugh! I thought you fixed that thing?" I'm so annoyed right now.

"Don't worry, it will be rectified in a few minutes." He says as he pulls out. He helps me stand up and places a kiss on my neck. "Get dressed, I'll get the door." I turn around and see that he never even undressed! Shaking my head, I spin and head to the bathroom to clean up.

JAX

I open the door to find Jill and Xavier standing there waiting, impatiently. Jill is standing with her arms crossed and her foot tapping on the cement, "It's about time, sheesh!"

"You have lousy timing. Do you know that?"

"Anytime is a lousy time with the two of you! At least you are dressed this time."

"Hey, when it's in the heat of the moment, you don't always have time to undress!"

Her cheeks turned bright red and know that my job is done for the day.

"TMI, Jax! Where is the little hussy anyway?"

"Probably cleaning up the mess I made, it was all over." I chuckle as the embarrassment once again appears on her face.

Xavier roars with laughter, slapping me on the back as he walks over to the couch, "That's my boy!"

Cassie is coming down the hall when she hears my cast comment to Jill. "You are horrible Jackson Michael Whitley! Don't taunt my bestie!" she slaps my ass as punishment, "Shouldn't you be fixing something anyway?"

"Oh yes, thanks for the reminder."

I walk over to the box on the wall that holds the doorbell chimer, reach up and rip it from the wall. Cassie and Jill are standing there with their mouths gaped open.

"What was that?" Xavier questions.

"Cassie asked me to fix the doorbell."

"It seemed to work when we used it."

"Exactly! Now it doesn't." I smile.

Cassie comes over to me and gives me a peck on the cheek, "Thanks, Babe!"

"Anything for you, Darlin," I smile down at her, "You can thank me properly later tonight!"

"It will be my pleasure."

"It definitely will!" I wiggle my brows at her.

"Oh, for the love of God, will you two stop already!" Jill is pretending to dry heave.

"Quit being a bitch and be happy that I'm having lots of sex! It means that I won't be molesting you anymore!" She laughs and then winks at Jill.

I shake my head and chuckle. Poor Xavier is over there looking between the two not knowing how to take Cassie's comment.

"Who wants a beer?" I ask as I'm heading to the fridge.

All three answer at once, "Me!"

Upon my return, Cassie asks Jill why she didn't use her key.

"I never got a key when He-Man over there put the new locks in."

"Oh shit, sorry about that!" I grab one of the spares from the drawer and hand it to her.

"So, what's up?" I ask Jill.

"I just figured I would come over here and get ready for the BBQ and then we can all go together."

"Sounds like a plan to me." Cassie replies.

"Duncan should be here anytime now, so I'll probably just take off, if that's okay with you?" Xavier directs his question at me.

"Fine by me, I'm here."

Xavier finishes off his beer and heads for the door. Opening it, there is Duncan, just standing there.

"What are you doing standing out here?" Xavier asks him.

"I rang the doorbell and was waiting for someone to answer."

All four of us burst out in a fit of laughter.

The four of us arrive at Cassie's parent's house at little before five. I thought it would be best if Duncan and I each brought our own vehicle, Cassie riding with me, of course, and Jill arriving with him. Not so much for security, but to make it look like Jill and Duncan are "together". Cassie didn't want to worry her parents and if they knew that Duncan was there for protection, they would have a shit load of questions and we want to keep them in the dark. So, Jill and Duncan are officially a couple, well, for tonight anyway. I am going to have fun with this! I am pretty sure they have the hots for one another, but neither one will admit to it.

Duncan and I both get out of our vehicles and go around to open the doors for the women, using this time to do a quick search of the area before helping them out. Cassie has made a fruit salad and Jill, a pasta salad to contribute to the BBQ.

Before reaching the front door, I turn towards Duncan and Jill, "Now remember, you two are a couple, so you have to act like a real couple."

"Meaning what?" Jill asks.

"Meaning," Cassie speaks up, "You need to hold hands, put your arms around each other, and even kiss every now and then."

"Hell, I was the star in most of our high school plays, Cassie! You know I will do a good job and if it means that I get to kiss a hot guy with a body built for a God, so be it, I'll take one for the team!" Jill turns and winks at Duncan.

He actually turns a little pink at her compliment, "What about you Dunc?" I glance his way.

"You know I never shirk on my duties. I've never been a star of a play, but I've kissed quite a few women without any complaints on their part. Kissing and molesting a fine piece of ass like her," nodding at Jill, "will be a walk in the park!" Duncan smiles over at Jill and winks back.

Cassie and I bust up laughing from the look on Jill's face. I bend down to whisper in Cassie's ear, "This ought to be good!" She nods her head in agreement and then opens the door to her parent's house.

CASSIE

I find my mom in the kitchen preparing the meat for my dad, who is outside getting the grill started. My parents started this Summer Bash the summer after my 9th grade year. She just thought that it would be something fun for us kids to do to kick off summer vacation.

Everybody would bring swimming suits to swim while the food was grilling. The party would go until at least midnight. As adults now, we drink and party until either people leave or pass out; my parents can party with the best of them!

"Hey Mom, need any help?"

Startled, my mother turns. "Oh Cassie, you guys decided to come!" She heads towards me for a hug.

"I told you this morning that we were coming over." I roll my eyes at Jax over her shoulder.

"I've been so busy; I don't know if I'm coming or going!"

"It's okay Mom. Let me introduce you to your guests."

"How rude of me, I am so sorry!" She reaches her hand out to Jax and then stops short; her eyes roam up to his eyes.

"Mom, this is Jax." Not sure if I should say what our relationship is, he finishes for me.

"Her boyfriend. It's a pleasure to meet you Mrs. Manson." Amusement lighting his eyes over her mother's gawking. How embarrassing!

"Boyfriend? You never told me you were dating anyone?" She looks at me.

"I don't tell you everything, you know."

"Well, you will have to tell me later. I want to know where you found this handsome man!" She smiles at Jax, and he chuckles.

"And this is Duncan, Mom, Jill's boyfriend."

"Oh goodness! Did both my girls go shopping at Handsome-R-Us or what?" She giggles at her own joke.

Duncan shakes mom's hand, "So nice to meet you Mrs. Manson. Thank you for having us."

"Stop with the Mrs. Manson. Please, call me Patricia, both of you." Looking between the men.

"Can you stop drooling over our boyfriends and give me a hug?" Jill chirps in.

"Sorry Jill. Didn't see you behind the giants! I see that my daughter's smartass remarks are wearing off on you." She gives Jill a hug as she grins.

We head out the French doors to go see my dad and to get the guys away from my mom's flirting. I am so happy that my parents like Jax and he seems to like them as well. Usually, my parents "tolerate" the guys that come through my life. To be honest, most of them turn out to be jerks anyway, but I will never tell my parents that they were right!

There are a lot more people than I expected here, and I have to weave in and out of the crowd to get to Jax and save him. No doubt my dad is boring him about fishing. I reach his side and sure enough, dad is asking him what kind of pole he liked to fish with.

"Sorry Dad, but I need to steal Jax for a moment." I grab him by the arm and pull him away. Finding a quiet area around the corner of the house, I push him against the wall and jump up in his arms, he just barely catches my legs.

"I've been dying to do this all night!" Smashing my mouth to his, I demand that he opens up, and he does.

"Mm..." is his response.

He spins us around, putting my back against the wall so he can tease me by grinding his arousal into my crotch.

I break the kiss, "You are such a fucking tease, Whitley!"

"What? You can attack me, but I can't defend myself by making you senseless?" He chuckles and pushes harder.

A moan escapes my lips just as a peel of laughter drifts over to us.

"We should probably get back to the party, Darlin."

"Do we have to?" I whine, "We can go home and make our own party!" I give him my seductive smile.

"I love the sound of that, but we should stay just a little longer at least." He pushes a strand of my hair back behind my ear and kisses my forehead before releasing me.

"Ugh, fine, but you owe me big time when we get home buddy!"

"It will be my pleasure!" Snatching my hand into his, he drags me back to the party.

As we turn the corner, there Duncan is, sitting in a lawn chair, with Jill in his lap. My mother starts walking their way and next thing I see is Jill slamming her mouth into Duncan's. I slap Jax's chest and point their way. He looks over and I see his eyes bulge! I look back over and from the looks of it, they are really enjoying swapping spit with each other. They are really good actors, because Duncan's arms slide around Jill's waist and pull her closer, as her arms go around his neck.

Jax and I step up behind the chair and clear our throats to get their attention, "My mother is gone; you can stop now." I chuckle.

They are slow at ending their kiss and then Jill looks up at us, "You said to make it believable."

"Yeah, well you both just earned yourselves some Oscars!"

"Told you I was good. My partner seems to be holding his own pretty well also."

"Given a little more time, I'd have you changing your panties!" Exclaims Duncan.

Shaking my head at them, "I'm going to run to the restroom," I turn to Jax, "I need to freshen up." He smiles at me knowing the exact reason.

On my way back outside, my mom stops me and asks me to run a garbage bag out to the curbside. I grab it and head out front. Just as I get to the sidewalk, I feel a tingling sensation on the back of my neck. Weird, I haven't felt that since….

One set of arms grab me, causing me to drop the garbage bag, as another shoves something into my mouth and then holds a cloth over my nose. I struggle, but I start to feel weak and woozy, just before everything goes black.

THIRTEEN

JAX

I go in search of Cassie to see if she is ready to head home. It has been a good half hour since she went to the restroom, but I know her mom is cleaning up inside, because she came back out and asked Jill if she could help "them" clean up a bit. I want to give Cassie some time with her mom, so I hold back for a bit. Then her father nabs me and decides to finish his fishing story, causing me to stay away longer than I want to be.

Finally, I'm able to get away, claiming I need to use the restroom and now here I am. I climb the stairs to the deck and head back through the French doors. Cassie's mom and Jill are preparing the dishes for the dishwasher when I walk in.

"Need any help ladies?" I ask, rubbing my hands together.

"That's so sweet of you," Patricia replies, "but we are just finishing up. Thank you for asking though. It is more than that daughter of mine did. She took the trash out for me and then went and hid!" She laughs and shakes her head.

"You mean Cassie isn't in here with you two?"

"I haven't seen her. I assumed the two of you went somewhere for a quickie." Jill teases. Turning to Patricia, "They do that a lot."

"Oh, to be young again!" Patricia reminisces.

"Jill, Duncan needs you for a second." I lie.

She looks at me and with Patricia's head turned the other way, I widen my eyes and nod my head, indicating to go outside.

She nods back and turns to Patricia, "Are you okay if I go see what Duncan needs? I can come right back."

"Oh, no honey, we are all done. Thank you so much for all of your help."

"Of course, and thank you for another fun Summer Bash!"

"I do put on the best, don't I?"

"You sure do, Ma!" Jill smiles at her and then follows me out the door.

We find Duncan still sitting in the lawn chair from earlier. I am really hoping to find Cassie here with him, but there is still no sign of her. Fear like no other races through me.

He sees us approaching and stands up, "What wrong?" He asks, becoming alert.

"Have you seen Cassie in the last half hour?"

"Last I saw her was when she was with you and then she left for the restroom. Why?"

"I assumed she was inside helping clean up, but she isn't. Patricia sent her to take the garbage out, but she never came back inside."

"Where did she take the garbage to?" Duncan asks.

Jill speaks up, "Patricia told her to take it to the curb."

"He has her!" I say.

"Have you tried calling her?" Jill asks me.

I can't answer her; I can't move. I can barely understand what is being said, the noise around me fades out. I have failed her! I need to do something, anything! We need to find her fast, before that sick fuck does something to her!

Duncan shakes me and pulls me out of my horrified coma, "Snap out of it Jax, Cassie needs you now!" He whispers loudly.

"Her phone keeps going to voicemail!" Jill reports, starting to sound a little hysterical.

Duncan is already on the phone to headquarters, "Tell Taven that we need every abled body searching for her!" I command Duncan and he nods in response.

"Jill, I need you to tell Cassie's parents that we headed out because she had too much to drink and then excuse you and Duncan as well. Whatever you do, do not leave the house without him at your side!"

All she can do is nod her head yes, tears filling her eyes. I grab her shoulders and make her look at me.

"We will find her. You and I are not going to lose her, okay?"

Again, she shakes her head yes.

I turn to Duncan as he ends his call to Taven, "Taven is calling everybody back in and wants us to head over to the Compound A.S.A.P."

"Good! I'm going to search out front to see if I can find anything that may help us. Take Jill back to the Compound with you. I don't want her alone at any time."

"Will do; I won't leave her side."

I walk around the side of the house to get to the front, so nobody is able to stop me for a chit chat and I find where Cassie had dropped the bag of garbage. It is laying on the sidewalk instead of at the curb. I'm searching the ground for anything that could help when I spot something in the road at the end of the driveway. I go and pick it up and see that it is a piece of cloth or rag of some sort. My vampire senses pick up the smell of chloroform!

"FUCK!"

I see a woman coming out of her house to walk her dog from across the street and I walk over to her, "Excuse me, ma'am?"

"What do you want? Don't come any closer!"

"I am not going to hurt you ma'am. I just wanted to ask you a question."

"Well, stay right where you are and ask; no need to come near me to ask."

"Did you happen to see anybody out here about a half hour ago?"

"I saw a few drunks messing around and then they helped one into a van. Why do you ask?"

"I am just looking for my friend that I came with. Thank you for your time, ma'am."

As I go to leave, the woman shrieks. I spin back around and see that her dog got loose. I give chase and catch up to it snatching up its leash. I hand the leash back to its owner and she lays her hand on my arm, thanking me for bringing her dog back. While she is touching me, I peer into her memory, not because I think she is lying, but because there is always something someone forgets.

I see Cassie walking to the curb with the garbage, then two figures appear, one grabbing her from behind, the other gagging her and holding the cloth to her mouth. Cassie struggles for a few seconds and then goes limp. A black cargo van pulls up and they lift her into it. Both men look to be vamps, but I can't be sure. I get the plate number and see that it's a Maine plate. Well, that limits the possibilities, not!

I thank the woman again for all her help and then walk back across the street to my truck. I phone Kole right away.

"What do you have for me?" he asks.

"I have a Maine plate number for you," I reply and rattle off the number to him. "It's on a black cargo van. I am on my way in now, see you in a bit."

"10-4, I'll have it ready for you when you get here."

I slam my hands down on the steering wheel and roar as I am shake like a leaf. I screwed up big time and now the woman that I love, my mate, is paying for it! Wait, love? I guess I haven't really put my feelings into word, but yes, I love her! Not because we are destined mates, but for who she is. I need to get her back. I have so much to say to her, to tell her.

CASSIE

I try to open my eyes, but my head is pounding, UGH, such a headache! I try to move, but I can't. My arms are stretched above my head and my legs are wide apart, like a spread eagle. My mouth is so dry, but it's hard to swallow because something is holding it open. I try to remember where I'm at. It feels like I'm on a bed, but I can't be sure. Did Jax and I go home and get kinky? I can't think straight. I hear footsteps and I pry my eyes open to darkness. A door opens and a figure of a man stands in the doorway for a moment and then he flips the switch, and the room is illuminated. I stare in horror as a pair of green eyes gaze back at me.

Zayne starts towards me smiling, "My beloved Cassie, at last we are together!" The bed dips as he sits beside me.

"I am sorry for what I had to do to get you here, but I had no choice. That vamp wouldn't let me get anywhere near you, so I had to come up with another plan. It took a little while for it to be just right, but now you are here with me and he will never come near you again!"

Man, this fuck face is crazier than I thought! I can't even comprehend the shit that he is spewing. I feel nauseated. I try talking, but the gag won't let me.

"If I take the gag off, do you promise not to scream? I mean, you can scream all you want, and nobody will hear you, but the noise just really hurts my sensitive hearing." He explains.

I nod my head yes.

He reaches around to the back of my head and unties the gag. Relief is but momentary because the nausea comes back full force.

"I-I'm g-going t-to v-vomit." I stutter. My mouth is so dry, it's hard to form words.

Zayne leaves my line of vision momentarily and then comes back carrying a bowl. He sits back in the same spot and holds the bowl up under my chin.

"There, there. It's going to be okay; chloroform tends to do this to a person." He informs me as if I am a child.

My stomach empties into the bowl. God this is embarrassing!

Once I'm done, he washes my mouth with a wet cloth and then bring a glass with a straw to my lips. Water. I suck down as much as I can before he takes it away.

"Careful," he warns me, "If you drink too much of it too fast, you will make yourself sick again."

"Why am I here? What do you want from me?" I can't help the crack in my voice.

"I already told you that you belong to me. We are destined mates."

"I belong to no one, least of all you! We are not mates!"

"Think what you will. After all you are just merely a human; you will see in time."

"Destined mates have a strong attraction to one another. I have absolutely none towards you!"

"Ah, I see your lover has taught you a little about our kind. Too bad he couldn't follow the rules and leave another's mate alone!"

"You don't get to talk about Jax that way! He is more of a man than you will ever be!"

"Are you going to tell me that you felt nothing for me that first day you saw me outside of your workplace?"

"Pfft, just because I thought you were a good-looking guy THEN, doesn't mean I felt anything for you. Now that I know you, even your good looks have vanished! You are nothing but a vile creature that has a bunch of screws loose!"

"Ah, Cassie," he tries to caress my cheek, but I yank my head back, "Such fire running through your veins. My fangs ache, I need a taste."

"Fuck you, jackass! You are not coming anywhere near me or my veins!"

"Shh, I will have your blood and I will have it now."

He straddles me, so I can't move. It's like he weighs a ton. I hold my head back as far as I can, but his strength is no match for me. He tightens his hold around my head and turns it to the side. I feel him lick my neck and I start to scream, only it doesn't faze him. I feel a sharp pinch as his fangs sink through my skin and into my jugular. I feel a pulling sensation as he draws my blood into his mouth and moans.

I feel like I'm going to be sick again. My neck is on fire, and it burns more with each pull. I can't help but scream and beg for him to stop. He ignores my pleas and tears burst from my eyes. I can't take the pain anymore and I pass out.

Waking up is a little easier this time; my head doesn't hurt, but my neck burns like son of a bitch! I look around, thinking that I am alone, but no such luck. Zayne is sitting in the corner reading a book. He looks up and sees that I am awake.

"You're awake, good, you need to eat something. I didn't take much, but it will still help with your strength."

I glare daggers at him, "I don't want any of your food or anything else for that matter!"

"You're just upset, and I understand. You feel as if I have hurt you, and in a sense, I did. Not on purpose, mind you. Once you stop fighting it, fighting me, and start accepting me as your mate, my bite will only give you sheer pleasure!"

"For the last time, I am NOT your fucking mate!"

"Why? Because your lover says that you are his mate?"

"What the hell are you talking about?"

"Don't play dumb with me, Cassie. Your lover, Jax is it? He has you believing that you are his destined mate just so he can have his way with you! I've seen the way you respond to him; how sexual you are with him! Do you think I liked watching him fuck my mate, not only in your pussy, but your ass as well?"

Zayne is really starting to scare me, so much that I'm trembling. I have to try and figure out a way to get away from him, but I don't know how, not being all tied up. "Could you please untie me, Zayne? I promise I won't try anything."

He glances at the ropes that are restraining me and his eyes light up. "Ah, I see now. I saw it on the video, you love being tied up and dominated in the bedroom. Why didn't you say so? I love role playing!"

He comes over to the bed and kneels between my spread legs.

"What are you doing?" My fear, rising.

"I'm going to give you what you like."

"No, don't you dare touch me!"

He ignores me and starts to run his hands up my legs. Struggling does me little good, but I'm not giving up without a fight. Oh, my God, I think to myself, I can't be awake for this, for what he is about to do.

His hands stop about an inch from my crotch, and then he changes tactics. His hands are now fondling my breasts and no matter how much I squirm, I can't shake them off. In fact, it only makes him squeeze them tighter. I can't fight anymore, so I just lay here, staring up at the ceiling, waiting for it to be over. I try tuning out everything, but I can still feel his vile touch.

Instead of just lifting my shirt, he tears it right down the center, but he leaves my bra intact. I feel his disgusting tongue licking at the globes above my bra and then it travels down my stomach. I hear a ripping sound and feel air where my jeans once were. Tears roll down my face and I squeeze my eyes shut for the next part of the assault.

His tongue drags over my underwear at the crotch. He stops and I hear him sniff a few times. He startles me as he jumps up and roars. My eyes shoot open and land on him. He is now off the bed, but still standing too close for my comfort. His hands are fisted and he is seething mad. I don't dare say a word. I am just glad that he stopped when he did, for whatever reason.

He looks at me with disgust, "Did you think you could hide it from me? Think that I would let you keep it and raise it as my own?"

"W-What are you talking about?" I'm way past confused.

"What am I talking about? I'm talking about that bastard kid of his that you are carrying, that's what I'm fucking talking about!"

Shocked by what he just said, I look down at my stomach. I'm carrying Jax's baby? "I'm pregnant?" Shit! I never thought to use a condom once during sex, since I'm on birth control.

"Yes, you are pregnant! I don't know how it is possible though."

"I hate to break it to you, but it happens when you have unprotected sex, LOTS of unprotected sex." I just needed to rub it in, piss him off. I don't care at this moment. I'm having Jax's baby!

"Don't be so smug! I'm talking about him getting you pregnant. The only way you're able to get pregnant from a vampire is if you are mates."

"Well, thank fuck, a vampire didn't get me pregnant then, Ass wipe!"

Staring at Zayne, he looks a little startled. He then begins to smile, creeping me the fuck out.

"He never told you."

"Told me what?"

He begins to laugh hysterically, "Oh, this is too much!" He states as he is wiping tears from his eyes.

"You are bat shit crazy Zayne; you know that? I'm so tired of these little games already, just let me go!"

"Oh, dear Cassie, I will never let you go. You may be ruined for me now, but I will never let him have you again. As for the bastard, I will take care of it once and for all after it's born! I will not have any reminder of another vampire planting his seed in what was mine! Yes, Cassie. Your lover is a vampire!"

I suck in my breath, "No." He can't be. "That is a lie!"

"Yes, he is. Along with the rest of the Elite."

I can't help but think that what he says is true. I need time to myself to think.

"Can you please untie me Zayne. My arms and legs are sore, and I really need to use the restroom. I swear to you that I'm not going to try anything." I plead with him, and I don't know if he sees the resignation that comes over me or what it is, but he nods. For a moment, I think I see sympathy in his eyes. He reaches down and unties my legs and then my arms. He even goes a step further and rubs my shoulders for a moment. Helping me to stand up, he points me in the direction of the bathroom.

"I need to go and see about something, but I'll be back," I nod at him, "And Cassie, don't try anything or else I will have no choice then to tie you back up." He turns and walks out the door, deadbolting it behind him.

I look at myself in the mirror. I don't even recognize this shell of a woman staring back at me. I pull back the bandage that Zayne must have placed when I passed out and see two puncture holes that are scabbed over now, so I pull it all the way off and throw it in the trash can. I look at myself again. Dark circles ring my eyes, my skin looks paler then normal, my hair is one big rat's nest and I'm pregnant with a vampire's child. Can my day get any worse?

My only other thought is why he didn't Jax tell me this himself? Did he think I would end it? Him and the rest of the Elite has shown me nothing but kindness, unlike Zayne and his cronies. Why couldn't he trust in my love for him?

Whoa, what? Do I really love him? Yes, I do. I am 100% sure of it! Zayne is just trying to get your feelings for Jax to change, I say to myself. It's not going to work; I love him too much and I tasted the happiness that I know I can only have with him. I believe that Jax loves me as I do him, and I'm going to trust in that love. So, if he is a vampire, I'm also going to trust that he has a good reason for not telling me yet. We are having a baby, a baby who will have the love from both its parents. I just hope that the Elite find me soon. I have never been so scared in my life as I am being here with Zayne!

FOURTEEN

JAX

Kole is pacing back and forth, impatiently waiting for me, when I get to the Compound. "I got what you asked for Jax," shoving a sheet of paper in my hands, "This was the easiest search I have ever had to do. Those dumb shits didn't cover their asses like they should have."

I examine the results, "Elliot's Moving Service? Do you mean to tell me that he used one of his own company vans and did nothing to hide it? Either he is way dumber than we thought, or he is planning a trap for us."

"My thoughts exactly!"

"Can you compile a list of all employees that work for him?"

"Already done." He hands me another sheet of paper.

Looking at the information, I see that not only does he have the names, but also, the head shots of each employee and the addresses as well.

"Thanks, great job! I owe you one bro!"

"No thanks needed. No one messes with one of ours!"

Hearing him say this makes me love my Elite brothers even more. Knowing that, as my mate, Cassie is considered one of us, and will be protected always. Once we get her back that is, and we will get her back!

"Have everyone meet in the conference room in 5." I command and go in search of Taven.

I find Taven leaving his private rooms and stop him. "Hey Tav, here is what Kole found on the plate number I gave him." I hand him the report.

Taven's eyes bulge and he scans the paper. "Are you serious? We are dealing with a bunch of dumb fucks!" He says incredulously.

"Looks like it, but it doesn't mean this is going to be easy. Kole and I think it may be a trap."

Shaking his head, "You may be right." Taven agrees.

"Kole is gathering everyone into the conference room as we speak, so we should head there ourselves.

Before I can turn to leave, Taven brings me in for a man hug. "Sorry, this is happening to you buddy. You know we will get her and bring her home, right?"

I can't help but to tear up at his words. I don't understand the emotions that I keep having since meeting Cassie. I shake my head and hug him back.

Everyone is already in the conference room when we arrive, Jill included. Kai, the youngest of the Elite, but not the newest, squeezes my shoulder as I pass. "Let's get your woman home, shall we?"

Being the youngest Elite, Kai is also the most immature of us all. His shenanigans irritate all of us, but we love him just the same and although he acts like a child, he is the deadliest of the Elite. I think he believes that he needs to prove himself, because he is the youngest, so he works the hardest.

I nod at him and then head to the front of the room to stand beside Taven. I notice that Duncan is sitting beside Jill, his arm stretched behind her, resting on the back of her chair. He really meant what he said when he told me that he wouldn't leave her side, unlike myself apparently.

I begin, "I am sure Kole has filled you all in on what this mission is. I can't thank each of you enough for all of your help in bringing Cassie home." I look over at Jill, knowing that what I am about to say next is going to shock her. "Cassie is my destined mate, the woman that I love more than life itself and I will not stop until she is back home with me, with us, where she belongs!"

Jill is shocked alright! Her hand covers her opened-mouth expression as she stares at me. She turns and looks at Duncan and then to everyone else in the room, landing back on me. "You are all vampires!"

I nod in response.

"Does Cassie know?"

"No, I haven't told her yet. I wanted her to see our character first and know that she could trust us with her life and that we do care about protecting the innocent. I had hoped that when I did reveal what we were, that it wouldn't matter to her. That she would still except me."

Jill shakes her head back and forth. "Man, she is going to kick your ass for lying to her! She can't stand liars!"

I sigh, "I didn't lie to her Jill, I just hadn't told her yet and if she would have come right out and asked me if I were a vampire, I would not have lied to her."

"Hey, just saying, good luck telling her!" she chuckles. I notice how she moves slightly away from Duncan and apparently, he does too, by the crinkle in his brow.

I turn back to the business at hand, "Kole has handed out the information that we have learned so far. I am hoping that since they did a piss poor job of covering up the get-away vehicle, that we will find Cassie at Elliot's business location. I am aware that this may be a trap, so I need you all to keep your eyes open and take caution!"

Kai speaks up, "Same protocol as usual, I'm assuming?"

"Yes, take out all threats! I believe that all of his employees are vamps and you can expect them all to be working as guards as well. I only ask one thing… leave Zayne to me!"

We go on to discuss the layout and everyone's positions before we adjourn the meeting and leave to suit up.

'I am coming for you, Love!'

CASSIE

I haven't been locked up in this room for more than a few hours, but it seems like it's been days. With me passing out from pain or just from exhaustion, I haven't been able to keep track of time. Zayne must have taken my phone because I can't find it anywhere. The abuse that I have received in what little time I have been here, will give me nightmares for a while, if not for life! If Jax doesn't find me soon, I will have no other choice then to try and find a way to end this nightmare. I have never been one to think about offing myself, but to be violated by a disgusting psycho over and over, I can't endure it.

The bolt on the door scrapes and in walks Zayne carrying a tray with food. It smells delicious, but at the same time, it turns my stomach. He walks over and sets it down on the table beside the bed.

"I thought you may be hungry." He says to me.

"I don't want your food, though it would be nice to have some new clothes to wear since you ruined mine."

"Oh, but I like you this way much better! Be happy that I left your bra and underwear intact. Next time I may not be so generous."

Next time? Dear God, no, not again! I take a step back and bump into the wall as he strolls over to me. He reaches up and caresses my cheek.

"By the look on your face I can tell that the thought of me touching you, feeling me against you, disgusts you." He grinds his arousal against me, "Do you realize that I can have anybody that I want? I am handsome, funny, and I can please a woman so much that she will keep coming back for more, but it's you that I want, and it's you that I will have."

"Why do you want somebody that will never want you?"

"Because Cassie dear, in time, you will want nobody else but me! Once I take care of your vampire lover and his brat once it's born, it will only be you and I."

"But you said yourself that I could only get pregnant by my mate, so you must see that I am not your destined mate like you thought!"

"I am past the whole mate thing; it no longer matters to me. Watching you on that video, seeing your unleashed passion, stirred a fire in me that I can't put out until I have you!" His one hand holds me at my neck, while the other roams down and molests my boob.

A sob slips past my lips as I close my eyes.

"That's it, just let go, give yourself to me." He says.

I think he thinks it is a sob of pleasure, because he brings his hand lower and slips it into my panties. I jump as his fingers touch my clit, but there is nowhere to go, I'm trapped. I start pounding at his chest with my fists, but he catches them and holds them above my head with one hand and resumes his fondling.

"I want another taste of you, Cassie," he says close to my ear, "Don't fight me, it only makes it worse."

"Please don't, it hurts too much!"

"Then don't fight me." With those words, I feel the slicing pain as he sinks his fangs into me again, moaning in pleasure and rubbing himself against me.

He pulls his hand out of my underwear and undoes his pants, his shaft springing out, hard with arousal. His fingers move my underwear to the side, and I feel him at my entrance. I freeze. Just as he is about to thrust into me, loud sirens start going off.

Zayne stills for a second, then tucking himself back into his pants, he continues drinking my blood. He is taking way more than last time, and I start feeling woozy. I hear a loud crash and feel Zayne pull away from me. Slumping to the floor, there is yelling and swearing, then it goes quiet except for footsteps fast approaching where I lay. I feel arms lifting me and my name coming from a familiar voice. I struggle to open my eyes. My vision blurs, but I can make out eyes the color of sapphires.

"Jax, you are here," I whisper, "You came for me and the baby…"

JAX

When we arrive at the location, all seems quiet. Kole is able to disarm most of the alarms from his computer, but there are a couple that he can't override. It's enough to get us into the building and sneak up on the unsuspecting vamps. As soon as they spot us, all chaos breaks loose. The Elite, armed with their usual arsenal of swords and knives, start slicing through the group of vamps, body parts flying everywhere. I search the room, but Zayne is nowhere to be found. He must be with Cassie, which makes my gut wrench.

I holler for Kai to come with me just as his sword slices downward, taking the head from one of Zayne's men. It comes rolling to a stop at my feet. I kick it away and run from the room in search of Cassie. Finding most of the rooms empty, Kai yells over his shoulder at me, "Jax, over here! There is a door at the bottom of these stairs."

Instead of taking the stairs, I jump, landing at the bottom. I must have tripped an alarm because loud sirens are now going off. There is a metal door with a bolted lock, but the lock isn't in place. I try the knob, but that lock is. I take a step back and kick the door in with my foot, taking in the horrific scene before me.

There is Zayne, his back to me, pinning Cassie to the wall and holding her arms above her head, his fangs lodged into her jugular. She is in nothing but her bra and underwear. She looks dazed as he continues to take blood from her. I move fast, and as he retracts his fangs; I grab him by his neck pulling him away from her. "You disgusting piece of shit! Stay the fuck away from her!"

I send an uppercut to his chin and send him flying across the room. Kai catches him and automatically breaks Zayne's neck, subduing him for the time being.

"Cassie!"

I drop to my knees and pull her into my arms. I can't help the tears that flow down my cheeks.

Her eyes strain to open, but finally she gazes at me and whispers, "Jax, you are here, you came for me and the baby..." and then she passes out.

I pull her into a tight hug, "I'll always come for you, Baby, I love you!"

Picking her up into my arms, I hurry over and lay her on the bed, to examine her. I see the ropes at all four corner posts and then her shredded clothing thrown on the floor a little way from the bed. Swallowing the fury that rises up, I turn my attention back to Cassie. She looks too pale, and I turn her head to assess the damage to her neck from his bite, make that bites. That bastard drank from her twice! Did he not realize that after the first bite, she was not his mate? She would have been screaming in agonizing pain! "I will definitely enjoy killing that sick fuck!" I quickly check for any other marks on her body, but all is clear, aside from the bruising the ropes gave her. God, what did she have to endure?

I check her pulse, it's there. It could be better, but that tells me that he didn't take enough to turn her, thank God! I take my own wrist and bite down, so my blood could flow. I bring Cassie's head up and put my wrist to her lips, urging her to drink. My blood will help her heal faster. After a moment, she grabs my arm, holding it herself and starts to suck harder. What the fuck? I've never had this happen. I've helped a few people, in need, out, but all they needed was a few drops of my blood.

I don't mind Cassie was taking what she needed, I'll always give her what she needs, but damn, my dick is so fucking hard right now! "Hey love, take it easy."

That being said, she slowly starts to pull away. When she looks up at me, she smiles and then bursts into tears.

"Shh, I've got you now. He won't hurt you ever again Baby." I softly whisper.

"How long have I been here?" she asks between sobs.

"Not quite 24 hours. I am so sorry that I couldn't get to you sooner!"

"It seemed like days! The things he did..." She breaks off.

My stomach drops at her words. What did he do to her? I want to ask, but now is not the time.

"I will never forgive myself for allowing him to get to you! I won't blame you if you never forgive me either."

"Oh Jax, I don't blame you! I was the careless one that left the house without protection, it's my fault!"

"Let's talk about this later, I want to get you out of this place."

"Yes, please take me home!"

"I will, Baby, I will. Here," taking off my shirt so she could cover herself, "lets cover you up." I help her slide it over her head.

Cradling her in my arms, I carry her over to Kai who is standing watch over Zayne's unconscious form.

"Cassie, this is Kai, one of my Elite brothers. I am going to have you go with him while I take care of something."

"No, please don't leave me!" She pleads.

"Baby, I don't want you to see what I'm about to do, so at least wait right outside for me, okay?"

She hesitates, but then nods her head. I hand her over to Kai and he heads for the door. "Take her to the top of the stairs and wait for me there." I command. He nods and then walks out, with the love of my life safely in his arms.

FIFTEEN

JAX

I don't have much time to prepare him the way I originally wanted to, but I think I will inflict more pain this way. I almost just killed him outright, before he ever woke up, but that would be going too easy on him. Just looking at him turns my stomach, and to think that Cassie was here, alone with him, for almost a full day, makes my rage spike to unknown levels.

He is starting to wake up; it's show time!

Zayne moans as he opens his eyes and stares up at the ceiling. Instantly, they snap to the restraints that I placed around his wrists and ankles, just like he had done to Cassie, only mine are reinforced to hold a vampire. He jerks at them trying to free himself.

"You are wasting your time." I step into his line of vision.

"Ah, lover boy is wanting revenge, is that it?" He lets out a deranged laugh.

"You thought you had gotten away with it didn't you? Did you think I wouldn't come after her? She is MY destined mate; I'd walk through the fires of hell just to get to her!"

He blows out a sigh, "Yes, I admit now that I had it wrong, but then once I tasted her, I knew I had to keep her! Mm, her blood is like silk chocolate. Made my dick hard at the first drop, but her pussy is to die for!"

"You sick son of a bitch!" I punch him across his jaw, making his head whip to the side and the fucker laughs.

"Now Jax, why so violent?"

"You dare touch what is mine and ask me why I'm violent? You are seriously sick in the head!"

"Maybe, but it was all worth it!"

"Is this worth it?" I use my claws, shredding his clothes from his chest to his thighs, skin, and all.

He howls in pain, but it turns into laughter. He is now tied, spread eagle, without a stitch of clothing on and soaked in blood. He will heal quickly, but I am not done.

"What about when you took her blood, and she screamed in agony? Did she pass out?"

"Oh, she screamed alright, and as a matter of fact, she did pass out. I was tempted to take her then, but what kind of gentleman would I be if I fucked an unconscious woman, huh?" He chuckles.

My claws draw blood as I fist them tightly at my side. He is just antagonizing you, Jax. Don't let him get to you like this.

I grab him by his hair and yank his head to the side, "Do you want to know what she felt? It probably felt a little something like this!" I sink my fangs deep into his jugular and he screams like a baby. Instead of just retracting them, I ripped my fangs out of his neck, taking a chunk of flesh with them and spit it out in his face.

He looks a little scared now, but it doesn't stop him from keeping his mouth closed.

"I really wish now that I had fucked her crazy the first time I fed from her, since you so rudely interrupted us by crashing down my door for my second feeding! I was right there, my tip against her waiting pussy. Maybe I shouldn't have fingered her for so long and just took what I wanted. Here, come see, you can probably still smell her on my finger!"

I grab my blade and slice it through his shaft, "That is for Cassie, you sick mother fucker!"

"ARGH!!!!!!!!! I should have killed your bastard when I had the chance!"

"And this is from me!" I pull my sword out of its sheath on my back and bring it down, severing his head from his body.

I drop to my knees, relieved that it is finally over. He will never again harm a hair on Cassie's head. As I stand up, it hits me, the words he said right before I ended him. Why did he call Cassie a bastard? Ugh, why am I even trying to figure out the word of a psychotic loon?

I go into the bathroom and wash the blood from my hands, face, and chest. I don't want Cassie seeing me like this, not when I am planning on telling her what I am. I walk back through the room and without even looking back, I race up the stairs.

Cassie is waiting for me at the top and runs to me, flinging herself into my arms. I hold her tightly and swing her legs up into my arms, so I can cradle her against my chest.

"You don't have to carry me; I can walk you know."

"Just humor me okay, Darlin!" Dipping my head, I take her lips with mine. She starts to respond, but I pull away, "Not just yet. I want to get you out of here first."

I turn to Kai and thank him for staying with Cassie.

"No thanks needed Jax, you know that. I'm going to go downstairs and take care of business; make sure everyone is out."

"Will do."

"What's he going to do?" Cassie asks as she looks over my shoulder.

"We don't need anyone finding the bodies, so we are burning the building."

"Oh." Her eyes are wide, "So, are they all dead?"

"Everybody that was in this building when we attacked is dead, yes."

I gave orders to Jayde, one of the other Elites, to make sure everybody was out of the building and to not leave until it was fully engulfed. I place Cassie into my truck and go around to the driver's side. Climbing in, I pull Cassie to my side, not letting her go as I start the engine. I sit here for a moment with my thoughts.

"What is it?" Cassie asks placing her hand on my thigh.

"I thought I lost you. I was so scared of what he was going to do to you. I was determined to get you back, but I feared that I would never hold you in my arms again. I don't know when it happened, but I have fallen madly in love with you Cassie!"

Her breath hitches and I see tears glittering her beautiful aqua eyes. She brings her lips to mine for a soft kiss and then pulls slightly back.

"I love you too, Jax! There is more that I would like to talk about, but I just want to get out of here first." Turning towards her prison, I nod my head.

Pulling up to the Compound, I glance at her, "It's late, do you mind if we stay here tonight and then head back to your place tomorrow?"

"I don't mind; I can actually use a shower A.S.A.P."

"By the way, Jill is here, and she is most likely going to maul you over as soon as you walk in the door." I chuckle and go to open my door, but she grabs my hand and I look at her.

"I want to talk to you quick before we head inside."

"Okay, everything alright? Are you in any pain?" I ask, shutting my door again.

"No, but I learned something while I was being held. Actually, I learned two things, but one is more important than the other."

"Sounds serious, what is it, Baby?"

"First, I want you to know that Zayne didn't rape me. Well, he didn't have intercourse with me that is. That isn't saying that other things weren't done, though, but I can't talk about that right now. I just want you to know that he didn't have a chance to do it."

"Thank fuck!" I kiss her forehead and then press it against mine, giving us both a moment. "Are you ready?"

"Not quite. There is more." She looks at me.

"The first time that he drank from me, he was going to, you know, have sex with me." She swallow and then continues, "I still had my underwear on, thank God, but he licked me... over my panties.

Something made him stop, though, he became enraged, and his molesting seized."

"What enraged him?"

Cassie is still holding my hand when she brings it up to the flat of her stomach and holds it there. I stare at our hands a moment, confused. Then his words come flooding back to me and it all makes sense. My eyes feel like they are going to pop out of my head!

"A baby? Are you sure?" Excitement makes my voice crack.

"I think so! I kept getting nauseous while I was down there and even vomited once. I mean, why would he say it if it weren't true?"

"He wouldn't have."

Excited about the news, I'm not thinking straight, not realizing that what I am about to do will give away what I am. "Here sit back a moment."

She follows my instruction and I lean over to place my ear to her belly. My nose is also close to her crotch and I smell it at the same time I hear a faint heartbeat. I jump up, smacking my head on the roof of the truck, "Ouch!" I laugh, but then I look at her and smile with sheer joy.

She smiles back, then it fades, but just a little, "You are one, aren't you?"

My smile fades completely and I just look into her eyes. She knows, he must have told her. I nod my head and wait for her wrath, but it doesn't come. She lifts her hand to my cheek and rubs my 5 o'clock shadow.

"As much as I'm upset and hurt that you weren't completely honest with me, I love you so much, I don't care what you are! As long as you love me and our baby, that is all the matters."

I let out the breath I've been holding in, "I would gladly give my life for you and our baby; I love you so much that it hurts! I am sorry that I didn't tell you everything, but I wanted you to see me for who I was as a person first, so when I did tell you, it wouldn't freak you out and you leave me."

"I understand, I truly do. Now, about that shower?"

I smile at her and give her a quick kiss before jumping out of the truck and helping her out.

"Are you ready for Jill?"

"Actually, yes. I could use a bear hug from my bestie." She giggles.

I grab her hand and walk her into the Compound.

CASSIE

I'm just stepping through the door as a body smashes into me. Jill throws her arms around me and bursts into tears. Wrapping my own around her, I hug her to me as well.

"Miss me much?"

"How can you be a smartass at a time like this?"

"I'm okay Jill, really!" I rub her back to calm her down.

She pulls away from me and looks me up and down to make sure I am really okay.

"Why are you wearing Jax's shirt?" she asks as she finally notices that he is shirtless.

"Oh, you know me; I was flashing someone on the highway and my shirt flew out of my hands. Jax was nice enough to lend me his." I chuckle.

Rolling her eyes towards Jax, "This has to be your fault. You would do anything to walk around half dressed!" We all laugh at her comment, but then she stops, "I expect the truth once you get some rest." She hugs me again and I let Jax lead me to our room.

Instead of showering, I decide a soak in the jacuzzi tub would be so much better. Jax fills it up for me and as I'm heading towards the bathroom, he is coming out.

"Aren't you going to join me?"

"As much as I would love that, I want to give you your space."

I wrap my arms around his waist and look up at him, "I need you in my space right now more than anything. I need your arms around me, and I NEED you to wash my back!" I wink at him and turn, walking into the bathroom and stripping at the same time.

I hear a growl right before I am lifted up off the floor, and I shriek. After undressing, Jax steps into the big tub and sets me down between his legs. I lean back against him, sighing. I lay here, enjoying the quiet, while Jax washes me in slow, smoothing strokes. He runs his hands over my belly and keeps them there.

"I know we have only known each other for a couple of weeks and it's way too soon to be having a baby, but I couldn't be happier!"

"I feel the same way, Cassie. Maybe it's because we are destined to be together, but it doesn't matter, because I wouldn't choose anyone else to bear my children. Do you think it's a boy or a girl?" he asks.

"I don't know. What would you like it to be?"

"I have no preference, as long as it's healthy."

"Me too." A thought occurs to me, "Who do I go see about my pregnancy? I mean, I can't go to a regular Doctor."

"That's a good question. I am assuming you want to wait to tell anyone until we have it confirmed right?"

"That would be ideal."

"Well, do you mind if I say something to Taven? He is the only one I know that may know of someone. It's not like I go knocking up women all the time." He chuckles.

"You better not be fucking any other women, never mind knocking them up!"

I tease.

"You are all the woman I need or can handle." He laughs louder this time.

"Great answer Casanova!"

"Okay all joking aside; tomorrow morning I will speak to Taven in private and get some information. God, I can't believe I am going to be a father!"

"Hello, I'm going to be a first time Mom!"

"I know, but you need to understand. I thought I lost my chance at having kids the day I was turned. Only destined mates can have children. Some vampires never find their mates."

"That is so sad." I frown, "Well, for as long as I live, I will give you as many as you want while I can."

"You do realize that once we are officially mated, you will have eternity to give me children."

"What do you mean? Do I have to become a vampire?"

"No, you have to remain as you are in order to have children, but after the mating ritual, you will stop aging."

"Well, that's not so bad then! I'd rather be a baby making machine for you than turn into a vamp! No offense..."

He laughs, "None taken. A baby making machine, huh?"

"It was a joke, don't get any ideas wise ass!"

"Let's get you out of here; you are turning into a prune! Good thing you will live for eternity, I don't want to be married to an old prune as you get older. I'll have to turn you in for a younger model!" He laughs.

"Do voodoo dolls work on vampires?"

"I'm not really sure. That's a strange question, why do you ask?"

"So, I can hurt you and not myself when I slap you whenever you make comments like that!"

We both go into a fit of laughter at that one. Man, it is good to be back with him. My world feels right again, and I can start living my life without always looking over my shoulder. I haven't asked him what all happened between him and Zayne, but I have a feeling that he wouldn't tell me anyway. All I know is that Zayne is dead, and we can now begin our lives in peace.

Jax takes me down to the kitchen since I haven't had anything to eat all day. Kai, Jayde, Cooper, and another Elite I have not met yet are all sitting around the table all having a few beers. Cooper looks up and smiles, "There you are gorgeous! So glad to see you back home!" He gets up and brings me in for a bear hug.

"Getting a little touchy feely are we, Coop?" Jax's jealousy shows through.

"Can't a guy give a gal a compliment and a hug?"

"Sure, they can, as long as it isn't my gal!"

"Alright you two, stop it right now!" I turn to Jax taunting, "Can't a gal get some attention after an ordeal she just went through?" I wink at Cooper and look back at Jax.

"You want attention? I'll show you attention and then some!" He tries carrying me out of the kitchen, but I grab the sides of the door frame giggling.

"Stop, I need food you big Oaf!"

"You are lucky I love you, minx!"

"No, you are lucky that you put me down so I can eat! You have never really seen me when I need food!"

"Isn't that the truth!" Jill adds walking into the kitchen, "She once stabbed me with a fork because I stole a fry, and she hadn't eaten all day!"

"But did you die, Jill!"

"That's beside the point. You still stabbed me!"

"You are such a Drama Queen, Bitch!"

The men are just staring at us like we are some nut jobs. Jax and Cooper, who are used to it, just stand back, and enjoy the banter.

"Is there going to be a cat fight?" Kai asks.

"My money is on Cassie." Jayde bets.

"Why Cassie and not Jill?" The nameless Elite asks.

"Because Cassie is hungry." Jax pipes in and Jayde agrees, there is laughter all around the table.

"What, so no cat fight?" Kai looks disappointed and Cooper slaps him behind the head.

"What?"

"You trying to see a little action between two women when one of them is my mate?" Jax asks, eyebrow raised.

"After the mess I saw of Zayne after you were with him? Hells no!"

All laughter stops including my own. Kai looks at everyone and then lands his eyes on me. "Hell, I'm sorry Cassie. I'm always putting my foot into my mouth."

"It's ok Kai. It's just a little too soon. I forgive you. As long as you make me a ham sandwich with lettuce, pickle, tomato, and mayo!" I smile.

"Coming right up!" He gets to work on my sandwich.

"So, is anybody going to introduce me to the new hottie?" I smile at my newest victim.

He blushes and looks at Jax before standing up to shake my hand. "I'm Dane, pleasure to meet you."

"Come on, you can do better than that! We are almost family, where is my hug?"

Dane looks to Jax and then back to me, not sure what he should do.

"Cassie, stop teasing my brothers, it's rude!" Jax slaps my ass like I did to him for teasing Jill.

"God, ruin all my fun! Sorry Dane, it's nice to meet you too! How about a kiss on the cheek?"

Dane bursts out laughing and heads for the door, "You got your hands full with that one!" He smacks Jax on the shoulder.

"Don't I know it!"

"Your food has arrived!" Kai informs me as he sets it down in front of me.

"Awe, thanks Kai, you shouldn't have!" I take a bite.

"But..."

"You never take anything Cassie says seriously, Kai. You will figure that out soon enough!" Jill heads for the door, "I'm heading to bed, goodnight."

"Night Bitch, see you in the morning!"

"We should head that way too, it's late." Jax rubs my back.

"Yes, and I am exhausted... night everyone."

"Night." They all say in unison.

Once we are in the hallway, my stomach starts getting nauseous again.

"Where is the closest restroom?" I ask.

"That door right there." Pointing to the one closest to me.

"Thank God!" I run to it and slam it shut behind me, making it just in time to empty my stomach.

SIXTEEN

CASSIE

I wake up with Jax planting soft kisses on my neck, while rubbing my belly. I smile and think about how this guy has changed my world around. Who would have thought that the man I fall in love with and who will be the father of my children will turn out to be a vampire? Being with him doesn't scare me. He is kind, loving, protective, and a pain in my ass some days, but I can be a bigger pain in his ass on most days. What can I say? I like to keep life interesting! Most of all though, he spoils me rotten and never asks for anything in return. He is the father of my child, my mate, my vampire.

What does scare me is the fact that I have no clue as to how my pregnancy will go. I pray that we find answers. There has got to be someone out there that can help us. Until then, I will just take it day by day, I guess. Maybe I will be able to get food down this morning. I am starving and I am craving pancakes and sausage topped with syrup and whipped cream, yum!

"Morning, love. How did you sleep?"

"Surprisingly good. I thought for sure I'd have nightmares, but I think I was just too exhausted."

He turns me onto my back and continues with his feathery kisses, this time on my belly. I run my fingers through his hair as desire starts to burn inside me. I moan and gently try pushing his head down further. He looks at me, questioning. I know he doesn't want me to feel pressured into any intimacy after my ordeal.

"Please, take the memory away." I plead.

I see understanding in his eyes and he continues with his kisses, slowly traveling farther down. He pulls my panties down; I lift my leg to help him get them off. His mouth is on my clit licking it in slow strokes, giving it a little suck and turning his attention to my heated core. His tongue runs through my folds finding my entrance and he slips it inside me, taking his time, he thrusts slowly. Pulling it out, he licks me some more, this time dipping lower to include my ass. I feel his fingers enter my pussy, plunging in and out as he continues the assault on my puckered hole.

He lubes my ass with the juices running from my opening above and then thrusts a finger in that hole too. With both my holes filled, fingers plunging in and out of them, he latches on to my clit, sending me over the edge. He removes his fingers from my pussy and inserts his tongue again, loving the taste of my cum, he laps up every last drop of it.

He repositions himself between my legs, his tip at my entrance, "Look at me Cassie. I want you to see who is making love to you!"

I watch him as he slowly enters me, "I love you, Cassie. You are my forever."

Tears start rolling down my cheeks at his words, he leans down and licks them away, knowing they are from his words and nothing more. Moving to my lips, his kiss is slow and passionate, just like his strokes are. I have never felt so loved as I do right now.

He lifts my leg and buries himself fully. Pulling almost all the way out, he stops and then strokes back in. He gives me long soft strokes striking every nerve until I beg for him to take me harder. He increases his speed until he is slamming into me over and over again. Feeling my orgasm building as well as his own, he rams into me one last time and erupts like a volcano inside, ripping my orgasm from me as well.

We lay spent for a little while. Rolling over, I put my head on his shoulder, "I'm starving." As if on cue my stomach rumbles and Jax laughs.

"What would my loves like for breakfast?" Kissing the top of my head.

"Pancakes and sausage if you have any. Maybe a little syrup with lots of whipped cream?"

"I can think of better ways to serve you whipped cream, Baby."

"Mm, I'll have to remember that!"

Jax slides out from under me, "Just stay right here. I'll go and see if Max is in the kitchen. He is our Elite chef of the compound. I will talk to Taven while your food is cooking and then bring it to you once it's done." He smooths my hair and then plants a kiss, "Be back soon."

I lay here for a while, thinking about his touch and the love I have for him. My stomach rumbles again and then does a flip flop and I am running to the bathroom to empty an already empty stomach. Pain slices through my gut and I cry out just as I hear a knock at my door. The pain is too intense for me, and I cry out again. Jill comes flying through my door and straight to the bathroom where I am curled up into a fetal position on the floor.

"What's wrong?" Jill panics.

"My stomach, it hurts so much.!" I barely whisper.

"What can I do? Tell me what to do!" She is freaking out which freaks me out even more.

What if I am losing the baby? I can't lose it, Jax would be so devastated! "Go get Jax for me, he is with Taven."

Jill nods and runs out the door in search of Jax. The pain keeps tearing through my mid-section not letting up. They feel like bad hunger pains, only multiply that by fifty times, at least. I don't feel any wetness between my legs, so I'm not bleeding, that's good. What the fuck... more pain!

I hear pounding feet speeding my way and then Jax is here, kneeling before me. "What's wrong, Baby?" There is fear in his voice.

"Pain, lots of pain!" I cry out, wrapping my arms around my stomach.

Jill and Taven show up a moment later, fear in both of their eyes. Taven pulls his cell phone out, presses a button and then puts it up to his ear. He turns and walks just outside the door to talk. Another bought of pain cuts through me, and I moan loudly. I am in Jax's arms being carried over to the bed. Instead of laying me down, he sits on the edge and holds me tight, rocking me back and forth as if I'm a child, it soothes me.

I lay my head on his shoulder, my face in towards his neck and I smell woods and spice, but there is something else there that I can't pinpoint. As if I am possessed, I bite him. It startles him and he looks down at me. I'm staring back at him and then at his neck while licking my lips. A claw that has grown from the tip of his finger is there, at is neck, cutting into his jugular. Blood seeps out and the smell hits me. That's the unknown scent I was sniffing! All of a sudden, my mouth is on his neck sucking and pulling. His blood is divine! The more I drink, the less I feel my stomach pains. Once the pain is completely gone, I pull away from his neck, licking any trace of blood that is still lingering and then I wipe my mouth.

I look up at Jax and then over to Jill and Taven. Jill has a horrified look on her face.

"Did that crazy son of a bitch, Zayne, turn you into a vampire?" Her voice is shrill.

"No, Jill, I'm still me."

"Then what the fuck was that?!" she points to Jax's neck.

"I don't know!" Freaking out, I look up at Jax.

"We need to tell her, Darlin."

I nod my head and turn towards Jill, "I'm pregnant."

"Say that again?"

"She said that she's pregnant!" Jax talks slow as if talking to a deaf person then smiles.

"I'm not deaf, I heard her the first time! I just wanted to make sure I heard right." Flipping Jax off and turning back to me, "Why didn't you tell me?"

"I just found out yesterday and I wanted to confirm it before we told anyone. Please don't be mad!"

"I'm not mad," she sighs, "just still a little freaked out from watching you drink his blood. What was that all about anyway?"

"I think it was the baby." Jax replies, looking at Taven as if to confirm.

Taven nods, "I just got off the phone with Dr. Howard. She specializes in vampire pregnancies."

"Is she a vampire?" I ask

"No, but she has been mated to one for over a hundred years and she has 6 kids of her own."

"So, she can help us?" I let my excitement show.

"Yes." He chuckles, "If fact, she wants to see you in her office at 4pm today for an examination."

I beam at Jax as he smiles back at me.

Taven speaks up again, "She explained to me what was happening, why you were in so much pain. Apparently, the baby needs Jax's blood as well as regular nutrition from food. You need to be taking Jax's blood 2-3 times a day or else you will become severely sick." He stops talking, but I can tell that there is more.

"What is it? What are you not telling us?" I ask, feeling a little anxious.

He hesitates, "All though you will get really sick, you shouldn't have the pains that you were having. Those are from something else."

"What do you mean? What are they from?" It was Jax who spoke this time.

"The pains will get worse, and she will need to feed more and more from you the longer you two aren't officially mated."

Jax nods at Taven, "Will you two give us some privacy? I need to talk with Cassie."

"Sure, of course." Jill replies and Taven nods.

They walk out the door as yet another new face appears, carrying a tray of food. "Someone order room service?" he smiles.

"Perfect timing Max, thanks."

He sets the tray down and walks over to me, his hand stretched out before him, "Hi, I'm Max. And you are the lovely hellion that everyone is talking about!"

I shake his hand and chuckle, "Yeah, what else is new? It's so nice to meet you and thank you for making my breakfast."

"It was my pleasure. Besides, I wouldn't want you to eat anyone else's cooking. That would be pure torture!"

"Thank you, Max!" Jax says in a warning tone.

Max takes it as a sign to leave and turns towards the door, "Let me know if you are in need of anything else, Cassie." He winks at me and Jax throws a pillow at him, but misses.

JAX

Cassie is just finishing up her breakfast when I turn to her, "I need to talk to you about the whole mating thing. I want to explain to you what it entails."

"Is it bad? I mean does it hurt?"

"No, nothing like that. I'm told that it is the best pleasurable experience between mates."

"Well, I can't see anything being more pleasurable than you fucking me senseless the way you do!" She gives me her seductive smile as she crawls onto my lap, instantly bringing my cock to life.

"Oh, love," I murmur to her, "I agree 100% with you on that one, but before you start making me lose my train of thought by wanting to take you right this instant, I need to finish the topic at hand."

"You can continue while I use my "hand" to help the little problem you have going on here!"

She slips her hand into my sweatpants and wraps it around my cock, taking my breath away. Slowly, she pumps my shaft while I'm trying to remember what I was talking about. I moan and start moving my hips in sync with her hand.

"Are you going to continue?" she asks, an evil smile upon her lips.

"What was I saying?" My eyes are closed, reveling in the way she feels holding me.

"You were telling me about the mating experience." I hear the smile in her voice.

"Ah, yes!" Not sure if my response is remembering what the topic is or because the molestation of my cock feels so fucking good! "Sex is involved, of course, but the most important part is that we need to take each other's blood while we are having sex."

Her hand stops and it takes me a second to realize that my dick isn't being pumped anymore. I open my eyes and look into hers. I can see that she is a little freaked out.

"You mean, you have to bite me?" her voice wavers.

I knew that would be the part that she would have issues with, so I go right in to explain.

"Cassie, when your true destined mate bites you, there is no pain, just instant arousal. A vamp can bite someone that isn't their mate and not cause them pain, but the person needs to be a willing participant."

She looks skeptical. "How do you know for sure? I mean, you have never performed the ceremony before."

"True, but I have taken blood from willing women before and never hurt them."

Her face turns red with my mention of taking another woman's blood. I don't blame her; I wouldn't like hearing about her ex-boyfriends.

"That's all in the past, love, you are it for me, forever!"

"I know this… doesn't mean I like hearing about it though." She pouts.

"I just need you to know that you will never feel that kind of pain with me. I'd kill myself before causing you any kind of pain."

"Everything is happening all at once, but I do know that I want you, and I want this baby. Can we just wait until after our appointment to discuss it further?"

"Of course, nothing needs to be decided right at this minute." Trying to take her mind off the topic, I smile, "Now, how about finishing that awesome hand job?"

We are walking into the doctor's office for our first visit and Cassie's examination. Both of us are a nervous wreck, not knowing what to expect. I still can't believe that I'm going to be a daddy, it's all so unreal! Will I be a good father? I have never been around babies before. Me being an only child and everything. I want to do everything right; be the best dad I can be!

My own father was a work-a-holic, so I never spent much time doing the whole father-son bonding with him. Maybe that is where I get my work ethics from, except my family will always come first. My family, I love the sound of that. I suppose I had better make an honest woman out of Cassie, but I'm not sure if she even wants to get married. Honestly, the mating ceremony is what makes it official, for vampires anyway, but I want to give that woman everything she deserves, and more. She is giving me the best thing I could ever ask for in life!

The receptionist gives us paperwork to fill out and Cassie hands over her insurance card before we take a seat in the waiting room. There is only one other person in the room with us and they get called back to see the doctor within minutes of us sitting. Cassie finishes the paperwork and comes back, taking my hand as she sits and fidgets.

"It's going to be okay, Baby, just calm down."

"I can't help it, sorry." She gives a nervous giggle.

The nurse opens the door and informs us that the doctor would see us now. My heart starts to race, and my nerves are on edge. Would the baby be more like a regular person, more vampire or would it be half and half? This is what I have thought about for the last hour or so. Wondering what all we were going to learn today. Will it freak Cassie out? How is she going to take the news? Argh, I am driving myself crazy!

We are led into a room where a nurse takes Cassie's vitals and asks her questions about her "woman issues", as well as the last time she had intercourse. I chuckle, not meaning for it to actually come out, but Cassie chuckles herself, "If you had a man like that at home, how would you answer that question?" She answers.

The nurse, who looks to be close to Cassie's age, looks me up and down, "So, you are telling me that you last had intercourse this morning?" The nurse smiles and jots it down.

I am pretty sure I am blushing right now. I have been doing a lot of things lately that I normally wouldn't do since meeting Cassie.

"I will go let Dr. Howard know you are here, and she will be in in a few minutes. If you would, please change into the gown that is lying on the exam table. You will need to undress from the waist down." The nurse leaves, closing the door behind her.

"You are such a little shit; do you know that minx?"

"Oh, did I embarrass you, Babe?" A mischievous smile on her face.

"Remind me to spank you when we get home!"

"Why wait?" she bends over the table, sticking her ass in my face.

"Oh no, I'm going to enjoy it way too much and I'll be damned if I'm sporting a hard on while we talk to the doctor, nice try though."

No sooner do I end my sentence, the Dr. walks in. Surprisingly, she looks young, maybe mid to late twenties. Her blonde hair is tied back into a ponytail and dark framed glasses over brown eyes. She is a pretty thing, but she has nothing on my hellion.

"Hi, I am Dr. Howard, and you must be Cassie and Jax." She shakes both of our hands. "First time parents, huh?"

"How can you tell?" Cassie asks.

"Well, Taven told me when he called this morning, said you had a little scare? Want to tell me about it?"

Cassie reports how she had been feeling really nauseous on and off for the last 24 or so hours and not being able to eat. She explains the pain she had this morning, how excruciating it is.

"I think we figured out the cause of the pain." I speak up, "When she got close to me, she craved my blood and once she drank, the pains were gone, and she was able to eat her breakfast. We know nothing about these kinds of pregnancies, and I guess we are a little freaked out."

"It's perfectly understandable Jax, may I call you Jax?" Doc asks.

"Yes, I prefer it."

"My mate, now husband, and I felt the same way with our first, it's natural. As you are aware, only destined mates can have children. The baby needs nutrients from both mother and father, and the blood has to be the mate's blood. Not any blood will do during the pregnancy and it's first six months after they are born. Cassie, you will have to drink from Jax 2-3 times a day while you are carrying and if you don't, your body will reject anything you try to eat or drink until the baby gets its blood first. They are devious little things." She laughs.

"Devious is not the word I would use!" Cassie admits.

"Have the two of you sealed your bonding?"

"No, not yet. Is that an issue?"

"Well, no, not really. Until you have sealed it, though, you will need to drink from Jax 5-6 times a day and when you don't, the pains tend to be more horrendous."

"Oh, I see." Cassie sounds a little disappointed at the news.

"You are planning on completing the bond, are you not?"

"Well, yes, I guess I just thought that we had time."

"It won't hurt the baby if you don't, but for your own sake, I would do it as soon as possible. My bonding was the best feeling ever. I had waited a year before finally getting up the nerve to do it, and now I wished I had done it right away."

Wanting to get off the subject, I ask, "So what else can we expect with the pregnancy Doc?"

"Aside from the whole blood issue, there is only one other thing that is different than a regular pregnancy. A normal pregnancy is forty weeks, whereas vampire pregnancies are only twenty weeks, so about five months."

I thought both mine and Cassie's eyes were going to pop out of our heads at that news. Only five months? We have so much to do before it comes!

"Let's do a pelvic examination and then an ultrasound, so we can determine when the little one will come."

Doc has Cassie lay back on the table and put her legs in some kind of metal holders. She then disappears between Cassie's legs, causing me to feel a little uncomfortable, like I am intruding on a private moment or something.

"Everything looks good on this end." She smiles and then instructs Cassie to take her legs out of the holders, that she calls stirrups. She rolls a machine over to the bed and lifts Cassie's gown, covering her bottom part with a sheet.

"This is going to feel a little cold, Cassie." Squirting some gel onto Cassie's stomach, she starts moving, what looks like a scanner of some sort, around on Cassie's stomach.

That's when we hear it. A little heartbeat drumming out of the speaker. The doctor points at what looks like a little bean, "There he or she is mom and dad! Would you like to take a picture home?"

I'm speechless, my eyes are glued to the screen that is showing our son or daughter. I feel tears well up but don't let them fall. I kiss Cassie's forehead and then look down at her and see that she is bawling like a baby.

"Yes, we would like a picture, if it isn't too much to ask." I finally answer the doctor.

"How long before we can find out the sex?" Cassie wants to know.

"Let me do some quick measurements here, so we can figure your due date and when we can determine the sex." She keeps clicking the keyboard and moving stuff around on the screen.

"It looks like you will be proud parents come November fifth, give or take a few days!" She smiles, "You can also set up another ultrasound appointment if you want to learn the sex, in about six weeks." She hands us our baby's first picture and tells us to call her if we have any questions and then she leaves the room, leaving us alone.

I sit on the bed beside Cassie and draw her into my arms as we stare at our baby's first picture.

SEVENTEEN

CASSIE

Going back to work on Monday after the long eventful weekend I had felt great! I am able to keep my mind occupied with work instead of the ordeal I went through. I've always been a strong person, so I know I will get over this, in time. Trying to keep my mind and excitement away from my pregnancy is a whole different matter! Jax made me agree to meet him on both of my fifteen-minute breaks so I can take his blood that the baby needs. My lunch is my own since both me and the baby need those nutrients as well.

Jax always parks in the back of the parking lot so anybody that passes by us will just assume we are having a quick make out session. Of course, there is a lot of fondling going on within these sessions, but never enough time for more. Taking his blood arouses him every time and I can't help but giggle every time I leave him sitting there with a hard on. I do offer him hand jobs to help release the pressure, but he always refuses, making me promise to take care of him after work. I never go back on my promises!

I walk into the breakroom at lunch time, and I see Jill and Jason, the new guy, with their heads together. Jason jumps and backs away, like I had just caught him with his hand in the candy jar. I give Jill a questioning look, but she turns her head and pretends to read the magazine laid out in front of her. I sit down across from her, not saying a word.

"Hey Cassie, I'd stay and chat, but my break is up." He stands and knocks the chair over in the process, "God, I'm such a klutz! I guess I'll see you ladies later." then he was gone.

"Okay Earnhardt, out with it!"

"Out with what?"

"You know exactly what I am referring to!"

"Can you please be more specific? I try not to read what you got going on in that crazy mind of yours." she shutters jokingly.

"Okay, you want to play it this way? Fine. What were you and klutz boy discussing when I walked in? It looked like you were having a very intimate conversation."

"Oh that? It was nothing, we were talking about this article here."

I lean over the table to look at the one she is pointing at, "How to Please Your Man in the Bedroom to Keep Him Coming Back for More? You were discussing this article?" I laugh as Jill's face turns beet red.

"Y-Yeah, we were!"

"Oh Jill, you have always been a horrible liar."

She deeply sighs, "Ugh, fine! He asked me out to dinner tonight."

"And what is so secretive about that? That is awesome!"

"I don't know, I said yes, but now I'm not sure."

"Why is that?"

She looks at me like I have grown a second head, "What will Duncan say if he finds out?"

"The two of you are not an item, are you?" She never came straight out and told me what was going on between the two of them, but I knew something was there.

"Well, no, not really. I mean, we hang out a lot, but nothing has ever happened between us. Not counting the night of the Summer Bash, because that was just for show."

"You could have fooled me and Jax!" I chuckle.

"Don't be a bitch, Case!"

"Okay, okay, I'm sorry! So, if you are only friends, what does it matter what Duncan thinks?"

"Because, I am pretty sure he has feelings for me, but is holding back due to the whole "destined mate" thing!" She pouts.

"Well, what if you are his mate? You have the blood type."

"Yeah, but he doesn't know that."

"You haven't told him? Why not?"

"I don't know if I want that life, Cassie! This whole vampire stuff still freaks me out a bit!"

"They are still human Jill and in case you have forgotten, my baby is half vampire!" I can't keep the accusation out of my voice.

"I know that and I'm not saying anything bad about them! It's just still hard for me to take in everything is all. You can't blame me if I want a chance at a relationship with a "regular" person, I'm not like you, Case!"

"What's that supposed to mean?"

"You are always doing your own thing, doing stuff that is outside the box. Yes, I'm usually right alongside of you, but that doesn't mean I'm like that."

"Fine, whatever. I am sorry if I want my best friend to be happy and when you are with Duncan, I see it. You know, you can't help who you love, and you can't mess with fate, but I understand what you are saying, and I'll stand beside you in whatever you decide. I just want you to promise me one thing."

"What is that?"

"If you find that Jason is not the right one for you, you will be more open minded and take a chance to see if Duncan is the right one for you!"

With a heavy sigh, Jill nods.

"Great! See, was that so hard?"

"Whatever," she chuckles, "I have to get back to work, I'll see you later."

I get home from work that night to find a note from Jax, informing me that he had to leave for a few hours on Elite business. We came back to my house after our doctor's appointment yesterday and it was so nice to have the house to ourselves. We christened every room in here and was not disturbed once! I can't get enough of my vampire, just thinking about him now is making me want him!

I get to work on fixing supper, hoping he will be home by the time it is done. It's weird, I'm usually a microwave or frozen pizza kind of person, but I find myself enjoying making an actual meal, using the stove like a big girl! Now whether or not the food comes out edible is a completely different story. I'm trying my hand at meat loaf and mashed potatoes, not too hard, right? If anything, the house will smell good, that's got to count for something!

Jax walks through the door as I'm taking my non-burned meatloaf out of the oven. "Mm, something smells good." He says as he comes up behind me.

"I made meat loaf. I hope it's edible."

"I'm sure it's fine, but I wasn't talking about the food, Baby." He rains kisses down the back of my neck. Luckily, I have already set the meat loaf pan down on the stove or it would be all over the floor! My knees go weak every time he kisses me like this!

He runs his hands around the front of my waist and rips the button off of my jean shorts. I am now down to two pairs that still have the buttons attached. I sigh and clutch the edge of the counter as his hand dips farther down, finding my hot spot. Forgetting all about the food, he has me panting for more and I grind myself into his hand, feeling my pressure building already.

"You like that, huh? You want more?" His husky voice near my ear.

I shake my head yes, but he doesn't like how I answer, and he stops, "You know what I want. Say it, tell me what you want me to do to your lovely pussy!"

"Don't stop! I want more, so much more!" I say breathlessly.

He eagerly resumes his play with my clit. Then in a matter of seconds, both my shorts and panties are gone, laying shredded on the floor. He spreads my legs wider and kneels behind me. His tongue is running through my folds, lapping up the wetness and moaning. I feel his fingers slide home inside of me and it's all I can do not to fall from the tantalizing sensation, but he holds me up, thrusting his fingers inside and finding my g-spot each time.

My desire is building as his tongue and fingers take me to new heights and my orgasm is ripped from me, sending waves of pleasure throughout my body. His mouth sucking the cum that drips from me. Before I can even recover, he grabs my hands and brings them behind my back, restraining them there. He bends me over the counter, holding me down as he slams is cock into me and starts fucking me good and hard.

"Is that all you got?" I ask, taunting him.

"Oh, you want more? I'll give you more, so much more. Just remember that you asked for this!"

He uses the dish towel to secure my wrists together, grabbing my hair tightly, he holds me in place, so I don't hit my head on the wall from the force of his thrusts. His finger is in my ass, increasing the pressure of my building orgasm. Feeling that I am almost there, he leans over me, and I just barely hear him as he speaks next to my ear.

"Don't you dare fucking come! I will tell you when you can release it, but not until then!"

I whimper, knowing how hard it's going to be. I need to let go now! My pussy walls suctioning his slick cock and him hitting the right spot with each thrust. I then feel his speed increase even more and I know he is almost there. Pulling his finger out, he uses my hair to pull my body up and against his chest. He untangles his hand from my hair and slides it around to my throat, putting pressure, as if he is going to choke me, but leaves me enough airway to breathe. God, I want to come all over his cock!

"Not yet, you can't come yet!"

I'm starting to tingle with the restricted airway and then I feel it, hot liquid shooting deep inside me. He thrusts deep within and stops, letting it shoot out, all the while chanting "not yet" to me. Just as I think I'm going to pass out from not being able to let go, he demands, "Come on my fucking dick now!"

"You want me to come now?" I ask, breathless.

"I said to come now!"

"No!" I can play this game too.

He pushes me back down over the counter and shoves his finger back into my ass while the other hand moves to the front and pinches my clit. Wave after wave rushes through me as I soak his cock with my juice. He starts slamming into me again, ripping another wave of pleasure from me. He continues his assault until I beg him to stop. I can't take anymore, I'm spent! He slows his movement until he stops completely but doesn't remove himself.

"You think you can disobey me like that and not have consequences?" He asks by my ear.

I can't help but giggle.

"Wrong answer, my little Minx!" He pulls out so quick, picks me up and lays me on the dining table on my side, my hands still tied behind me. Lifting my leg, he takes me again!

"I can't possibly come again! I have nothing left!"

"You will come for me again and I won't stop until you do! I'm going to fuck your pussy until my cock is drenched in your juice and then I'm going to fuck that pretty little ass of yours while my fingers fuck your pussy and are coated with your come so I can lick them clean! Hold on, Baby, you asked for this!"

He did as he promised and tore another orgasm from me while fucking me with his mighty shaft and then pulling out and shoving his come soaked cock into my ass while his fingers took my pussy. He is slamming into my ass so hard, I can barely breath. One last orgasm rips through me as he erupts into my ass, and I literally pass out.

JAX

I'm carrying Cassie to the bedroom as my phone starts vibrate. I quickly lay her down and walk back to the kitchen as I see it's Taven and I answer.

"Please tell me that he talked!" I say.

"We didn't get much out of him I'm afraid." Taven replies, "All we know is that there are Hunters out there that know about Vamps and are out to kill us all."

"Shit!" This is not good I think to myself. "Well, do what you have to do to get him to talk some more!"

"Um, it's a little too late for that. Kai kind of went ape shit on the guy and accidentally broke his neck."

"How the fuck could you let that happen?!"

"Hey! I needed to step out and take a call. I was gone maybe 30 seconds and came back to a dead Hunter! Believe me, I came unglued on kai's ass!"

"So, we are back at square one then?"

"Not necessarily. We now know that there are Hunters searching for our kind, but they know nothing of the Elite. The dead guy said as much."

"Well, that's good news, I guess. That means we are one step ahead of them." I point out.

"That is exactly what I was thinking. I want to call a meeting in the morning. Can you be here after Cassie leaves for work?"

"Sure can. I'll see you then."

I pocket my phone. God dammit! Just what we need now, a bunch of people thinking they are all big and bad and wanting to kill the vile creatures of the world. They have no idea what they are getting themselves into. They are not strong enough to take us on. We have two choices, one, we watch them and step in when they attack other vamps just so they don't get themselves killed. I am not sure if I would call them evil people, they don't know any better and they think they are doing good. Or two, we take them out just like the evil people of the world, which I am not liking one bit, but if it means keeping the innocent vamps safe, then so be it.

Headquarters received a call this morning from an upstanding pillar of the community, who is also a vampire. He reported that he and his mate had been attacked by two people in the early hours before sunrise. Unfortunately, one was killed during the ambush and the second was being held by the vamp himself. Cooper and Jayde went and collected the other one and brought him in for questioning. I spent all morning interrogating him but got nothing. I am not one for torturing a person who can't heal themselves like we can, so I finally gave him over for one of the others to take over and I came home. I will give the guy until nightfall to talk, before using my abilities to take the information myself!

When I came home and saw Cassie standing over the stove looking so hot in her short shorts, tight t-shirt, and her hair down, I couldn't help but take her right there! Helping to relieve the frustration of the day, and then the new frustration of my arousal, I gave her what we both needed. That woman is my life, along with the precious life she is now carrying. With this new threat hanging over us, I will not stop until it is taken care of, and my family is safe again!

I crawl into bed beside her and draw her into my arms, smelling her sweet chocolate and strawberry essence. She snuggles into my chest, her head between my neck and shoulder, mumbling something in her sleep. I smile, not understanding what she is saying. Then I feel her nipping at my neck. Now knowing what the mumbling is about, I reach up and slice my jugular. Her mouth moving swiftly to drink the only blood that our baby can survive on right now. Taking her fill, she snuggles back into me and falls fast asleep.

We both get woken up by a pounding on the front door. I bolt up in bed, looking for Cassie right away. She is sitting up looking just as confused. Another pounding comes and I am on my feet. "Stay right here, sweetheart. Let me see who it is first." She nods in understanding, and I head for the door. I look out the peep hole and see Duncan on the other side. I sigh and open the door.

"What the fuck, man? What is so urgent that that you are pounding on my door?"

"Have you seen or heard from Jill? She isn't answering her phone and she isn't at her place. I was hoping she was here!" Panic clearly in his voice.

I step aside to let him in. "No, I haven't seen her, but maybe Cassie knows something. I'll go get her."

"Thanks, man."

"Yeah, no problem."

We are back in less than a minute.

"Cassie! Have you heard from Jill since work?"

She sighs, "No, not yet, but she should be calling me anytime now."

"Why is that? Where is she? Is she okay?"

"Slow down Duncan and let her answer your questions, sheesh!" I chuckle and shake my head.

"She is okay. At least as far as I know. She is supposed to call me after her dinner date tonight."

Duncan looks a bit confused. "A dinner date? Who with?"

"She went out with a co-worker of ours." She replies.

Relief sweeps over Duncan's face, "Oh good. I wonder why she didn't tell me she was going to dinner with a girlfriend?"

"Umm, probably because she went with a male and not female." Cassie scoots closer to me, as if she expects Duncan to explode on her.

"Oh, I see." Disappointment evident on his face. I kind of feel bad for the guy.

"Duncan, what are your feelings for Jill?" Cassie inquires.

"What do you mean? She is a good friend, why?"

"Really? Because the look on your face tells us different." I speak up.

Hesitating, he runs his hand through his hair as he takes a seat on the couch, "It doesn't matter what my feelings are for her. It doesn't matter that she smells like a field full of wildflowers in the Springtime, and it doesn't matter that I want to go mad when I'm not with her! We can never be together; I can't do that to her. What if my mate comes along while we are together, I'd have no choice but to give her up!"

I look over at Cassie and I see that her eyes are glistening with unshed tears. I grab her hand and squeeze. It breaks my heart to see the big guy this way, but I agree with him, there is no future for them.

"What if your feelings for her did matter?" Cassie asks him.

"They don't so there is no point." Duncan has his head hanging down.

Cassie mumbles, "She is so going to kick my ass when she finds out I said anything, ugh!"

"What is it, Cassie?" I ask.

With a long, drawn-out sigh, Cassie walks over and sits beside Duncan. "Jill's blood type is O positive."

"What?" He looks up.

"Jill, she is able to mate with vampires."

All of a sudden, Cassie is picked up and tossed in the air by a laughing Duncan before he sets her back on her feet, "You're not fucking with me, are you?"

"No Duncan, I'm not."

"Then why didn't she tell me this? Did I pick up the wrong signals from her?"

"I am surprised you didn't know. I thought all vamps could tell by the smell or something? And no, she does have feelings for you, BUT unlike me, she doesn't like jumping into the unknown and being with a vampire kind of freaks her out. You need to give her time, Duncan."

"So, I'm supposed to sit by while my mate dates other men?"

"If you truly care about her, yes! You sit by and watch her realize things on her own. Besides, Jason isn't for her, so you have no worries."

"Jason?"

"Yes, her dinner date tonight. His name is Jason, and he has nothing on you, so no worries big guy!"

Duncan grunts and sits back sulking. I pat him on the back, "All in good time, man. You don't want to scare her away." I try reassuring him.

"One thing though, Duncan. Please don't let her know that you know her blood type. I wasn't supposed to say anything, but she can be pig-headed, and someone needs to interfere when needed!" Cassie states.

Duncan nods his head in understanding, "I'll try my best, but I am not one to stand back and let other men paw all over my woman!"

"Spoken like a true mate, Dunc!" I chuckle.

Once Duncan knows that Jill is home safe, he heads home himself. God, it's been a long day and all I want to do is spend a quiet evening with my girl. So much for that! Just the two of us again, I head to the kitchen and start heating up our cold dinner. It actually did smell pretty good walking through the door, but my thoughts had wandered away from the food.

"I am not sure it was edible to begin with, never mind being reheated." Cassie looks skeptic.

I dish some meat loaf and some potatoes onto our plates and grab some forks, on my way to the table.

"Let me be the judge of that. I'd rather be the one to keel over if it's not." I wink.

"Ha, ha, it can't be that bad, ass!" She shoves my arm.

I take a bite and move it around in my mouth, "It's actually pretty damn good!" Shoveling another forkful into my mouth.

"Seriously?" She asks as she takes a bite. "Mm, I did good for my first time at meat loaf!"

"You are good at everything you do." Giving her a lopsided grin.

"Speaking of… you are so hot when you are demanding like that! You need to do that more often!" I am graced with her seductive smile.

"Well then, I demand that you finish your dinner so I can do some more pounding in that vagina of yours!"

EIGHTEEN

CASSIE

Jill calls me as soon as she gets home from her date with Jason to tell me all about it. It almost sounds like she is trying too hard to make me believe that she enjoyed herself, but like the best friend that I am, I keep my judgements to myself for the time being. Maybe I am just being biased, because I really like Duncan and I think he is the best for her. I don't know, there is just something about Jason that I can't put my finger on and I have felt this way since that day he almost walked into me when I was in the break room at work. The same day that I met Zayne. Ugh… to be rid of that memory would be awesome!

I just want my best friend to find her happiness like I did and I really don't think Jason is it! As she goes on to tell me about the restaurant he took her to and then the movie they saw at the theatre, it all seemed like a normal date, but there was just something nagging me about the whole situation. I shrugged it off and tried paying attention to what she was saying at the moment.

"He wants to go out again Friday night."

"Oh yeah? Do you want to go out with him again?"

"I guess so. He is really nice and I would hate to not give it another go since tonight went really well."

I don't know what I was thinking, but I couldn't stop my mouth from having diarrhea, "Duncan was here looking for you tonight."

"Oh? What did he need? I saw that he tried calling me... like five times, but I didn't want to be rude while I was on a date and I haven't had a chance to call him back."

"What did he want? He was freaking out because he couldn't reach you, or find you for that matter!"

"Isn't that a little bit stalker-like?"

"I'm just going to come out and say this because it needs to be said! I truly believe that the two of you are destined mates and that is why he was freaking out!"

"Don't go there, Case! We already discussed this earlier."

"I know we did, but I'm just saying...."

"Well, don't. You don't know for sure that we are mates, and I am going to continue dating Jason until I decide that he isn't the right one or until I decide that I want to give the vampire thing a whirl!"

"Okay, I get it! Just know that he cares deeply for you and it's going to kill him seeing you date another."

"I am sorry, the last thing I want to do is hurt him, but I have to do it my way."

"Alright! Why don't Jax and I host a game night tomorrow night and you can invite Jason? It will be fun, and it will give me a chance to get to know him better outside of work."

"I don't know. Isn't it a little soon?"

"Good God woman, it's only game night! Orgy night is next week!" I can't help but laugh and I get a chuckle out of Jill as well.

"Okay, I'll ask him tomorrow at work."

"Great! I'm gonna go have hot kinky sex with my vamp, so I will talk to you tomorrow!"

"TMI, Cassie, TMI!" She ends the call.

I go ahead and invite a few others from work to game night and Jax invites a few of the Elite who had the night off, Duncan being one of them. Jill isn't too happy, but I explain to her that Jax had as much right to invite his friends as I had to invite mine. I know it was a shitty thing to do, but hey, all is fair in love and war! Besides for the whole love triangle, everything went well. At least in the beginning anyway.

We start out with Cards Against Humanity and then end up going to drinking games. I, of course, sit those out and become the gopher whenever someone needs a refill, but I'm having a blast watching them all get smashed! The Elite men don't get quite intoxicated since their metabolism burns most of the effects of the alcohol off, but even being tipsy, shows their lighter side and I love it.

I keep seeing Duncan stealing looks at Jill from across the room and my heart hurts for him, but I know all will be right in the end. I know my bestie and she will make the right decision as soon as she is done being pig headed. A few times, I think I see Jason giving Duncan the evil eye when he thinks no one is looking, but I can be wrong. Just as that thought crosses my mind, Jason grabs Jill and kisses her full on the lips, taking her by complete surprise. Next thing I hear is glass breaking and I look over at Duncan's broken beer bottle in his hand. Jill looks his way embarrassed and then turns and leaves the room.

I go and follow Jill as she walks into the bathroom, and I shut the door behind us, "What the fuck was that all about?"

She looks at me and shrugs, "Apparently, he wanted a kiss. We are on a date you know."

I can see that she is trying to cover up the little shake she has going on, "Yeah, well all I saw is someone trying to prove something to someone else in the room!"

"This was a bad idea, Cassie."

"If he wants to date you then he is going to have to be able to hang with all your friends too! Last I knew, you and Duncan were good friends."

"I don't know if we can be friends like that while I'm trying to figure things out."

"I see. So, now that you have a boyfriend, you are just tossing Duncan to the side, because you don't need him anymore?" I don't hide my anger. Jill is being a snobby little bitch and I will not have it.

Duncan has been nothing but kind and a good friend to her. I know she is acting this way because of her feelings for him, but that doesn't mean I will tolerate it.

"It's not like that and you know it!"

"What I know is that you care for Duncan, but you are scared and so you are acting like a bitch! I know you are not meaning to, it's really not in your nature, but you are and as your best friend, it is my duty to point it out to you!"

Jill bursts out crying, "I do care for him, more than you know, but I am scared! How do you handle it?"

"I handle it just like any other normal relationship. They ARE human too, I've told you this, and they are good men, Jill. If you are mates, he will love and cherish you always! There is nothing to be afraid of, not from him."

"I know all this. Remember that one time at work, when I cut myself on the box cutter? I fainted at the sight of my own blood! Blood freaks me out and I don't know if that is something that I can get passed."

I pull her into a hug, "Hey, did you ever think I could ever drink someone else's blood? No, but look at me now, trying to bite through his skin just to get to his!" I laugh, "Granted, that is mainly the baby causing me to do it, but It's still me taking someone else's blood."

"It was pretty gross watching you do that." Jill chuckles.

"I will make a deal with you. If you can try seeing past the whole blood thing, I will try getting passed the whole excruciating pain part and finally go through my mating ceremony."

"I thought that Jax's bite won't hurt you?"

"That is what I'm told, but when Zayne did it, all I felt was burning and blinding pain, it's hard to get passed that."

"So, how would you go about letting down a guy who is really into you, because you want someone else?"

"Oh no, you got yourself into this one against my wishes, and you can get yourself out of it!"

"Some friend you are!"

"Use it as a learning experience. You are learning how to break it off with a guy AND you are learning how I am always right!" I smile and then walk out of the bathroom, leaving Jill so she can get herself together.

As I walk back to the others, I see that Duncan is grabbing himself another beer, that isn't the problem. The problem is walking up to him like he is on a mission. Jason stands at least a half foot shorter than Duncan, but apparently, he isn't intimidated by it. He stops Duncan as he is walking by with his beer by reaching out and grabbing Duncan's arm.

"Hey buddy, I think you are making my girl uncomfortable by being here, so why don't you excuse yourself and leave?"

Duncan is about to respond when he notices me standing here. He looks back at Jason, I am an invited guest like yourself, and if Jill or you are too uncomfortable, then maybe you should leave." He tries walking away, but Jason isn't having it.

"I would love to but for some reason Jill is friends with that crazy bitch, Cassie, so I have to deal with it!"

Jill chooses that moment to walk in on the conversation, "That "crazy bitch" is my best friend, and you don't get to call her that!"

I decide to sit back and watch how this plays out. Sure wish I had some popcorn right about now! With his magnified senses, Jax must have heard the comment too and comes walking over. I catch hold of his wrist and shake my head no, meaning for him to stay out of it, so he just stands here beside me and watches. Leaning over and whispering, "Do you have any popcorn?" I can't help but giggle.

"I'm sorry Jill, I didn't mean it to sound that way. I like Cassie, but even everyone at work thinks of her that way."

"They have known Cassie for years and have earned the right to call her that. You have not and I don't think that you're sorry either."

"I was only trying to get this guy to leave," pointing at Duncan, "because I could tell he was making you uncomfortable."

"This guy," she now points to Duncan, "has a name and it's Duncan. He also happens to be a really good friend of mine and is not making me uncomfortable. If anybody is, it's you! Why the fuck would you kiss me like that in front of everybody? We have only been on one date. It is like you are trying to claim possession of me and wanted everyone to know it!"

Go Jill, I am so proud of you! Let him have it! I glance over at Duncan and can see a slight smile on his face and sheer pride for the woman standing in front of him, defending him.

"I just got caught up in the moment and it felt right, so I kissed you. I didn't mean to embarrass you in front of your friends. Can we get out of here and talk about this?"

"I am not ready to leave yet, but I am pretty sure that you just overstayed your welcome! I'll see myself home, goodbye Jason!" Jill walks from the room leaving Jason with his mouth hanging open.

As I am walking by him to join the others, I reach out and help him by closing his open jaw, "Goodnight Jason. So glad you were able to come, I will see you tomorrow at work." I smile and leave, Jax and Duncan following me. I hear the front door slam close a moment later.

JAX

Standing back in the living room beside Duncan, I look over at him, "Those two are a force to be reckoned with! Are you sure you want to go there, buddy? It's too late for me, but you still have time." I chuckle.

"I'm pretty sure after that little show, I'm a goner!" Duncan replies.

"Well then buckle up cowboy, because it's going to be a wild ride!"

"I sure do hope you're right!" He smiles back at me.

I give a hearty laugh and slap him on the back. Staring over at my little hellion and her best friend, I can't help but think how much more interesting our lives are going to be. There are no dull moments when those two are around!

Once everyone else says their goodbye's, Jill and Duncan are the only two guests left. "Jill, you are more than welcome to stay in the spare room if you want." I inform her.

"I think I am going to have Duncan give me a ride home, that's if you don't mind?" She looks up at him.

"Why, it would be my pleasure, little lady." He smiles down at her and looks over at me and winks.

Shaking my head, I grab Cassie's hand and start leading her to the bedroom, "Lock up on your way out, Dunc!" I holler over my shoulder.

"Will do!"

I have just barely closed the door when I'm mauled. Cassie shoves me against the wall and attacks me, ripping my shirt form my chest literally! She then starts on the button of my jeans and to my surprise, yanks on them, popping the button off, and then sliding them down. It is such a huge turn on that I am instantly hard, and my cock springs out, full staff.

"Hm, to what do I owe this pleasure?"

"Just call it a pregnant woman's hormones and to the fact that you are so fucking hot, I can't keep my hands off of you!"

"What do you want from me?" I ask in a low deep voice as I begin to slowly undress her.

"Where do I start? I want you to fuck me with that huge cock of yours, for starters!" she begins kissing and licking my chest, "Then I want to drink your blood as you sink your teeth into me and drink mine."

I stop dead in my tracks. Did I just hear her right? Did she just agree to mate me tonight? I grab her shoulders and push her slightly away.

"Cassie, are you saying that you want me to make you my mate?"

She looks right at me, "It's time to rip the band-aid off, so yes, I want you to make me your mate."

I crush my mouth to hers and pick her up, carrying her over to the bed. Laying her down, I follow. I break my lips away from hers to look down at her and I can tell she is still a little nervous.

"I am not going to fuck you tonight, Cassie. I am going to make love to the woman I love, the woman that is carrying a precious gift; I am going to make love to the woman who gave me my life back and who I am honored to protect until my dying day." With that said, I begin our mating ceremony.

Using my tongue and my lips, I cherish her body from head to toe, taking my time and making sure I taste every inch of her luscious form. She shivers with anticipation beneath my touch. I spend extra time on the part that is holding our precious cargo, noticing that she has a slight bump. I smile to myself. Reaching my hands up, I gently massage her breasts, taking special care of her nipples. She moans and arches into my hands.

I dip my mouth lower, finding the bud that ignites the fire within her. It doesn't disappoint. Her hips start to move with the rhythm of my tongue and her moans get louder. Bringing one hand down, I slide my fingers into her warm sheath, finding it soaked. My other hand joins in the play below, taking over for my mouth as I move down to her wet folds. Tasting her essence and bringing her first wave of pleasure down on her with just my gentle touches. My tongue wants her cum, so I insert it inside, along with my fingers. She cries out and moves her hips faster as, yet another wave of desire fills her.

Needing to be inside of her, I move up her body, sucking on a nipple as I go. Her pussy invites me in, and I make love to her in long slow strokes as her legs wrap around my waist, bringing me in deeper. I thrust a little harder and faster, but still keep it gentle. I turn to my back, taking her with me, never leaving her warmth. She sits upon my shaft and starts moving up and down with the same rhythm I am using. Kneading her breasts with one hand, I give her clit some more attention with the other. The time is nearing, I can feel my pressure building.

I sit up and capture her tits into my mouth once again. After a moment, I move her hair to one side and then then using my claw, I slice my jugular, so she can latch on. My cock hardens even more, and

I begin licking and sucking above her jugular. Without warning, I sink my teeth into her soft flesh and moan myself, tasting her blood for the first time. I get no scream of horror, but when I pull a mouthful of her sweet blood into my mouth and swallow, I am lost forever. Her blood is like pure spun silk as it slides down my throat. Her taste is like heaven on earth! She screams in pleasure as I continue to pull on her neck while pumping my cock in and out of her.

I feel little pin pricks on my neck. Fangs? Can't be and I ignore all thoughts except for one; pleasuring my hellion. I feel a strange sensation run through my body, as if fusing it to something. It feels as if my body has become whole, like something that has been missing has found its way back home to me. At the same time, I sense the same reaction from her. That must be it, our bodies are now fused as one. Sheer joy spreads through me and I start thrusting harder and harder until I feel her climax and mine shoots out imbedding itself deep inside of her! I retract my fangs and lick the puncture wounds so they can heal up, not leaving a trace of evidence. She stops her drinking as she finally comes down from her climax.

"I promise to love, cherish and protect you forever, Cassie." I whisper to her.

"I promise to love, cherish and protect you as well, Jax."

With the words being said and the uniting of our bodies and blood, we are now mated for eternity, and I am finally home.

NINETEEN

CASSIE

I wake up feeling different, not too much, but definitely not my usual self. Opening my eyes, everything looks clearer, as if I have beyond perfect sight. I can smell the cleaning products I used yesterday before our guests had arrived, like I have just cleaned in the last ten minutes. I also pick up the traffic on the highway that is a few blocks away. What the fuck? Did this happen because of the mating? If so, this rocks! Suddenly, I hear Jax say, 'God, I love you!'. I turn towards him as he is looking down at me.

"I love you too, Vamp!" I say back.

A strange expression comes across his face, "You heard me say that?"

"Of course, I did, I am not deaf you know." I snuggle into him.

"But I didn't say it out loud."

"Yes, you did." I laugh at him.

"No, I didn't Cassie. I was thinking it."

"So, what does that mean? I can read your thoughts now too?"

"Too?"

"Well, yeah, I mean, all my senses are better than they were before and now I'm reading your thoughts."

"Hm, that's interesting. I was never told that part of being mated."

"What part?"

"Our mates must take on our traits once we mate. All of our magnified senses and with me, reading people's thoughts. I can also use mind control, but I hate doing it. It takes too much energy and I want people to make their own decisions. I wonder though…"

"Wonder what?" I ask.

"Move to the other side of the bed, where we cannot touch each other."

I pout at him, because I am nice and warm all snuggled up with him, but I move anyway. I want to see where his madness is going.

"Okay, now I want you to think of something to say to me, but don't say it out loud. Just think it." He instructs me.

'This is getting weird; I think maybe we should get his head checked out!' I think to myself.

Jax rolls his eyes, "My head is fine, minx. No need to reserve a room at the psych ward just yet," he laughs.

"Oh my god! You totally just read my mind!"

"I did and usually I need to be touching the person in order to read their mind!" he explains. Then I hear, 'Now get that sexy ass of yours back over here!', except his lips don't move.

I smile and scoot over and back into his arms. As we are snuggling, I feel a slight pain in my gut and then, somehow, I slice my lip open, "Ouch!" I bring my hand to my mouth, "What the fuck?" I feel sharp canines.

Jax lifts my chin up to examine me and then smiles, "I thought I felt those little buggers last night!"

"Are these fangs?" I ask, starting to freak out.

"Calm down, Baby. Yes, those are your fangs."

"I thought you said I wouldn't turn into a vampire! It's plain to see that you were wrong!" I'm shrieking at this point.

"You are not a vampire, Cassie! The only times your canines will grow is when you need to drink from me for the baby, and then when we make love, for a more pleasurable experience and to keep us connected as mates. You do not have to live off blood the rest of your life."

I calm down a bit, but I am still freaked out a little. Jax drops his head to mine and swipes the blood on my lip with his tongue.

"Mm, you taste divine, my little Hellion!"

Smiling at him, "Well it's my turn to taste you now; baby needs his daddy."

"Him, is it?" Jax's eyes smile down at me.

"Or her," I shrug my shoulders, "Now bring that gorgeous neck of yours to me!"

Jax leans down and turns his head to give me access. My little fangs bite into his neck and his essence washes over me, I hear him moan. Then I feel a little pinch as he sinks his fangs into my neck and my body starts to flood with arousal.

Before I even know what's going on, he is inside of me thrusting his cock in and out of my wet pussy. The bonding between our bodies is like ecstasy and is beyond amazing, I lose control, taking him with me. Coming together so hard while drinking from one another is like nothing I have ever felt. I can't explain it, I can't even think. We retract our fangs from each other and the next thing I know, we are out cold.

I wake up 2 hours later, "Shit! I'm late for work!"

"Call in sick today, Baby, and stay in bed with me."

"As much as I love the sound of that, I can't." I chuckle, "I'll need to take time off here soon for when the baby comes. Besides, the bills aren't going to pay themselves, you know."

"You don't have to work, sweetheart, I have enough to last us an eternity."

This is the first time I am hearing of his wealth, and I'm stunned. I'm not sure how to take it. I have always taken care of myself, never needing a man to support me financially. I don't know if I want to start now.

"That's good to hear, but I like to pull my own weight. Maybe once the baby is born, I will think about staying home."

"It's your call. Just know that you have the choice of either going into work every day or staying home with this!" He yanks the blanket away from us to show me his very hot and enticingly naked body. His cock rock hard… again.

I groan and crawl out of bed before he changes my mind. "I have to go, but know this," I cock a brow at him, "You will pay for this little tease later tonight!"

He smacks my ass, "I am looking forward to it!"

I arrive to work an hour and a half late, explaining to my boss that I haven't been feeling the greatest. Even though it was a lie, it gets me thinking about my condition. I am going to have to tell them soon that I am five months along, since I'm due in a little over four months. Maybe I should start wearing baggier clothes to make me look a little bigger. Ugh, I really hate lying to people, but what do you do?

Jill is in the break room when I walk in, "Hey, Hooker, how's your morning going?" I ask.

"A lot better now that I know Jason isn't in today! I was really dreading coming into work and having to deal with him."

"Hm, maybe he felt the same way, so he stayed home to lick his wounds." I chuckle.

"Yeah well, either way, it's for the best."

"So, you going to tell me how the ride home went last night?"

"There is nothing to tell. I did apologize for hurting him, but other than that, it was the same as usual. I think you have it wrong about him liking me."

"Nope, I promise you, I am not wrong. Have you thought that maybe he is just giving you some time, or that he is a little shy? You should initiate it."

"No way, I can't do that!"

"Why not? I initiated the mating ceremony last night and it worked like a charm!" I smile.

"Shut the fuck up! You did not!"

"I sure did! Took my own advice and just jumped in. You are now looking at half of a mated couple!" I can feel myself beaming with pride.

"I am so proud of you!" She brings me in for a bear hug, "So, did it hurt?"

"Not at all. The sheer pleasure it brought is unexplainable!"

"Well, it's about time he made an honest woman out of you!" Jill laughs.

"It's not like we are married yet, so technically, I'm not an honest woman, yet."

"Technicalities, it's all it is."

"He did tell me; I could quit my job. That he has enough to last us an eternity."

"Are you serious? Then why are you still here?"

"I don't know. I am just used to taking care of myself, not depending on a guy. I know I will probably have to quit once the baby comes, but I don't know if I can do it before."

"Well, you don't have to decide anything right now."

"I know. As if I don't have enough on my plate. We had better get back to work before a search party comes looking for us!"

"Hey, I thought you needed to meet with Jax during break to feed the baby?"

"I fed this morning and since we are now mated, I should last until my third break."

"That must be a relief!"

"It's really not that bad. I actually love the taste of his blood and when we share during sex, it is phenomenal!"

"Um, that's a bit much to be sharing with me, but I am glad to hear it." She laughs.

The rest of the day goes by uneventful, except for when Jax visits on my break. We decide to park behind the building and have a quickie while I feed. I love the excitement it brings when you know that you can be caught at any given moment. Luckily, we aren't. Other than that, I can't wait to get home to my vampire!

JAX

I'm on cloud nine as I walk into the Compound, whistling and all! I get quite a bit of strange looks from some of the guys, but I don't care, nothing can sour my mood today! I go in search of Taven, finding him in the kitchen, finishing off his breakfast.

"Oh, hey Jax. There are some leftovers if you are hungry."

"No thanks. I drank my breakfast this morning." I reply smiling.

"You didn't! Well, I'll be. She finally caved in, huh?"

"Well, she referred to it as "ripping the band-aid off"." I chuckle.

"Either way, congratulations, man!" He slaps me on the back.

"By the way, I thought I should tell you that when we mate, our mates take on our traits. Cassie's senses are magnified, and she can read my mind. I can also read hers without touching her. I don't know if that part is because of my own abilities or if it happens to all mates."

"Damn, that's good to know."

"I thought you would find it interesting. So, tell me, do we have anything new on these so-called Hunters?"

"I'm glad you asked. The men have been keeping close watch on all activity and I had Kole go through all the town's activity during the night hours from the past week. It seems as though these "Hunters" believe that we only come out at night." He chuckles, "The dumbasses want to be heroes, but they don't even know their asses from their elbows!"

"Bunch of idiots! We are going to have our hands full trying to keep them alive." I exclaim.

"Exactly my thoughts, too! But there is something else. One of the Hunters seem to look familiar to some of our men, but they can't pinpoint where they have seen him. It's not a good caption of him though, because he seems to stay in the shadows. I am still waiting on Cooper and Duncan to come in so they can look him over as well."

The door opens and in walks Duncan, "Ah, we were just talking about you big guy!" I state.

Taven repeats to Duncan everything he just told me. We both walk around Taven's desk and look at the computer monitor, watching as he replays the video. He stops it on the image of a man. I look at Duncan and it looks like his head is about to explode! There, on the screen, is that little weasel, Jason.

"Hold on, Duncan, don't go storming off! We need to come up with a plan." I inform him.

"Well, this plan had better include me killing that bastard!" He seethes.

"What am I missing?" Taven asks.

"The reason why some of the men say he looks familiar, is because he was just at my house last night for game night! Jill brought him as her date!" I explain to him.

"Jill is dating this guy?"

"No, not anymore. He tried telling Duncan that he had to leave last night and then called Cassie a crazy bitch, so Jill let him have it and threw his ass out." I end with a smile on my lips.

"I see. Damn, I'm surprised you didn't kill the bastard for what he said!" He laughs.

"Cassie wanted Jill to handle it and she did a good job of it, so there was no need to step in."

"So, do you think Jill told him about us?" He asks.

"There is no fucking way Jill would tell anybody about us or vampires period!" Duncan exclaims.

"Okay, sorry I asked, but I needed to be sure!" Taven says, holding his hands up.

"What are you thinking our next move should be?" I ask.

"I think we need to just sit and wait until they make a move again."

"I think you are right. I'm going to go drive around for a bit and do a little watch detail until it's time to feed the baby."

"Man, it's still hard to believe that you are going to be a daddy! It does give all of us hope that someday, we will have a family of our own as well!" He smiles at me.

"It's the best feeling ever, I tell you!"

As I am driving around on my detail, my thoughts go to Cassie and our future. I think it's time to pop the question. I mean, we don't have to wed right away or anything, but come on. We are mated for eternity, so why wait to get her a ring? Even though I know she won't and can't turn me down, I am still nervous. Will she be happy? Will she get scared? Will it piss her off because I'm assuming it's going to happen? I can't stop myself from my thoughts, even as I am pulling up to the jewelry store.

After looking at different rings for forty-five minutes, I lay my eyes on the perfect one. It's a two-carat, French-Set Halo diamond band in platinum, with matching wedding band. I truly believe she is going to love it! Tucking it in my glove box until I get back to the Compound, I pull out and start driving around again. After about an hour, I decide to head over to Walmart and meet Cassie, but as I drive by a little hunting store, I see Jason in the front window, sizing up a crossbow. I shake my head, seriously? I quickly send Cassie a text letting her know that I am running behind and that I will let her know when I get there.

Finding a parking spot, I cut the engine and get out, walking over to the store. A bell chimes as I walk through the door, alerting the clerk that there is another customer. I raise my hand in greeting and signaling that I don't need help. I walk over by the window that I last saw Jason at, but he has moved down another isle, still carrying the crossbow. I come up behind him.

"Going hunting anytime soon?" I ask and he jumps before spinning around.

"Jesus, fuck! Don't come up on a guy like that!"

"My bad, I'm sorry." I give him a cheesy smile.

"Didn't think you were the type of guy to shop in these stores." He states.

"I'm not. I actually saw you in the window and thought I'd pop in and say hi. I didn't take you as being any sort of hunter. What is it you hunt?"

"Oh, you know, whatever is in season." I see his fingers are on the trigger even though it isn't loaded.

"I see. Maybe I will have to tag along and try it out some time. If you don't mind that is?"

"Anytime, I'd be happy to have you tag along."

"While I have you here, I hope there are no hard feelings. Last night got a little out of hand and a lot was misconstrued."

"Yeah, it did. I didn't mean any harm by anything I said. I guess I get nervous around people I don't know."

"Great, so we will let by-gones be by-gones." I stretch my hand towards him to shake.

"Yes, let's." His smile doesn't quite cut it for me, but he takes my hand anyway.

"I got to run, but I'll see you around soon." I walk out of the store with a big ole smile on my face.

TWENTY

JAX

I decide that I want to propose to Cassie in the place that we first met, Bar Harbor. I know it isn't her best vacation spot, because of what all happened with Zayne, but I am hoping to give her happier memories of the little town. Besides, I really should go back and retrieve my belongings before someone comes across them and thinks that something bad happened to its owner. They will have a search party out looking for someone who is perfectly alive and well. That will be the excuse I use to get her to go with me.

After packing an overnight bag and a few other items for both Cassie and me, I sit waiting for her to walk through the door after work. Just like clockwork, three-twenty rolls around and I hear her car pull into the garage. She smiles at me as she walks through the door and right into my waiting arms. I kiss her long and hard.

"Mm, what is that for?" she inquires.

"Just because."

"I'd like to see the kind of kiss I get once I've been a very good girl then!"

"I guess you will never find that one out, since you are never a good girl." I tease.

She slaps my chest, "You're not funny! I was a good girl last night, you said so yourself!"

"Ah, but there is a difference with being a good girl and being a good girl at doing bad things!"

"You enjoy the bad things I do in the bedroom, so that should count for something!"

"I'll have to think it over. Now, I need you to go get changed. I need to take a road trip and I want you to come along."

"A road trip? To where?"

"Bar Harbor. My stuff has been up on the mountain for weeks now and I would like to go get it. Do you mind going with me?"

"Oh my God, I guess I didn't realize that you left all of your stuff there! Of course, I will go with you."

"I figure we can get a room for the night as well, so you don't have to be sitting in the truck for five hours straight."

"Oh, did you now? What if I had a hot date with a drop-dead gorgeous guy planned for tonight?"

"Well then, you better cancel, because you are stuck with this ugly mug for the night!"

"I think I can handle looking at you for the night, as long as it's more than your face that I get to look at." She seductively presses her body to mine.

I grunt at my arousal and then push her towards the bedroom, "Go get changed before I take you right here and now!"

"Fine! Just so you know, I wouldn't mind a quickie before we leave." She smiles at me.

"Oh, I can guarantee that it won't be a quickie if I take you now! Now go, before I throw you over my shoulder and into the truck without letting you change!"

"Sheesh, so demanding!" She starts sashaying away while dropping her clothes to the floor, causing my arousal to become a full blown, aching hard on.

We arrive in Bar Harbor a little after six. My plan is to ask her as soon as possible and then we can have the whole night to celebrate and then grab my stuff in the morning before heading out for home.

"How about we grab a quick bite at the café? I could also use a large cup of coffee after that drive."

"Ooo, yes, I have missed their chocolate chip muffins!"

I pull the truck up to the café and as soon as I get out, I am bombarded with hellos from every passerby. It is the peak season, so there are crowds of tourists walking around as well. Luckily, I called the café ahead of time to reserve a private patio table for us, because the business is packed.

There is a line of people waiting to order, so I tell Cassie to wait in line and I go on ahead to talk to the manager and make sure everything is ready. I walk back and grab Cassie's hand, pulling her through the crowd to get to the patio. Customers glare at us as we pass, but I don't let it bother me. I would be pissed too.

"How did you get us this table so fast with it being this packed?"

I shrugged my shoulders, "I told them that you were pregnant and needed to sit down before you over heated. They are going to bring you a water and take our order."

Cassie looks around, taking in the scene before us. "Do you realize that this is where we first met?"

I look around, "Yeah, I guess it is."

"Good Lord, are you one of those men who couldn't care less about sentiments?"

"I never really thought about it. I have never had anyone in my life to have to worry about it." I am getting really good; I should become an actor myself!

"That is so sad to hear." She grabs my hand, "To never have had a special someone in your life as long as you have lived."

I squeeze her hand, "I have you and our baby now. That is all that matters." I smile warmly at her. It's the truth. It has never bothered me before I met her and now, I can't imagine my life without her in it.

The waitress walks over to our table and sets down two glasses of water and takes out a note pad and pen. "What can I get for the two of you?"

Cassie orders her white chocolate, mocha Latte and her chocolate chip muffin and I order my large black coffee. After the waitress leaves, Cassie stares at me and cocks an eyebrow.

"What?" I ask.

"I think that is the first time that we have gone somewhere, and the server didn't gawk or smile at you. That's weird."

"What are you talking about?"

"Casually look around. You will see quite a few women staring openly at you! You are very easy on the eyes, Babe! I'd claw their eyes out, but I know you only have eyes for me, so I won't be needing bail money."

I lean over the table and brush my lips against hers, "There, that will give them something to gawk at!" I laugh, "I love you, Baby."

"And I love you, now stop with the PDA before you embarrass me!" She giggles.

I hear the waitress making her way over here, "I love the sound of your laugh, Cassie. I love everything about you. I was truly blessed to have you crash into my cart at the grocery store, but even before then, I smelled your sweet essence and followed it. I was coming out of the clothing store around the corner when I smelled you. Me showing up that day here at the café was no coincidence. I came for you. I didn't realize what it was, but when I did, it scared the shit out of me. That's when I jumped up and almost spilled my coffee. I had been staring at you the whole time, but when you looked up at me, I lost it. I knew you meant something to me right then. That is why I brought you back here, to where we first saw each other."

The waitress puts down the drinks and Cassie's plate, which had a cover over it, and then walks away.

"Why haven't you told me all of this before?"

"I was waiting for the right time. Cassie, you are my life now, there could never be anyone else for me, ever!" I slide out of my chair as I lift the cover off her plate. Sitting there, beside her muffin is the open ring box, I drop to my knee, "Cassie Jo Manson, I want you by my side for eternity. Will you do me the honor of becoming my wife?"

The look on her face is priceless. With tears streaming down her face, she shakes her head and throws herself into my arms, "Yes, Jax, I will marry you!"

A roar of laughter and clapping come from the customers who witnessed the event. I can't help but kiss her, and kiss her thoroughly I did, before pulling away from her and placing the ring on her finger. She stares at it a moment, "This is too much, Jax!"

"You don't like it?"

"No, I love it, but it didn't need to be this big!"

"Well, you deserve bigger, but I thought this ring was perfect for you. That's why I chose it."

"I love you Jax!"

"I love you too! How about we take your muffin to go. I am hungry for my own muffin and only you can give it to me!"

"Oh no! I can't have my future husband starving! What would people think?" She smiles and kisses me again, "Thank you Jax."

"For what?"

"For making this vampire's hellion the happiest woman alive!"

CASSIE

When Jax said that he had gotten us a room, he meant a quaint little cottage on the beach, hot tub and swimming pool included. It's in a beautiful setting, surrounded by trees on one side and the ocean with a private beach on the other side. I can't believe he did all of this just to propose. The man surprises me at every turn! I normally don't like all this kind of fuss, but then again, I have never had it happen to me before. He is way too good to me! He says he is the lucky one, HA, being saddled with a smartass, little hellion is not lucky! I am the lucky one. Yes, he may be a vampire, but he is the best damn guy on this earth! I don't deserve him, but the fates seem to think otherwise.

He carries me over the thresh hold when we get to the front door and does not put me down until we are in the bedroom. Even then he doesn't want to let me go, as if I will disappear if he does, "Cassie," he says in his low husky whisper, "Tell me what you want."

His words send chills down my body, not because I'm afraid, but because I know what kind of lovemaking night this is going to be, "I want you raw, wild, and untamed. I want the beast inside of you to come out and show me how he loves me. He is part of you and like you, I love him just as fierce. Don't hold back, I want it all!"

I could swear I see his sapphire eyes glow a bright blue for a second once I speak those words. Seems he is still holding back on my account. "Stop holding back, Jax. I want all of you, nothing less."

His eyes begin to glow the bright blue that I saw, and his fangs extend. His body is tense. "Is this what you want, Cassie, to see my monster?"

"No, I see no monster. Just the man I love letting his vampire out to love me." I run my fingers over his fangs and the tension leaves his body as he stares at the truth in my eyes.

I bring his head down, and his lips to my lips, sliding my tongue over his fangs. He moans and grabbing my ass, lifts me up. My legs wrapping around his waist as he slams me into the wall and rubs his hardness against my heated core. Using his teeth, he rips my shirt right off of me, doing the same with my bra. Latching onto my nipple, he sucks while his fangs scrape against them causing a thrilling sensation to run through me.

Not completely sure how or when he does it, but I am naked from the waist down as well, him rubbing my clit while nibbling at my tits. There is a pinch above my nipple and my desire swirls throughout my entire being, crippling me of all thoughts and reality. Heat continues to build as his fingers claim my pussy. Aching and wanting more, I start moving my hips to the tempo of his hand. One more pull from my tit and I'm sent over the edge, coming hard. He lifts me up high, so my pussy fills his mouth with my juices, my legs now wrapped around his neck.

He turns and without taking his mouth away, slams me down on the bed, undressing himself while lapping up the last of my cum. He stands up and flips me to my stomach, turning my head so it's facing the wall. "Don't you dare fucking move, Baby!" He moves away but is back within seconds. Everything goes dark as he slides something over my eyes. My arms are pulled up and metal cuffs are put into place around my wrists and somehow attached to the frame, but still giving me some pull to be able to twist.

I feel a strap of some sort running down my back and over my ass. WHACK! It stings my ass cheek and repeats on the other side. I moan because it feels so good. He roughly pulls my legs far apart and fastens something around each ankle and I can't close my legs. I am stuck like this for his taking. I am completely at his mercy.

I feel a sting as he slaps the strap against my pussy, causing instant wetness. I can't help but moan.

"Ah, my little hellion likes to be tortured, does she?"

"Jax, please!"

"Begging isn't going to get you anywhere with me, love. You wanted the vampire to come out and play, well, here he is, and he shows no mercy. Now be a good girl and don't make a peep. I wouldn't want to have to gag you unless it's with my dick."

Oh my God, he doesn't know how turned on I am at this moment! I don't know if I can go on without making a sound, but I'll play the vamps little game for now. Paybacks are a bitch!

Suddenly, my ass is pulled up in the air and he is eating me out, thrusting his tongue in and out of my opening, lapping at my folds and sliding his tongue up to my ass. I am being stretched as his fingers come into play, slamming into me as he nips my ass with his fangs. I feel the pressure and turn my head into the pillow to muffle the scream that comes as he rips the orgasm out of me.

I'm panting, trying to catch my breath. He slips something around my mouth and a ball is put into place in my mouth. He whispers by my ear, "I warned you not to make a peep. Next time it will be my cock and I may not be so nice with it." He kisses my forehead lovingly.

His hands are on my hips, his cock thrusting inside of me hard and fast. "No coming for you this time, this is all me. I need you to make me come, so I can lube up that fine ass of yours and abuse it! Slamming into me so hard, I can feel his balls hitting my clit. Just as I am not able to hold back anymore, he pulls out and I feel hot fluids drenching my ass hole. He rubs it all around and into my ass, then he Inserts something cold and hard, which then starts to vibrate. I moan because it feels so fucking good! He slaps my ass, "Not a fucking peep!"

He takes the gag from my mouth and slides himself under me, filling my mouth with his dick. "I want you to suck me off until I come again, and you take every last drop of it!" I take him in as much as I can and suck him off as he starts to eat me out at the same time. "Remember, do not come until I say so!"

I moan, because it's going to be hard when he is going to town on my pussy, and it feels so fucking good! He slaps my ass hard and shoves his dick in further as punishment for making a sound. I start sucking harder and deeper, swirling my tongue around the girth in my mouth. I feel his dick swell and know that he is close. Continuing my assault, I feel my canines throb and smile to myself. Being careful not to nick him, I extend my fangs and gently scrape his shaft, "Jesus fuck!" he roars, and his orgasm explodes into my mouth.

Licking the last drop, he moves away, leaving me hurting with pent up pressure. He removes the restraints from my ankles and wrists then rips the blind fold away. He is still in his vampire form, staring down at me, still hungry for me. He moves between my legs and enters me in one hard stroke and then stops. The vibrating plug is still in my ass, making me feel so full with him in me as well.

"I'm going to finish making love to my soon-to-be-wife and I want to hear you screaming my name as you come all over my cock. He starts thrusting into me slowly and then speeds it up as he nips at my tits.

With the plug in my ass on high speed and his cock filling my pussy, I scream and let go, coming all over him.

Without losing a beat, he flips over, and I am on top, riding him. The plug in my ass now vibrating his balls. As I reach for my climax again, I sink my teeth into him as his sink into me, tumbling us both into oblivion.

TWENTY-ONE

JAX

It's ten o'clock at night and I'm wide awake, listening to Cassie's labored breathing as she sleeps. I have my hand laying on her little baby bump, imagining what she will look like as it grows; I can't wait until she is big with my child and glowing. I wonder if it's a boy or a girl and who they are going to take after in looks. Just a little over four months now and we will know. I've been thinking about buying a new house, but I am not sure how to broach the subject with Cassie. She seems really content in her home now. Argh, I have to get up and do something, these thoughts are going to drive me crazy.

I carefully pull my arm out from under Cassie, not wanting to wake her, and slide out of the bed. The nice thing about this place is that it's so private, that I can walk around naked, inside, and out without any neighbors seeing. I walk out the sliding back doors to the pool and dive in. I break the surface and tread water, looking around and enjoying the view. I wonder if the owners want to sell? I would love to have this house as a vacation home.

I hear a noise by the door and watch as Cassie walks out like I did, bare ass naked. I will never get tired of looking at her, she's so damn beautiful! She walks into the pool using the stairs and swims over to me. Reaching out, I pull her to me, and we float, watching the night sky. I love having these moments with her. She surely keeps me on my toes, but then there are rare moments like this when we can just relax and enjoy just being with each other, no need for either of us to talk.

My hand is splayed across her stomach as I hold her. "Have you noticed the little bump that you have?" I ask smiling.

"Is that a fat joke?" She teases.

"Hey, take it how you want, Baby, but I for one, love it! In fact, I can't wait to see you big with my child."

"Why, so you can make fun of me when I can't put my own socks and shoes on because I'm so fat?"

"You know it! Or when your ankles get so big that they no longer look like ankles!" I laugh.

She turns around and shoves me under the water. I come back up sputtering because I'm laughing so hard. Grabbing her again, "Oh, Baby, you are beautiful no matter how fat you get! We will work it all off once the babe is born anyway." I give her a mischievous smile.

"Now that, I can handle, but any other form of exercise, forget it!"

"We should think about heading back in. I want to get an early start and I want to grab some breakfast before heading up the mountain. I must feed that belly of yours." I tease as I poke at it.

"Yes, food must get in my belly." She says in her Fat Bastard from Austin Powers voice. We laugh and then head inside.

We are up by seven in the morning, showered and out the door by eight. Cassie is a little sad to be leaving, but what she didn't know is that while she was showering, I was buying this little get-a-way cottage from the owners. I plan on surprising her once all the papers are transferred over to her name.

"Can we just grab some breakfast to go? I'm anxious to get home." She asks.

"Whatever you want, Darlin."

I take us through a drive-thru and head up the mountain. It would have been faster if I left my truck below and used my speed to get up to the top, but I don't want to leave Cassie by herself for too long. It is bad enough that I can't take the truck all the way to the top to where

I was staying, but at least I only needed to leave her for 5 minutes top. Yes, I am that fast.

For the past month, we have been living in prewedding bliss. We decided on a March wedding and that is less than a year away, so Cassie and Jill have been busy planning that while I have been working longer hours with the Elite, trying to get to the bottom of these so-called Hunters. It's been quiet since we brought in the first guy for questioning. We figure that it's only a matter of time before we get another lead.

I am watching the clock anxiously, waiting for three in the afternoon to roll around. Cassie and I have our ultrasound appointment at three thirty and we are excited to see what we are having. Cassie has finally started to really show and so we have to let the cat out of the bag with her parents and co-workers. Of course, being her parents, they are worried for her, thinking that we are moving too fast by getting married and that I may leave her. We can't tell them the truth to help ease their worries, we can only continue as we are and in time, they will come to realize that I am not going anywhere. Her co-workers on the other hand already have her baby shower planned, they are thrilled.

I stop at the house to pick Cassie up and it looks like a tornado has come through it, the women are nowhere to be seen, "Hello, are you ladies underneath all of this debris?" I holler out.

Cassie pokes her head out of the kitchen, "Hey, babe, I'll be ready in just a minute."

"What's all this?"

"I am sorry. I was hoping to have it all cleaned up, but time got away from us. It's all the wedding samples and what-nots. I'll pick it up as soon as we get back, I promise."

"No, it's fine. I just wondered if I needed to send in a search party, I still don't see Jill."

"Funny man you are! She left 5 minutes ago. I forgot that I am supposed to have a full bladder, so I am chugging some water down now."

"We have a few minutes yet, take your time and don't drink too fast."

We get to the clinic with five minutes to spare. After checking in, we go to wait in the waiting room, but we are called just as we are sitting down. My palms are sweaty, and I am so nervous, but excited at the same time. Grabbing Cassie's hand, we walk back together.

Cassie is ready and laying on the table when Dr. Howard walks in and greets us, "How have things been going? Any more pains like last time?"

"Nope, we have been good about getting her fed on time." I respond.

"How often do you take his blood in a day?"

"Usually about three times, but sometimes more when we are intimate."

"So, I take it you two have mated since our last visit?" She smiles at us.

"We sure have!" I grin and Cassie shakes her head at me.

"Okay, let's see if baby will cooperate and show us what they are, shall we?"

Once again, the doctor pours the gel on Cassie's stomach and uses the wand. The heartbeat comes through loud and clear. I don't think I will ever get enough of hearing that! Then we see the baby. It has grown so much in the last six weeks! You can now see the arms, hands, fingers, legs, feet, toes, and a little button nose.

"Well, mom and dad, looks like you are going to be the proud parents of a beautiful baby girl!"

"A girl? Are you sure?" Cassie asks.

"I thought it didn't matter to you?" I question.

"Oh, it doesn't. I just don't want to decorate and buy for a girl, and it turns out a boy."

"I can promise you that it will not be a little boy, Cassie." Dr. Howard giggles.

I grab Cassie's hand and squeeze, "We are having a little girl!"

"I can see it now! She is going to have every Elite wrapped around her little finger and be very spoiled!" she laughs.

"Well, this Elite will love being wrapped around her little finger, just as I am around her mother's." I lean down and kiss her forehead.

"Here are the pictures of her and I want to see you back here in three weeks." The doctor tells us as she hands me the pictures.

"Thank you, Dr. Howard." I shake her hand.

"It is a pleasure as always!" She replies.

CASSIE

The next three weeks flies by, and everything checks out great with the baby. Our next appointment is in two weeks. Aside from my growing belly, I feel great. The wedding plans are coming along, and we are looking at new houses. Jax had brought it up to me a week ago and as much as I love my home, I have a growing family now. He also gave me a set of keys to our new get-a-way cottage in Bar Harbor. Boy, did I really thank him for that one... we didn't leave the bedroom for a whole day!

Jax isn't home as often as he was in the beginning. With the Hunters out there, they have been on watch constantly and have found that the Hunters have grown in numbers. Jax had told me about Jason being one and at first, I had thought it best if I didn't say anything to Jill, but I couldn't keep her in the dark. Even though Jason never came back to work, I didn't know if she would ever run into him again. Of course, she freaked out about it, but over time she had gotten over it.

Her and Duncan have grown closer, but neither one have yet to say if they are official or not, but I still believe it's only a matter of time. We all know that they are destined mates, as well as Duncan, but Jill, being her sensible self, has to be completely sure before she jumps all in, unlike me.

Mid-August is now fast approaching, and I have yet to get my wedding dress. Jill and I plan on going dress shopping today if she ever gets her ass over here! It's not like her to be late, if anything, she is always early. I try texting her and get no response, but she is the responsible driver between the two of us and will not respond if she is driving, so I wait.

Finally, 15 minutes late, she pulls into my driveway. I don't give her time to get out of the car, as I hurry out the door and over to her car, "It's about time, you slow ass!" I joke.

"Don't even go there. I am usually the one that is waiting on you!"

"Fine. I'll give you this one pass." I smile.

"Why are we even doing this now? You are pretty big to be able to get an accurate size?"

"Because the wedding is only seven months away and at least I can get it ordered now and then have 3-4 months to get it altered. Besides, I am wanting out of the house. It sucks when Jax isn't around."

"I know what you mean. I am usually hanging out with Duncan when I'm not with you and now, with them taking on extra patrols, I am bored."

"So, how is that whole thing going with him?" I glance over at her.

"It's going well. He is really sweet and patient with me." She leaves it at that, but I know there is more.

"Why were you late, Jill?" Smiling, I already know the answer.

Jill hesitates before answering, "Duncan brought me lunch, so we sat and ate together."

"And…"

"Ugh, you are so nosey; do you know that?"

"No. I am your bestie and I know when you are holding back on me, now spill!"

"Fine! He kissed me before he left."

"And that made you late?"

"I might have kissed him back, which then turned into a heated make out session." She giggles.

I shriek, "I knew it, you little skank!"

"Don't be getting any ideas! Just because we had our tongues down each other's throats, doesn't mean it's happily ever after for us!"

"No, not yet anyway." I give her a smug smile.

We pull up to the Bridal Boutique just in time for my appointment. The dresses are all amazing, but it still takes me about two hours to find "the one". With an off the shoulder, plunging neckline, hourglass figure and a mermaid tail flare at the bottom, I know it is the right one. Even with my protruding belly, it is still gorgeous on me! Jax had told me not to worry about the price and gave me his credit card, so I bought the dress without looking at the tag.

As we are leaving the Boutique, we are talking about stopping for a Latte, when a blacked-out SUV pulls up quick, taking us by surprise. Two figures jump out wearing masks and grab Jill. She screams and I jump into action, grabbing hold of the back of her shirt with one hand and continuously hitting one of the figures. He finally let's go of Jill and grabs hold of me, flinging me into the vehicle behind Jill.

Kicking, hitting and screaming, trying to get out, Jill and I both fight against our abductors, but there are four of them and only two of us. All I can think about is not seeing Jax again. They were after Jill, not me, but I'd be damned if I let anyone take my bestie! We are better off together than just her by herself. I see Jill take a punch to the side of her head before I feel pain burst through my own and then darkness.

I gain consciousness, thinking déjà vu, except this time I am blindfolded. I remain quiet and still, so I can focus on my surroundings without the kidnappers knowing I'm awake. I can hear voices coming from another room, so happy for my new magnified hearing, I strain to hear them clearly.

"What the fuck are you doing, grabbing Cassie too, you dumbass?"

"What else was I supposed to do? She wouldn't let go of Jill and I couldn't do anything that would end up hurting her, she's pregnant for Christ's sake! I did the only thing I could do! Besides, we didn't need any witnesses to run back and tell the Elite. Not before we are ready."

"I couldn't care less if something happened to that monster bastard! It's an abomination!"

"Jason, you don't know that for sure!"

What? Jason is behind all of this? No wonder they were after Jill and not me. My God, I knew there was something not right with that guy!

"Yes, I do! Do you think I sit around on my ass all day doing nothing? No! I have been scoping out the possible threats, and let me tell you, you just unleashed the biggest threat of them all! Jax and Cassie are mated, and you NEVER touch a mate! We are as good as dead now!"

I can't help but smile at that. He knows his facts; I'll give him that. This still doesn't help us with our situation though.

"Well then, since we are as good as dead, we might as well take out what we can before we see our maker!" another guy speaks up.

"Meaning?" Jason asks.

"Meaning, we yank that creature out of Cassie and call it good!"

I can't help the horrific sound that comes out of my mouth. Take my baby? Never will I allow them to take her! I will die fighting if I have too! My first kill will be that vile monster, the one that dares to take what is mine!

"Well, looks like someone is awake." Jason speaks up, "Sorry Cassie, you weren't meant to be part of this, but you did it to yourself! You should have thought of your baby's safety before getting involved."

"I am not one to stand around and let my bestie be kidnapped by the likes of you or anybody else for that matter! What are you wanting anyway, Jason?"

"Ah, so you know who I am. I guess there is no need for the blindfold anymore." He slips it off my head and I adjust my eyes to the bright light.

Looking around for Jill, I don't see her. "What have you done with Jill? Is she okay? Please don't hurt her!"

"I would never hurt her; I am in love with her!"

"Ha! This is a funny way of showing it!'

"I just wanted to get her away from that monster that is always by her side. What is his name, Duncan?"

"Well, you signed your death warrant with that one too, not just with Jax!"

"It is what it is, and we shall see who is standing in the end!"

"How long do you plan on keeping us locked up?"

"As long as I have to! You are safe here, no need to worry. We protect humans from those vile creatures."

"They are human too, Jason. It's just a little something in their DNA that makes them different. The Elite protect the innocent, just like you!"

"Oh, do they now? They already killed one of my men, an innocent!"

"That was an accident, and technically, he wasn't innocent. He attacked an innocent vampire and his mate. Therefore, making him a monster who needed to be taken out!"

"I don't have time for all this. Just know that you are here for a while, possibly until you have that thing, and we decide what to do with it!"

Oh my God, NO! I need Jax's blood to keep us both alive! "Please!" I beg, "I need to be let go! I can't stay here more than a few hours! My baby, she needs her father's blood 2-3 times a day!"

"And how is that my problem? You will be better off if you lose it anyway."

"You don't understand! I will suffer horrendous pain and if we go too long without it, we both die!" I am bawling at this point, too scared to care.

"Hm, I'll think on it and will be back." He leaves me tied in a heap.

I have to get a hold of myself and think! I'm going to need to feed in the next two hours, tops! I look down at my belly, "Hold on little one, mommy will figure something out."

I look to see if I can find anything to cut the ropes from my hands, but the room is pretty much bare. I close my eyes to think. Think,

Cassie, think! Oh My God, that's it! Think! Maybe if I call out to Jax with my thoughts, he will hear them! I don't know if we need to be close or if he needs to be trying to listen, but it's all I have right now.

"Jax, Baby! If you can hear me, I need you now! The Hunters have me and Jill! Please find us!!" I sit and listen for a response. Nothing. I keep chanting it over and over again, in hopes that he will hear me soon!

TWENTY-TWO

JAX

It's been a long day of patrolling and I'm beat. Just when we think we have a good lead on the Hunters, it turns into a dead end. There have been three vampires murdered in the last two weeks, two of them innocent and the third one had it coming. These guys are learning quick and need to be stopped, but they are good at hiding themselves.

I just want to get home, relax and feed my girls. I speed dial Cassie to see if she wants me to pick anything up for dinner. I don't think I can do frozen pizza again this week. Love her to pieces, but the woman can't cook to save her life! Her phone goes straight to voicemail, so I wait a couple minutes and try again. Again, straight to voicemail. Guess we will order delivery once I am home.

Ten minutes later I'm pulling into the driveway. Walking into an empty house, I try Cassie's cell again, nothing. I am not liking this, so I call Jill and get her voicemail. I speed dial Duncan and he answers on the second ring.

"What up?" he answers.

"Have you talked to Jill in the last two hours?"

"It was about two hours ago when she texted me while Cassie was trying on one last dress. I'm almost to her house now. Why, what's up?"

"I just got home, and Cassie isn't here. I've tried her cell three times now and Jill's once, I keep getting voicemail." I am starting to panic.

"I'm pulling up to Jill's place now, but I don't see her car. That's strange, she told me she would be home by now."

"Maybe they stopped for dinner somewhere. I'll try again in a bit, thanks buddy. Let me know if you here from Jill."

"Will do."

I grab a beer from the fridge and sit at the table, an uneasy feeling in my gut. I close my eyes, "Where are you, Cassie?" I think to myself.

Then, as if she is standing next to me, I hear, "Oh my God, Jax! You are there, I can hear you!"

I open my eyes and look around, but no Cassie. Shit! She is in my thoughts, communicating! This is freaky! "Cassie, Baby, is that really you?"

"Yes! I have been trying to get you to hear me for a little over an hour! I was about to give up! I need you Jax!"

"What's wrong, Cassie? You are scaring me!"

"The Hunters, they took me and Jill as we were leaving the Bridal Boutique! That mother fucker, Jason, is in charge. I wasn't supposed to be taken but I fought them as they tried to take Jill, so they grabbed me too!"

"FUCK!" I roar, "Baby, do you know where you are being held?"

"No. They knocked both Jill and I out when we wouldn't stop fighting them once we were in the SUV. I don't even know where Jill is at. I am in a room by myself still tied up."

"What do they want with Jill?"

"All I know is that Jason said he loves her and that he wants to keep Duncan away from her. He doesn't plan on hurting us, though, but Jax, he knows what you are, along with the rest of the Elite."

"Okay, don't worry about that right now. It's good that they are not planning on hurting either of you. That gives us some time to figure out where he has you at."

"Babe, I haven't fed since this morning. I'm okay right now, but it won't be too much longer."

"Shit!" How could I forget about my daughter? "I need you to try and get any kind of clue as to where you may be at."

"I will see what I can do. Jason knows that our daughter needs your blood. He wasn't too concerned about letting her die without it, but he didn't like hearing that I would die too. I don't know what his plans are for us and that scares me."

"It's going to be okay, Baby! I will find a way to get to you. Be strong and do what you do best, cause some hell! I love you, Cassie, and I will be seeing you soon!"

"Love you too, Jax, and please hurry!"

Before I could call Headquarters, I receive a text from Cassie's phone.

"If you ever want to see your mate and child again you will meet me ALONE at the coordinates that I will be sending you! If I see anybody with you or within a 10-mile radius I will gut your mate and rip out that monster that you call your child!!!"

I can't breathe. All I can do is stare at the text and read it over, and over, again. Another text comes through which are the coordinates and it says to be there in an hour. I run out to my truck and google the coordinates as I squeal out of the driveway. I call Duncan and inform him of the events, hearing him cuss and throw shit.

"Duncan, you need to listen to me! We will get them back, but we have no idea where they are. I am on my way to meet the asshole now, but I have to be alone! I am sending you the info of where I'll be meeting him, but you have to stay away, you cannot be within 10-miles. Do you understand?"

"YES, I understand, but I don't like it!"

"I know buddy, I know. I don't like it either, I smell a trap. Promise me something."

"Anything."

"If something happens to me, you need to save my girls. Find a way to feed my daughter until she doesn't need it anymore." I'm choking up just thinking about it.

"Of course, I will, but you will not let anything happen to you. You have too much to live for!"

"Yes, I do!"

Hanging up with Duncan, I try making contact with Cassie, "Can you hear me, Love?"

"Yes, I'm here."

"Are you doing okay?"

"I'm okay. Just a few twinges here and there."

Shit! I need to get to her soon! "I'm coming for you! Someone texted me with your phone, telling me to meet them at a specific area. I don't think it's where you are at, though, but I am going to do what I need to do to find you. Just please hang in there!"

"Jax, it has to be a trap! Don't go!"

"I have to, it's my only choice if I want to find you!"

"Just please be careful and stay alert. I can't lose you Jax!"

"Ditto, my little minx!"

I pull up to the rundown house forty-five miles south of Augusta and turn my engine off. I have about fifteen minutes left to spare. I get out of my truck and start pacing. After ten minutes a black SUV pulls up and three men get out, all armed with crossbows. A fourth man climbs out of the vehicle, and I immediately recognize Jason, also holding a crossbow.

"Ah, Jax! Glad to see you can follow directions! I am terribly sorry to bring you and Cassie into this mess, but it's done. It's not like I wouldn't be coming after you at some point anyway, but I was hoping to leave you for last."

"Get to the point you son of a bitch!"

"I understand why you are pissed, but make no mistake, I will kill them if you try anything. We protect innocents and even though Cassie is mated to you and is pregnant with that abomination, she is still an innocent, caught in your little web! I do not want to harm her, as crazy as she is, but I will."

"So, what do you need from me?"

"I don't need anything from you, it's what your mate needs. Now, just to show that I am not a horrible person, I am going to bring you to her. You will also be my captive for the duration of her pregnancy, only seeing her long enough to give her what she needs to stay alive."

"You are bringing me to her? What's the catch?"

"No catch. I don't want her blood on my hands if need be. You will do what is told of you or they will suffer the consequences! Do we have an agreement?"

"Of course, just take me to her now!"

"I give the orders here, not you!"

"Just please take me to her."

"Of course, but first, you must put these on." He holds up neck, wrist and ankle shackles all chained together.

I yank them from his hands and put them on. Two of the guys help me up into the SUV and the third guy gets into my truck to follow us. Before leaving, a hood goes over my head, turning everything black. Fuck! How am I going to get us out of this one? I'll think about that later, for now, I need to concentrate on the direction that they are taking me.

CASSIE

The pains are strong and doubling me over, causing me to lay in the fetal position. My hands are still tied behind my back and my legs are tied together, making my muscles ache on top of the stomach pains. I've called out to Jax a few times but I have gotten no response. That alone is making me freak out! What did they do to him? Is he dead? Why hasn't anyone come to me in hours? My mind is about to explode with all these unanswered questions and thoughts. I can't even try to sleep, to push them out, because of the horrible pain I'm in!

Finally, I hear the locks on the door move and it opens. I look up from my position on the floor and I see Jason enter, but another bout of pain rips through my gut, making me cry out and curl myself up as best as I can.

Jason runs over to me, "What's wrong?" He asks me, moving my hair out of my face.

With a scratchy voice, I whisper, "Need Jax..."

He stands and runs for the door, ordering someone to bring something into my room. I hear chains and think of how cold hearted he is if he plans on putting them on me, but I have no strength to fight. I close my eyes. Let them do what they must.

"CASSIE! What the fuck, why is she still tied up?" A familiar voice roars and I lift my tear-streaked face up.

"Jax?"

"Yes, Baby, I'm here!" Jax says in a soothing voice, then yells, "Let me go to her, she needs me!"

I see him scuffle over to me, all chained up from neck to ankles and my heart cries for him. He let himself be captured so he could get to us, "Jax, you shouldn't have come! They will end up killing you!"

"I've told you, love, I'd die for you! I couldn't leave you here knowing that you and our daughter would die without me!"

I start to cry as another pain starts in my gut.

"Keep me in the chains, I don't care, but please untie her. She is not a threat locked in here!" Jax pleads.

"Fine, but if she tries anything, I will use the shackles on her." Jason warns and I hear Jax growl.

"Can you please take the neck shackle off of me so she can feed? Keep the wrist and ankle cuffs on, but she needs access to my jugular." Jax is begging now.

Jason comes over to me and unties all of the ropes, causing a moan from me as I try and get circulation flowing again. Then he heads towards Jax and takes a key off from around his neck. He positions himself behind Jax and then there is a click before the neck cuff is removed.

Jax shuffles his way over to me and leans over to grab my hands and help me to stand up. Pulling me over to the only metal chair in the room, which is bolted to the floor, he sits and brings me down on his lap.

"Do you mind? This is kind of a private moment?" He asks Jason and his men.

"Fine, you have 5 minutes, and we will be right outside the door. Don't forget, you try anything, and they will suffer." He points to me and the baby. Jax nods his head in understanding.

"Cassie, you must feed from me before the pains get worse and while there is still time. They are keeping us separated."

"What? Why can't they keep us together?"

"It's too risky for them, but don't worry, we will figure something out, I promise." He kisses me quick and then turns his head, giving me access.

I hesitate for a mere second and then sink my teeth into his delicious vein as he moans. My stomach starts to settle, and I relax and then Jax sinks his own into mine. I feel the desire start building, but I try and push it away, knowing that we can't do anything about it. After a moment he pulls away, but holds my head to his neck, urging me to keep drinking. A few more pulls and I lift my head.

"How long is he going to keep us here, Jax?"

"I don't know, love. I think he plans on keeping you until our daughter is born and then getting rid of her and I."

"What? No!"

"Shh, I'm not going to let that happen, Baby! You know that. In the meantime, we can still communicate with each other."

"Okay. I know you won't allow any harm to come to us, but it hurts to see you like this, just because of it."

"Please don't worry about me. Let me worry about me and you worry about you and the baby. Promise me."

"I promise to take care of us, but I can't promise not to worry about you!"

"Fair enough I guess." He kisses me long and hard until we hear the door open.

"Time to go Jax. You will see her again in a few hours." Jax nods and like a good little boy, puts the neck cuff back on.

We stand together and give each other one last kiss before he is taken away. Jason stays behind and turns towards me, "How do you do it?"

"Do what?" I ask.

"Be with him, knowing what he is?"

"Tell me Jason, what do you think he is?"

"He is a monster. One who preys on innocent people and drains them dry, leaving them for dead!"

"Do you know what he did when we first met? He saved me! Saved me from a vile monster who kidnapped me, because he thought I was his mate. He did unspeakable things to me and Jax saved me, a person that he could have walked away from, but didn't, because he has vowed to protect the innocent. He protects them from the vile vampires AND the vile people!" I take in a breath and go on, "They are not all bad, Jason. The Elite? They are the good guys; they don't kill heedlessly. They kill the ones that do! I know I can't change your mind; you believe what you believe, but I had to inform you of the truth. Do with it what you want."

"Well, I didn't expect all that, but I asked for it I guess."

"Jason, when can I see Jill? I am sure she is scared."

"I'm sorry Cassie, but I can't allow you to see her. You two do too much damage when you are together."

"Is she okay?"

"She is as good as you can expect someone who has been kidnapped to be. I keep trying to soothe her, but she wants nothing to do with me right now. That will change though."

I can hear Jax trying to communicate with me, so I need to try and get rid of Jason.

"Okay. I wanted to thank you for bringing Jax to me, also."

"Yeah well, it's one thing to get rid of vamps, but I don't want an innocent's blood on my hands."

"Well thanks anyway. By the way, do you think I could get a bed or air mattress in here so I can sleep? I'm exhausted."

"I will see what I can do." He walks out of the room, locking me in.

TWENTY-THREE

JAX

I've lost track of how long we have been held prisoners here after the first couple of weeks. At first, it was easy, because they would take me to Cassie's room three times a day, but they started taking me to see her more throughout the day and that screwed with my mind. If I were to guess, I would say it's been close to 2 months now and going by how big my little girl has grown, I'd say that Cassie could possibly go into labor in about two weeks, maybe three.

I have had these damn shackles on the whole time, my skin is raw from the restraints, but I have kept Cassie and the baby safe by acting like a good little vampire, and that is all that matters. Everyday Cassie and I communicate, trying to come up with how we could escape, but it never works out. I am scared to death what will happen if Cassie goes into labor here. Not only do we not know what kind of labor it will be, but also, what Jason will do once she is born.

I never thought that we would be here as long as we have, especially since every Elite has a tracking device on their vehicle. My thinking is that my truck never made it here. Duncan has got to be going out of his mind, not knowing what happened to us, to Jill. In all this time that we have been here, I have never seen Jill. I don't even know if she is even here. Cassie has been sick with worry over not knowing where her best friend is being kept. At least we have each other, Jill has no one.

I swear on my life that when I am free of these chains, the beast will come out and no one will survive that wrath. I just need to hold on a little bit longer. I need to keep being the obedient prisoner and continue hoping that it will work in my favor. That they will trust me enough to release the chains and in doing so, release the beast.

My thoughts turn back to Cassie, "Good morning, love. Did you sleep well?"

"Not really. I have been having a lot of back pain, making it uncomfortable. What about you? Have any wet dreams about me?" she jokes.

"You know I do every night, Baby."

"It's been too long, Jax. I need you so bad, my body aches for you."

"As mine does for you, love. We just need to hold out for a little longer."

"It's been months and our daughter will be born soon. I can't have them take you both away from me. Something needs to be done soon."

"Do you have anything in mind?"

"Kind of, but you are not going to like it at all."

"Tell me what crazy scheme that little head of yours has come up with."

"Promise you will not be furious and really think it over?"

"Uh oh, I don't think I'm going to like this."

"I hate it, but what other options do we have?"

"Cassie, stop procrastinating and just spit it out."

"I am going to start acting indifferent to you when they bring you in to me and I'm going to start flirting with them…"

"NO, YOU ARE NOT!"

"Please just listen to me!"

"Absolutely not! You are mine and I don't want anybody thinking otherwise!"

"But if I can get close enough to them to be able to grab the key, then you can free yourself and kill the bastards!"

I have to admit that it's the best plan that either of us have come up with in all this time that could actually work. I can't stand to think of another's hand touching my woman, the mother of my child!

"And what if they try something and you are helpless to stop them? Or they are bold enough do touch you while I'm right there? I don't think I cannot show my rage at seeing that!"

"I know, babe, but we have to try. This baby is coming soon!"

There is nothing else to do, but to agree with this insane plan and pray that it works. It's our last shot. Resigning to this crazy plan, I give a long sigh.

"Fine, but don't take it too far! I will try my best not to react."

"I love you Jackson Michael Whitley, always remember that."

"I do, love."

They come for me shortly after I break communication with Cassie. I can't believe I agreed to this, but it's too late to turn back and it really is our only option at the moment. As we walk down the hallway, the guy named Dan, makes small talk with me just like every other time he takes me to Cassie. I pretend to listen and throw in a sentence here and there for good measure. It's like we are old pals.

I act as if I'm bummed out about something, so he questions me. "What's got you so grumpy today, besides for the obvious, that is?"

"Women, they never know what they want, changing their mind whenever they feel like it!"

"Ah, problems with the Mrs. I see."

"Ha! That's putting it mildly. She is all gun-ho about being mated to a vamp but have her around a bunch of regular guys for a few months and her tune changes!" There, maybe that will help get things started in the right direction.

"I'm sure things will work out for ya, Jax."

"I'm at the point where I don't think I want to work it out anymore. I've tried these past few weeks, but I'm not doing it anymore. I'm here for the baby now, that's it. That woman is crazy, and I don't need that in my life."

"Sorry to hear that. Does she really find the guys here attractive?" he asks.

"Apparently." I can't believe he is falling for it!

I communicate to Cassie letting her know that I got the ball rolling and quickly inform her of mine and Dan's conversation, so she needs to act accordingly. We stop outside of her room so Dan can unlock the door and then we step in.

"Well, it's about time! Your child is starving, and I want to get this over with." She says, acting irritated.

"Keep your pants on, I'm here, aren't I?"

"Oh, I'll be keeping my pants on when you are around, that's how we ended up here to begin with!" She points to her belly.

"Whatever! Just do it, so we can be done already!"

Dan comes over and unlocks my neck cuff and instead of sitting with her on my lap, I remain standing. Dan goes to leave, and I call back to him, "No need to leave, this will only take a moment."

He nods his head at me and then just stands there watching, like he was at a fucking peep show.

I lean over a little bit so she can reach my neck and with only her hands on my shoulders, she bites down and I bite back my moan. What I would give to be able to wrap her in my arms again. It seems like forever ago that I last held her, always having these damn chains on.

Once she has her fill, she retracts her fangs and steps away. I put the neck cuff back on and start towards the door.

"Oh Dan," I hear Cassie call in her seductive little voice, "Can you be a sweetie and get me something to wash down the awful taste in my mouth?" She runs her hand up and down Dan's arm.

"I sure can. Let me get Jax back to his room and I'll grab you something." He winks at her and I roll my eyes.

"Perfect. Thank you so much!" She smiles.

Dan takes me back to my room without saying a word. I'm pretty sure he knows that I witnessed his flirting with my mate. I communicate with Cassie as soon as the door closes behind me.

"Well, that was some great acting on your part!" I accuse.

"Jax, don't be this way, please. Did you see how he acted towards me? He is going to be an easy target."

"I know he will, but I still hated every minute of it. It hurts me not to be able to hold you during those private moments and now not even to have your closeness by you being on my lap? It's torture!"

"It's torture for me not to have you drink from me! Shit, he's back already.

Please remember that it's only you!" And then she is gone.

CASSIE

Dan is back with my drink in a matter of minutes. Damn, he didn't waste any time at all! Luckily, he is the most gullible of the bunch and seems to be the horniest as well! As much as I hate to admit it, that works perfectly in our favor.

"Oh God, thank you so much for this! I have such a bitterness in my mouth now!" I take a drink of the soda, "Mm, so good!"

"I wasn't sure what you liked to drink, sorry."

"I usually don't have a preference, as long as it tastes good in my mouth." I lick my bottom lip slowly.

"C-Can I get you anything else?"

"At the moment, no, but stay close. I may need you for other things. Oh, would Jason happen to be around?"

"No, not until this evening. He took a group with him to patrol. Looks like you are stuck with me until they come back."

"Oh, I wouldn't use the word stuck. I like your company. Maybe after my little nap you can come keep me company?"

"It would be my pleasure, Cassie. Just knock on the door when you wake up."

"You are too sweet, Dan, Thank you." I give him a quick peck on the cheek, making him blush and then he leaves.

The tank top they provided me with is stretched tight across my swollen breast, showing a deep cleavage and working into my plan great. I knock on the door and call for Dan. He is there opening my door in seconds, his eyes landing on my chest. Typical guy doesn't matter who you are, ugh!

"Hey Dan, could you bring Jax to me? I think this kid wants another feeding already. I'm starting to get stomach pains. Oh, and after, I would like to play some cards. Would you like to play poker with me?"

"What kind of poker do you play?"

I lean into his ear, "Any kind you like!" Then I lick the rim of his ear, ugh gross. It does the trick though.

"I'll go grab Jax, so you can get this over with." He smiles at me.

He leaves to go get Jax.

"Jax, it's show time! Dan is coming for you, and we are getting out of here."

"So, what's the plan?" He isn't sounding very enthused, but can you blame him?

"Just keep your eyes on my every move, no matter what, okay?"

"It's not like I have a choice."

"It has to be now. Jason is gone with a big group out on patrol, so it's the best time!"

"Okay, okay! He's here, see you in a minute."

Dan walks in with Jax and closes the door. He takes the key off from around his neck and unlocks the neck cuff, but before he can put it back on, I put my hand on his wrist and my body snug up against his. Rubbing at his peck area and slowly moving my hand down, stopping right above his jeans. I feel his nasty arousal against me, nauseating me, but I rub just a little against it, turning it into a full hard on. I lace my fingers through his, the ones that have the chain to the key in them. Not paying any attention to anything else, but me rubbing against him, I quickly, but carefully, lace the chain through my own, taking it from his.

"Dan, as much as dickhead over there likes an audience, I am a little shy when it comes to people watching. Could you possibly step out for the allotted time?"

As he gazes into my eyes, I start rubbing his stomach with my hand as I unlace my other hand from his and pocket the key quick. He looks at Jax and then back at me skeptically, so I whisper in his ear, "But don't go too far, because you owe me a game of cards and I want to collect!"

I look back at him as I bite my lower lip seductively.

"Okay, 5 minutes." He agrees.

"Not a minute longer." I continue to smile as he smiles back and closes the door behind him.

I quickly go to Jax without looking at his face, because I don't want to see the hurt in his eyes. I slide the key into the hole of the cuffs and turn. It clicks open and I do the same at his ankles.

"Stay still so they stay in place and looks like they are still on when he comes back in. I'll get him so his back is to you, and you come up and snap his neck, got it?"

He is just standing there with a tick in his neck. Oh yeah, he is livid! "Please Baby, don't fall apart now, you are free! Now take some of my blood to get some of your strength back."

Snapping out of it, he bends down sinks his fangs in, taking what he needs. I quickly bit him to grab some for the road. Sure enough, the door opens and in walks Dan as I am wiping my mouth. I smile and head over to him, lacing my arm through his as I turn his back to Jax.

"Dan, please hurry back after taking him back to his room. I am in need of your company."

"No worries. I'll be back in a jif..." he never gets to finish his sentence.

I stare as he crumbles to the floor, not a tear to shed. Then I'm running into Jax's arms, and he folds me into a tight embrace.

"I pray I never have to watch something like that again!"

"I am so sorry, Jax! I hate that it hurt you so much!"

He smashes his mouth to mine briefly and then let's go, "Come on, love. Let's see who else we can kill!"

I giggle like a schoolgirl at his words. How psychotic is that!

There are only four other men standing guard, which I think is weird, but if Jax did also, he didn't say. From the looks of it, we are being held in some kind of warehouse. After making sure that all of the guards are dead, we go in search of Jill, but she is nowhere to be found. There are no other rooms with locks on them, aside from ours. Which means, she was never here! Before I could allow myself to freak out over that notion, Jax goes and grabs the car keys from each of the dead bodies and goes in search of a get-a-way car for us. We find a dark blue Camry that goes with one of the sets of keys. Jax helps my fat ass into the passenger side, buckling me up and then jumping into the driver's side, peeling out as he takes off down the road.

Once we are miles away, I let myself breathe normally again. It takes me a few minutes, but then everything sinks in, and the flood gates open up. I feel Jax's hand over mine, squeezing it gently. I can't look at him. I still feel horrible at what I had to do, even though it got us out of there. I don't know how he can even be touching me.

"Hey, Baby, it's going to be okay. We won't stop until we find Jill, I promise!"

"As much as I am freaked out about Jill not being there, I'm thinking about you and what you must think of me!"

"Cassie, you were great back there! I couldn't be prouder of you. You did what needed to be done and I let my emotions get in the way! Don't ever think that I feel less for you, because of what you did!"

I look at him with swollen eyes, "You are? I mean, proud of me?"

"Yes, Baby, very proud!" He lifts my hand and kisses it, "Now let's get you back to the Compound so you can get some good rest. I want to have Dr. Howard come and check you over."

"How are we going to tell Duncan that Jill is lost to us at the moment?"

"Let me worry about that. Like I said, we will find her."

With that, I close my eyes and let exhaustion take me into a deep slumber.

TWENTY-FOUR

JAX

As I pull up to the Compound, something feels odd. There are no vehicles or any kind of activity; it feels vacant. I don't wake Cassie right away, because she needs to sleep, and I don't want her worrying about anything else at the moment. I pull out the burner phone that I bought on the way here and dial Taven's number.

"Who is this and how did you get this number?" He answers.

"Tav, it's me, Jax."

"Holy Fuck, man! I never thought I'd hear from you again! I thought those fuckers killed you!" He explodes.

"Come on, you should know I'm not that easy to kill!" I joke.

"Jesus, Jax. Where the fuck have you been?"

"Let's just say that Jason was gracious enough to put Cassie and I up for an extended vacation of solitude."

"So, what happened?"

"I will explain everything, but first, where the hell are you guys? I'm at the Compound, but it's vacant."

"Yeah, we thought it best that we relocate, just in case we were compromised."

"Good thinking. Text me the coordinates of the new location to this burner phone. I'm going to grab some new clothes for us and get rid of this vehicle in case any of it is bugged."

"Sounds like a plan. Man, it's good to have you guys back! The men are going to be ecstatic! How are the women holding up?"

"Cassie is exhausted and due to have the baby almost any day now." I hesitate and then continue, "Jill isn't with us. We haven't seen her this whole time. I think he kept her somewhere else, because there was no sign of her anywhere when we did a sweep of the building before taking off."

"Shit! Duncan is going mad as it is! He isn't going to take this news very well."

"I know it, but like I promised Cassie, we will find her. I won't stop until she is back safe with us."

"You got that right! I'm going to go ahead and send you the new location and then I better go find Duncan and give him the news privately."

"Thanks, man. I'll see you soon!"

My next stop is my bank. Luckily, Jason never took my wallet from me, so I still have all of my credit cards and bank card, but I don't dare use any of them in case they are being traced. I pull up to the bank and gently wake Cassie up, "Hey, Baby, I need you to wake up."

"Where are we?" She asks as she looks around.

"I need to grab cash from my bank, and I don't want to leave you alone. Are you ready to go in?"

"Yeah, sure, let's go." She says as she rubs the sleep from her eyes.

I help her out of the car and put my arm around her waist as we walk in. We have to wait about ten minutes before I can talk to the manager. Taking out a hundred grand isn't that easy. Finally, we get in and have the money within twenty minutes.

"Why take out so much?" Cassie asks.

"We need to get rid of the Camry, so I'm going to buy a new truck. I also want us to buy new clothes, because we aren't going back to your place until this is all over. It's too dangerous and we don't know if there are bugs planted anywhere."

"So, are we going to the Compound?"

"Yes, but it's been relocated, and I don't want to lead those fuckers to the new place. I don't think it was luck escaping that place with so much ease. Jason set it up that way for a reason."

"I thought the same thing too." She makes a face but tries to hide it from me.

"Hey, are you okay?"

"I'm fine. Just a little pang, but it's gone now, I can wait a bit longer."

"I don't want you waiting, you need to feed now." I insist as I pull into a dead-end alley.

I pull her to me and offer my neck. The second she bites down; my embrace tightens as arousal hits me. Just like every other time, I follow suit and sink my fangs into her, tasting her sweetness. Her hand goes to the bulge in my pants, and I groan. It feels so damn good to feel her touch, but this isn't the place, so I pull away from her.

"Good god woman, you are killing me over here!" I close my eyes, trying to get my senses in order as I pull her hand away from my cock.

"I want you so bad, Jax. It's been way too long!" She pleads.

"I will not take you here. I want you in a bed, on your hands and knees and I won't settle for anything else." My voice is strained with arousal, "Besides, I don't think it will work out so well, as much as our daughter has grown."

"I think you are right." She chuckles.

"Let's go get this shit taken care of, so I can get you home and in bed."

"Well, why are we just sitting here then? Get moving or I'm gonna take over driving!"

"No, you won't. I want to get back in one piece." I joke and am rewarded with a slap to my chest.

"No one likes a smartass, fuck face!"

I laugh. "Glad to see that my Hellion is back!"

"I do have a lot to make up for so watch out." She smiles.

After ditching the car, purchasing a new truck, and shopping for new clothes, we pull up to the new Compound just before three in the afternoon. I haven't even gotten Cassie's door open before a horde of men come flying out of the front door right towards us. Smiles on all their faces; we are passed around to each Elite for bear hugs. The only one I don't see is Duncan. When I look around, I see him standing back by the door with a forlorn look on his face. Cassie runs, well, more like wobbles fast, over to him and throws her arms around his waist.

Duncan embraces her and they have a moment together, tears flowing down Cassie's face and wetness glistens in Duncan's eyes, but do not fall. I walk over to him and squeeze his shoulder, "We will find her together and then you will kill the mother fucker!" I swear to him. He nods as he pulls away from Cassie to bring me in for a man hug.

"How about we bring this inside before we attract attention?" Taven speaks up.

"I agree."

"Hey Max, I sure hope you have some food for me and the baby, and lots of it!" Cassie addresses him.

"I'm on top of it right now." As he runs past us and back inside.

We all laugh, "Yep, wrapped around their fingers!" I wink at her.

CASSIE

Max cooks me up a nice twelve-ounce, medium rare, ribeye with mashed potatoes and gravy and a side of bacon wrapped asparagus, yummy! Talk about being spoiled! As I finish the last bite, I sit back and rub my belly.

"Max, if I wasn't so in love with Jax and about to marry him, I'd definitely marry you!"

"I'd except in a heartbeat, honey!" He smiles and winks at me just as Jax comes strolling through the door.

"I leave you alone for ten minutes and you are already propositioning a marriage proposal to one of my brothers?" He leans over and kisses the top of my head.

"Can you cook me a meal like Max just did?" I cock my eyebrow at him.

"You have a point. Maybe we should have a three-way marriage, except only one of us get the conjugal rights." He laughs.

"What, and I get none of the benefits? I think I'll pass!" Max replies as he walks out of the kitchen.

It is so good to be back among the Elite. I just wish Jill were here with us, where she belongs. I yawn, showing my exhaustion and Jax helps me up out of the chair.

"Let's get you cleaned up and into bed, so you can rest. Jayde and Dane are going to bring the Doc by after a while, so she can check you over. It's too dangerous to take you to her."

"I will feel so much better once I know for sure that she is doing well." I massage my tummy, "I don't think anything is wrong but going all that time without check-ups worries me a little."

"That is why I want her here as soon as you get some rest, love." He rubs my belly, "You know, we haven't picked out a name for her yet. Do you have anything in mind?"

"I have been playing around with a few different ones, but I won't pick until I see her tiny face. How about you? Do you have any suggestions?"

"I will love whatever you choose." He smiles.

Jax escorts me to our room, where a hot bath awaits me. I sigh and wrap my arms around his waist, "Just what I need, babe. Thank you!"

"Oh, yes, your stench is horrific!" He says plugging his nose.

"And you think you smell any better?" I joke.

"Guess we had better take one together, huh?"

"Are you going to keep your hands to yourself then?"

"Probably not." He replies as he starts undressing me.

I grab his wrists as he starts pulling my shirt up, "You promise you won't laugh at my fat body?" I worry, since this is the first time he has seen me this big.

"Baby, there is no way I could ever laugh at your body! Whether it be your normal curves or big with my child, I will worship it always!" He lifts my shirt over my head and just stares at my naked form.

Starting to feel self-conscience, I try using my hands to cover up, but he holds them down at my sides, "Don't ever hide your body from me, Cassie." He kneels down in front of me and starts planting kisses on my stomach, then puts his cheek and ear to it, so he can listen to the heartbeat.

"God, Cassie. This never gets old, listening to the heartbeat of the life that we created together." Just then, she kicks her father right in his face and he jumps back, "Whoa! Looks like we have a fighter on our hands!" He laughs, making me laugh, too!

"That was the strongest one yet, that I've felt!"

"Just a little longer and she will be in our arms." He says, "Speaking of," he picks me up and walks over to the tub, sets me down to undress himself and then has me in his arms again as he steps into the tub and sits with me in his arms, "it feels so good to have you back in my arms like this!"

I lay my head on his shoulder as we just sit there letting the hot water soak in. He grabs the soap and starts lathering me up, but I have different motives. I turn myself so my back is facing him. Instead of sitting between his legs, I sit on his lap, rubbing myself against him until he rises, which is an instant reaction.

"Mm, does someone want some loving?" He asks as he lathers up my back and then moves his hand around my girth, just to dip down lower.

As his fingers move over my clit, it ignites sparks that I haven't felt in months and I moan, "Yes, please! I can't wait any longer." I lift myself without warning and plant his cock deep into my starving pussy.

"Fuck, Baby, that feels so damn good!"

I start moving my hips up and down as he plays with my clit, but then he slides a finger into my ass and my desire breaks free, along with the scream that I can't hold back.

"That's it, Baby, let it all out…Fuck, you are so God damn wet and tight!" He thrusts himself into me harder and harder, "FUCK CASSIE!" He roars as his load explodes within me, causing another orgasm to rip through my body.

He remains inside of me as we catch our breath. Jax wraps his arms around me and lays his head on my back, "I can never be apart from you again, Cassie. I just can't!"

"I feel the same way, Jax. I need this closeness to you always. I will never feel whole unless I have you here with me."

"Ditto, minx!"

"Jax?"

"Hm?"

"Can you help me turn around?" I can't help but giggle a little.

He chuckles back but helps me to turn so I can face him, "Are you ready for round two?" I ask.

His eyebrows raise up, "Round two?"

"Well, yeah. You pulled out, so now it's round two." I give him an innocent smile.

He goes to impale my pussy, but I stop him, "You have already pounded my vagina, Mister, it's time my ass gets a little action!" He growls as he places his cock at my ass hole and I slide right down, moaning as I go.

"Jesus, Cassie, your ass is so tight, it almost hurts too much to be in it!"

"I can remove myself if you need me too."

"Don't you fucking dare! I said almost!" He pounds my ass as hard as he did my vagina.

"Oh… oh… oh, my God… faster Jax! Fuck my pussy with your fingers… fill me up!" I demand and he does just that. Slamming three fingers into me over and over as his cock is fucking my ass, he starts rubbing my clit with his thumb, causing my own pussy to explode with cum; then comes his own eruption into my ass.

Again, we lay spent. This time, Jax pulls the plug to release the water. My own holes remaining plugged with his cock and fingers. As the water finishes draining out, he pulls his fingers out of my pussy. They are coated with so much cum, it looks like he dipped his fingers in icing. I watch as he licks his fingers, moaning at the taste of my essence. I grab his hand and bring my own mouth to his middle finger and suck it deep, tasting my own sweetness.

Jax gazes at me with heated eyes before bringing his mouth down on mine, heating me to the core with just this one kiss. Picking me up, he carries me to the bed and continues to love on me.

TWENTY-FIVE

JAX

For the next two hours, Cassie and I make up for lost time, taking turns loving one another, or what other people may consider, torturing each other, but twisted minds like ours are never understood. Laying sated together, Cassie fast asleep, I'm here with my thoughts. Thoughts of revenge for those who think they are innocent and doing good, but in reality, they are but monsters, disguised as do-gooders. Taking innocents against their will, keeping them from their loved ones and killing those because they are different.

We Elite will fight for our rights and fight for our loved ones, starting with Jill. She is our first priority and there isn't a rock that we will not overturn in order to find her! Duncan can't live without his mate, now that he has found her and Cassie cannot live without her best friend, her sister. I just pray that when we find her, all will be well and we can all move on, but my gut is telling me that it won't be so easy.

A light knock has me tip toeing over to the door, as to not wake Cassie up. Opening it slowly and slipping out, Dane is here to inform me that the doctor is waiting out in the Rec room. I thank him and sneak back into our room, but Cassie is already awake and sitting up.

"What time is it?" The glow from the bathroom light illuminates the room just enough to see her hair all is disarray. Ah, sex hair is gorgeous! I can't help but smile.

"It's eight thirty at night. Dane just informed me the Doc is here, so if you are ready, I can go grab her and bring her here."

"Are you shitting me? You can't bring her in here…it smells like a whore house!" She laughs.

"It's only a one-woman whorehouse, babe." I smile, earning me a pillow to the head, "Get your lazy ass up and freshen up. I'll bring her to the empty room next door." Grabbing a clean shirt, I leave and go retrieve the Doc.

Cassie enters the spare bedroom just as I finish reporting what all had taken place in the last few months to the doctor. She stares in utter shock through it all and then sympathy appears in her eyes.

"You poor dear! How could they keep a pregnant woman prisoner? Only cruel, uncompassionate people would do that!" she goes to Cassie and hugs her, "At least they didn't make her suffer and they held you as well, so they could both survive, but still. I feel for both of you! I am going to talk to my husband and make sure we stay well protected while these vile men are still at large!"

"That would be for the best. It may be better yet, if you close the clinic for a while and just work out of your home and only with certain patients. Do not take on anybody new for the time being. We don't know if they ever followed us to your office and if they did, they may put two and two together and figure out that your husband is a vampire, along with your kids."

"Oh my! I didn't think about that, thank you for bringing it to my attention. I think I will take your advice and close down." She turns back to Cassie, "Well, look at you! You are glowing and your daughter has grown so much!"

"So, in other words, 'look how fat I've gotten'?" Cassie chuckles.

"Pregnant women are never called fat, dear! They are glowing and healthy and don't you ever forget that!" Doc chided her.

"Don't mind her Doc, she has a fat complex about herself apparently." I laugh and I get another pillow to the head!

Watching the play between Cassie and I, the doctor shakes her head and smiles, "Well, let's see how our baby girl is doing, shall we? I am going to perform a vaginal exam, where I use my fingers to check the inside of your uterus. I can also tell whether the baby is head down or still in the process of turning; It's all precautionary."

Cassie lays down as the doctor instructs and I sit up by her head, holding her hand. Dr. Howard instructs Cassie that she is going to feel a little pressure and that it is normal. Watching the doctor's face, I see her crinkle her brows together and then she clears her face of all emotion as she looks at me.

"Cassie, have you lost your mucous plug yet? It would be kind of like discharge."

"Not that I'm aware of, why?"

Doc pulls her hands away and takes off her gloves, throwing them in the waste basket. Ignoring Cassie's question, she asks another one of her own.

"Have you been having any kind of pain or pressure? Maybe some back pain or pressure around your abdomen?"

"I had trouble sleeping last night because of a little back pain, but it was more like discomfort, and I haven't felt any kind of pressure. Why?"

"Well, I'm asking because you are 3 cm dilated. Your water hasn't broken yet, but probably will soon. The baby's head is down, so that is great news."

"Wait, what do you mean I am 3 cm dilated? I am not due for another 2 weeks, at least?"

"It's nothing to worry about. Babies can come a few weeks early or a few weeks later, it's when they are ready, and it looks as if she is ready!" Doc giggles.

Cassie squeezes my hand and looks like she is about to cry. "She can't come yet; we don't have Jill back home! I can't have her without my best friend here!"

"I am sorry Cassie, but there is nothing we can do about it. The baby will be coming at any time now."

Cassie turns her head into my waist and cries. I smooth her hair down and try to comfort her.

Dr. Howard looks saddened as she looks at me, "I am not that far away. As soon as she starts having contractions that are about 5-7 minutes apart, call me and send your men. We should have plenty of time, so don't freak out."

"Yes Doc. Thank you for coming and for everything!"

"You take good care of her. Oh, and no more intercourse for the time being." She smiles at me.

"Aye, aye Doc!" Jokingly, I salute her.

I take Cassie back to our room so we can feed the baby and get her settled back into bed. She is quiet the whole time, not wanting to talk, just nodding in response to any questions I ask her. I'm worried about what this ordeal with Jill is really doing to her. I think it's time to call her mom. She has been afraid to call her parents since we got back, but she needs the familiar and without Jill, her parents are the next best thing.

I grab Cassie a little snack from the kitchen and hold her while she watches a little tv, before drifting off to sleep. I quietly slip from the bedroom and go to find Taven and Duncan to talk about our plan of action. Finding them in the gym, I pull my shirt off and join them in their sword and knife sparring session.

Duncan has a lot of pent-up anger and is showing it in his strikes. I am literally working to protect myself, almost as if he is pissed at me for not bringing Jill home. I don't blame him, I wouldn't let him come with me to meet up with Jason, but I had no choice.

This sparring is getting out of hand, so I throw down my weapons to show that I'm done.

"What, two months being locked up turned you into a pussy?" Duncan sneers.

"No. Your emotions are getting in the way and I'm not going to get killed because of it!"

"Come on, you need practice."

"No, what I need is for you to put down the weapons and talk to me! We need to come up with a plan. You want to get Jill back, don't you?"

He steps up to me and puts his face into mine, "Don't ever doubt that I would give up on finding her!"

I let out a sigh, "I don't doubt that at all. If anything, I'm the only one that knows exactly what you are feeling right now. That is why I am standing here."

Duncan hangs his head, and his shoulders sag, "I am at a loss as to what to do or where to go from here."

"Well, I may have an idea of the area that he is keeping her in."

His head whips up and he grabs me by the shoulders, "Why the fuck did you wait this long to tell me? We could have left earlier and had her back already!"

"Calm down Duncan!" Taven orders, "Let Jax explain everything."

Duncan let me go and steps back.

"I just thought of it as I was laying with Cassie and that is why I am here now."

"Pfft, while you are lazing around with your mate, mine is in who knows what kind of danger!"

"Fuck you, Duncan! My mate has been held prisoner for just as long AND she is pregnant! Jill has been her best friend since high school and she is worried sick over her being gone, which in turn also puts my child at risk! So, I am sorry if this didn't come to mind as I have been trying to settle my pregnant mate down! Did I forget to mention that she can go into labor at any moment? So fucking excuse me for thinking about things that are just as important! And if you want to be mad at someone, be mad at Jill for dating that son of a bitch to begin with! He's doing this because he thinks he is in love with her and wants to keep you away from her!"

"I am sorry man; I know this isn't easy for Cassie and I know you will do all that you can. My mind is just kind of letting go and it's making me crazy."

"Fine, all is forgiven. Now, can we get down to business?"

"Yeah, what do you have for us?"

We gather the Elite up and all meet in the rec room. There are some new faces among us, which Taven informed me that he hired new recruits to help with the numbers that the Hunters have. They are all tall and big mother fuckers, just what we need, as long as they can fight.

"Okay, listen up everyone. For those of you that are new, I am Jax. My pregnant mate and I have been held prisoner for the last two months by the Hunters. The same Hunters that have Jill. The leader's name is Jason. Kai is passing around information that I have on some of Jason's men, some pictures are included."

"So, if you and your mate were able to escape then why didn't you break Jill out as well?" This coming from one of the newbies.

"Do not question another Elite like that! If he could have, he would have. That's what we do here, nobody gets left behind!" Taven argues in my favor.

"It's alright Taven, I've got this. To answer your question, I'm sorry, what's your name?"

"Stephan."

"Okay, to answer your question Stephan, I searched that warehouse from top to bottom and there was no sign that Jill had even been there! Jill is my mate's best friend, and you better believe that if Jill were there, she would be here with us right now." I am getting irritated with the young pup the more I have to explain myself to him.

"On to the next part. My mate and I were being held at a warehouse in Yarmouth. Now, Jason told my mate that he was in love with Jill, and we know that Jill wasn't kept at the warehouse, but Jason was there every day. So, I have reason to believe that Jill is close to that area and that we need to concentrate searching in a 10-mile radius of Yarmouth. There is no way that he would stay away from Jill too long, so this is where we start looking."

"No one goes in alone! You find something, you call and wait for back up. I want to keep at least 4 of you here at all times. My mate will be going into labor at any time. She cannot be moved anywhere, and she cannot be left unprotected. Taven has assigned each of your details, so talk with him in a few minutes. Starting right now, everybody is on overtime until we bring Jill home! As always, kill every threat, no innocents! If you find Jason, bring him to Duncan… alive!"

TWENTY-SIX

CASSIE

I wake up and look around for Jax, but he isn't here. The tv is still on with the weather guy saying that the next few days are going to be mild. I can't believe that it's already mid-October, it's almost Jill's birthday. I start getting depressed all over again. I feel bad, because Jax was trying to sooth me earlier and I just wouldn't have any of it. This isn't his fault, and he is only trying to help me get through this. Why do you have to be such a bitch, Cassie! I get out of the bed to go use the bathroom before heading to search for Jax.

I find him and every other Elite in the rec room, but I don't go in. I'm just going to stand here and listen to what they are saying. I don't really call it ease dropping, since the door is wide open for all to hear. I just don't want to disturb them. Jax is talking to them about not going in alone and to call for back up and to bring Jason to Duncan alive. Oh my God, did they find Jill? I step into the doorway.

"Did you find Jill?" My hope is high.

Jax holds his hand out for me to join him at the front, so I wobble my happy ass over to him.

"Sorry, love, not yet. We do have reason to believe that she is near, if not in Yarmouth, like we were. So, we are going to start there. Half the men are going out within the hour to start looking."

"Oh, thank God!" It makes me feel so much better.

Jax begins introducing me to all the new faces, embarrassing me because I don't look cute.

"Excuse my appearance boys. If I had known that all you hotties were here, I would have put on something a little sexier!"

All the Elite who know me, just shakes their head and chuckles, including Jax, but the looks on the new faces are priceless!

"Awe, come on boys, haven't you ever seen a girl in a pregnant outfit before? Yes, I'm huge. I'm as big as a whale, and about to set sail!" I look around. "What, nothing? Oh, you guys are no fun!"

"Baby, stop teasing the new guys."

"Fine! Anybody that doesn't know the song Love Shack isn't worth my time anyway!" I smile at him and crook my finger, causing him to follow me to the kitchen.

I walk into the empty kitchen turn and throw myself at Jax, smashing my mouth to his. He accepts my assault and opens up for me. After playing tonsil hockey for a moment longer, I pull away.

"I guess someone is feeling a little better." He states.

"I am so sorry for being a bitch earlier. I don't know what came over me."

"Don't apologize, you have a lot going on right now. I completely understand. I know how to keep my mouth quiet when you are in a mood." He winks.

"Thank you for everything Jax. Your love, your understanding, your protective nature, your compassion, your baby…." I threw the last one in for good measure.

"Man, she really is messing with your hormones, isn't she?"

I burst out laughing, "Yeah, she really is!"

"I don't mind so much, although it's like dating Dr. Jekyll and Mr. Hyde at times."

"And there you go ruining the moment with those dick comments!"

"Come on, Baby, what kind of fun would we have if we didn't get a rise out of each other every once in a while?"

"Every once in a while? Pretty sure I get a rise out of you multiple times a day!" I say as I grab his package.

Max comes strolling in, "Get a room! None of that stuff in my kitchen!"

"Maybe you should have warned us sooner, before we christened the room earlier! We bad, sorry!" Jax winks at me as he grabs my hand to leave the kitchen. I'm covering my mouth, trying to cover the laugh that I so want to let out. Max will be cleaning the kitchen the rest of the night!

I have been tossing and turning for the last hour, my back pain is keeping me awake. Not wanting to wake Jax up, since he has to be up early for detail, I climb out of bed and leave the room. I'm wandering the halls, because it helps with the discomfort, when I hear a voice. Sounds like they are talking to someone on the phone. I just continue on, not paying attention, until I hear Jill's name.

I stop, not sure of where the voice is coming from, and I listen. The voice is low, but I can make out most of the one-sided conversation.

"Yes, they will be starting with a 10-mile radius around Yarmouth."

"They already have men swarming the area. It's best if you and Jill stay put for now. I don't think they have even considered the Island, because none of the patrolling was assigned to that area."

"Jason, will you just listen to me? You are safe for the time being and it will be stupid if you try moving her with so many patrolling the mainland!"

That fucking cock sucker, he is a mole! I need to find out who it is and maybe he can lead us to Jason. I hear him end the call; I hear movement towards the end of the hall. I straighten up and pretend that I am just walking down the hall. One of the new guys come out from the room that I heard the noise in. He spots me and I pretend to spot him at the same time.

"Oh, thank God! I am trying to find the kitchen, but I'm not sure of where it is. I'm not use to this Compound. Hey, you are one of the new Elites, aren't you? What's your name?"

"I am Stephan and of course, you are Cassie."

"Yes, I am Cassie. Could you possibly point me in the direction of the kitchen? I am always craving the pickles in the middle of the night."

He chuckles and points, "Second door on the left."

"Thank you, Stephan, you are a life saver!" More than you know!

I quickly grab a snack and as fast as my big ass can wobble, I head back to our room to wake Jax up. I'm not understanding how Stephan can be working for Jason, when he is clearly a vampire. Not unless Jason promised to let him live if he helps him by becoming a spy. Either way, it's a shitty thing to do, betraying your own kind and he will suffer for it for sure! Oh God, what if he has bugs planted throughout the Compound? Fuck! The guys could be walking into an ambush!

Slipping back into our room, I go straight to Jax's side of the bed and nudge him. He wakes up and is about to speak when I place my hand over his mouth. He instantly becomes alert. I grab a pen and notebook from the bedside table, along with my phone for light, and tell him to go to the bathroom and search for any kind of bug that may be planted. He questions me with his eyes, but I shoo him towards the bathroom.

Several minutes had pass until he gives me the all-clear. I join him in the bathroom and shut the door.

"Don't talk above a whisper, nobody can hear what I am about to tell you!"

"You are scaring me, Cassie. What is it?"

"Stephan is a spy for Jason!" I blurt out.

Looking confused, "What are you talking about?"

I go on and tell him what I overheard and everything leading up until now. The more I talk, the more his anger rises, and I have to talk him down from going to murder the bastard.

"I'm going to kill the son of a bitch with my bare hands!" Jax whispers.

"Babe, let's think about this. We can use this to our own advantage, but we need to keep all the new recruits in the dark, since we don't know who to trust!"

"You are right. You, my little minx, are a genius!" He says, kissing my forehead, "By the way, you do know you could have just mind-linked me, right?"

She waves her hand dismissing my comment, "You are just now figuring out that I'm a genius?"

"You are such a sassy ass; do you know that?" He smiles.

"It's all part of my charm, Baby!" I chuckle. "Now, do I get some kind of reward for this information? I don't give this stuff away for free you know!" I rub myself against him as I wrap my arms around his neck.

"I could have tortured it out of you." He smiles down at me.

"Hmm, I'll have to remember that for next time!"

"Have I told you how much I love your demented mind?"

"No, but I will allow you to show me." My hand slides down to grab is growing arousal.

Growling, he pulls my hand away, "You know we can't be naughty right now… Doc's orders, you little minx!"

"I understand that there can be no pounding of my vagina, but who said anything about that hole?" I cock a brow.

He backs me up into the wall and slams his mouth against mine fervently, taking my breath away. Shoving his hand down my sleep shorts and attacking my clit the same way he did my lips. Instant wetness causes him to run his fingers throughout my folds, coating everything in my juices.

"Is this what you want, my dirty little mate?" he asks.

"You are getting closer." My voice is strained with arousal.

He pulls me over to the sink and makes me grab the sides of the vanity. Yanking my shorts down, he kneels behind me and spreads my legs and ass cheeks wide apart before shoving first his tongue and then his finger into my ass. Mixing his saliva and my juices together for lube, he stands up behind me.

"Look at me Cassie."

I see his smoldering reflection in the mirror and as our eyes lock, he thrusts his cock into my ass, causing me to moan in pleasure as I close my eyes.

"Open your eyes, I want you to keep your eyes on me as I fuck your ass and make you come! I want to watch your desire build within them and watch as I make you explode!"

God, his words turn me on every time! I gaze into his sapphire blue eyes as he fucks me from behind. My pleasure is building and as his begins to build, his vampire joins in. Bright blue eyes stare back at me as his fangs erupt from his mouth. I'm close and he starts thrusting faster, bringing his hand around to rub my clit. My orgasm bursts forth and his fangs sink into me, but his eyes never leaving mine.

My orgasm keeps coming with each pull he takes from me. He thrusts one last time and holds it, erupting into my ass. I feel it shoot into me like hot lava. As the last of my quivers end, he retracts his fangs and kisses my neck. He is thrusting his cock slowly now and leans his head forward. I twist my neck so I can reach him, and I sink my own fangs into him, reigniting his own desire.

Once again, he his slamming into my ass as his pressure builds and on my last long hard pull from his neck, he erupts again, this time stronger. I feel his cum seeping out of my ass, reveling in the feel of it running down my legs. He pulls out and grabs a towel to wipe my legs and my ass.

"I shouldn't have taken you like that, but God damn woman, I lose all restraint when it comes to you!"

"You better take me like that more often!"

"So, you like that, huh? I'll have to remember that. Now" he says as he picks me up and carries me to the bed, "try and get some sleep. I'm going to go talk to Taven and Duncan about this issue we have. I love you, Baby."

"I love you too! Don't leave without coming to see me!"

"You know I won't. Sweet dreams, love."

I close my eyes and fall fast asleep.

TWENTY-SEVEN

JAX

I can't believe that ass fuck thought he could pull a fast one over on us! In all reality, he did, but to think he could continue, and nobody would catch on. My girl is the shit! She handled the situation like a pro, even when she returned to tell me, she had the right way of thinking by not saying a word until we knew it was safe. Even though, technically, she could have mind-linked me, but we will leave that to pregnancy brain; she still did well, and the fates definitely chose well for me, that's for sure!

Duncan is already awake, because he is on the early shift with me, but I had to drag Taven's ass out of bed. Both Duncan and I file into Taven's room, me motioning for them not to say a word. I do a quick sweep of his room and find it clean.

"What is this all about?" Taven asks when I give the okay.

"Cassie overheard Stephan on the phone a little while ago."

"And?" Taven is becoming annoyed.

"She wasn't trying to listen in, but then she heard Jill's name come up, so she listened."

This gets Duncan's attention.

"Stephan was talking to Jason. Seems as if we have a spy in our midst!"

"Are you fucking kidding me?" Taven explodes.

"Sh, we don't want him knowing that we are on to him! I think he could possibly lead us to Jason and Jill." I look at Duncan.

"Cassie said he mentioned something about them being safer where they are at than to try moving, because we are only searching the mainland. So, we have to be on track if he was getting spooked."

"So, what are your thoughts? How should we go about this?" Taven questions.

"I say we don't trust any of the new recruits yet, until we can investigate them further, but we need to inform the rest of the men. We will need all eyes watching Stephan as well."

"So, we go about our business as usual? Keep everyone on the original detail I assigned?" Taven asks.

"Yes. Everyone sticks to the original plan, except for Duncan and I."

"What are we going to do?" Duncan is looking a bit more upbeat.

"You and I, my friend, are going to Cousins Island. My gut is telling me that she is there!" I smile mischievously at him.

"Yes, with only you two searching there, nobody will catch on. I will keep your names up with the original detail." Taven informs us, "I will also have Cooper and Jayde on that detail when you two are not. That's if we don't find her right away."

"Let's meet out front in an hour Dunc. We will get a head start before everyone is up and moving around."

Duncan nods and exits the room while I stay behind to talk to Taven.

"Who do you have staying here at the Compound today? I'm worried about Cassie going into labor. She was already 3 cm dilated when Doc checked her, and she has been having back pain the last two nights."

"I haven't the slightest clue as to what any of that means Jax. I'm assuming it's what happens right before they go into labor though, right?" He chuckles.

"Yes," I smile, "I am worried about being so far away if it happens while I'm gone. I'll need two men to go pick up the doctor and the other two to stay here. Now that we know Jason is aware of our new Compound, I definitely need the protection here with her."

"No worries, man. I have Max, Kai, Dane and Kole staying behind during your shift and I will be in and out all day long."

"Great! Aside from me, they are your best men." I wink at him.

"Yeah, yeah, yeah, get out of here!" Taven shakes his head and shoves me out the door.

I return to our room and see that Cassie is still asleep. I crawl in beside her and snuggle her to my chest for a while. I enjoy the feeling of her wrapped in my arms and I never want to release her, but duty calls. After about a half hour of holding her, I leave her cuddling my pillow and jump into the shower, but she is awake when I step out of the bathroom.

"Mm, I love the smell of you when you just get out of the shower! Your woods and spice scent are the strongest."

"Well, yours is the strongest right after I make you come." I sniff her and can still smell her scent, mixed with mine, it's delectable!

"Always with your mind in the gutter! Just how I like it!" She wraps her arms around my neck. "Do you mind if I feed before you go?"

I turn my head for her, "It's all of yours for the taking, love."

My arousal is instant as she sinks into my neck, I love it! I bite into her a second later and feel her desire as well, but it's gone all too soon as we pull away from each other.

"There will be two bags of my blood in the fridge if you need any before I get back. It won't be the same as drinking from my neck, but at least our baby girl will be fed." I lean down and kiss her, hating that I have to leave at a time like this, but we need to strike now, while we still can.

"Kole, Max, Dane and Kai will be here while I am gone. Remember what Doc said, 5-7 mins between each contraction and you call her.

Two of the guys will go get her. They will call me if you go into labor, and I will fly back, okay?"

"Okay. I'm nervous, Jax."

"I know, Baby. Maybe you should call your mom and have her come to be with you."

"I think that will only make it worse. She will ask too many questions and I'm not ready to answer them yet. I'll be fine; besides, I have these men here wrapped around my finger. I will not be too bored." She smiles at me before bringing her lips to mine.

"I love you, Cassie."

"And I love you, Jackson." She watches me walk out of the room and out of sight.

Before leaving, I go in search of Raven, the closest we have to a doctor here at the Compound. He is of Native American heritage and knows the Shaman ways but has also done some studying of our medicine. I had him take some of my blood a few months back in case Cassie ever needed it and I wasn't around. I need to have him take more, just in case. Finding him in the kitchen, I pull him aside and ask this favor of him. He obliges and I follow him to the medical ward where he fills two bags with my blood. Thanking him, I go to meet Duncan outside.

"Buddy, you ready to go find your woman?" I ask Duncan, as if I didn't already know.

"Let's go get this mother fucker!" He jumps up into the passenger seat of my truck.

"Remember, if we find them, we need to wait for back up. You are not going to do her any good dead."

"Yeah, yeah, yeah, let's go!" He taps on the dash to get me going.

We make it to Cousins Island in a little under forty-five minutes. People are just starting to get motivated, so there isn't too much traffic. The island isn't very big, just under two miles, one mile being land, the rest water, and maybe five hundred in population. It is connected to Chebeague Island, but you must take a fifteen-minute ferry ride to get to it. I doubt Jason would have taken her that far. If Jill is here, we will find her, otherwise, we will try the next island.

With the sun rising, our first stop is a little diner. We take a table in the back, so we can see everyone coming in. The waitress stops at our table to get our orders, "You boys new to town?"

"Nope, just out sight-seeing. We are from the mainland." Duncan uses a gruff voice.

"Well, it's a beautiful time to do it. We get a lot of mainlanders in, doing the same thing."

We give her our orders and she leaves, letting us know she would be back with our coffee. I take that time to look our surroundings over. Nothing out of the ordinary. There are three elderly guys sitting around drinking coffee, probably a daily tradition for them. A young man, maybe in is mid-twenties sits alone eating his breakfast, but overall, it is quiet. The waitress makes her way back with our coffee.

"Not too much goes on around here, huh?" I ask the girl.

She smiles at me, "In this bitty ole town? The most excitement we have seen are the new people that moved in about two months ago. Other than that, nothing."

Duncan sits up straight, "New people?"

I kick him under the table, warning him to watch his questioning.

"I mean, I didn't realize there were any houses for sale here. I had thought about coming over and looking for something seasonal but was told there was nothing."

"Oh, we don't. This house was left for the old couple's grandson and has been sitting empty for about five years now. All of a sudden, he and his wife are here, with a whole horde full of men fixing the place up."

"I see. Any children or are they newlyweds? He might have been waiting until he got married before moving in." Duncan shrugs his shoulders as if it is a passing thought.

"I didn't see any. I haven't met his wife yet, only seen her in passing. I couldn't even tell you what she looks like, but the husband, I believe his name is Jay, he has been in here a few times. The nicest guy I have ever met, and easy on the eyes too, I might add!"

"Maybe we should see if he is looking for any more help?" I look at Duncan.

"I can always use the extra money." He says to me.

I turn to the waitress, "Where did you say this house is? If he has a lot of work to do to it, he may be looking for more hands."

"Oh my God, you have no idea how run-down this house is! He could probably use you!"

"We will definitely look into it, thank you… Jenny." I had to look at her name tag, but she smiles any way.

"Well, if you go down two blocks that way, take a right and go down half a block, you will see a hidden road on the left. There is a mailbox there so you shouldn't miss it. The house is nice and secluded from the road."

We hear a bell ding, "Oh, that's your order, I'll be right back!" I watch her walk away.

"You thinking what I'm thinking?" Duncan asks me.

"Sure am! Let's say we eat our breakfast and then do a little stakeout."

"I'm all for that."

We finish our breakfast and then leave, leaving the waitress a twenty-dollar tip. She doesn't know it, but she helped us more than she knew.

We find a nice, secluded spot to park my truck where we can see the road leading up to the house. I speed dialed Kole to have him look up information on the house and see who the family is that owns it. Once I give him the address, I hang up and call Taven to inform him of our findings. He is very impressed with how quick we were to get this info. I don't like to toot my own horn, but I am one of the best!

I excuse myself, telling Duncan I need to stretch my legs and to check in on Cassie. I get out of the truck and walk around to the back, leaning against the tailgate, I reach out to my girl.

"Hey, Sexy, what are you wearing?"

"Why hello handsome, what would you like me to be wearing?"

"Nothing, but since I'm not there and you are with four other Elite, you better be wearing two layers of clothing!"

She laughs, "You leave me alone with four very good-looking guys and expect me to be fully dressed?"

"If you all know what's good for you… yes!"

"Oh babe, you know you are it for me! How is it going over there?"

I go on and tell her what the waitress had told us, and she starts to get excited.

"Calm down, don't get your hopes up just yet. We are staking the place out now and we don't know if it's them or not."

"What does your gut tell you, Jax?"

I hesitate a moment, "My gut says it is, but that doesn't mean anything!"

"Well, it means something to me! I always trust your gut, so you should too! She is there, I just know it!"

"I just don't want you to be disappointed is all, just in case it isn't them."

"Okay, I promise I'll wait for your confirmation first."

"That's a good girl. Now, how's my other girl doing?"

"She is insisting on sitting on my bladder, so I'm having to go pee every ten damn minutes."

"It won't be too much longer, love."

"I know, it's just frustrating is all. Speaking of, I got to go use the bathroom again. I will talk to you later, babe, I love you."

"Love you too, minx!"

I had just gotten back into the truck when a SUV comes down the drive that we are watching. We can't see jack shit through the tinted windows on it, but it looks just like the one that I got into when Jason took me as his prisoner.

"I think it may be time to call for back up." I look at Duncan, "That looks just like the SUV that they put me in when they took me to Cassie!"

"I'm on it!" He says as he speed dials Taven.

With any luck, we will have Jill back with us by nightfall.

TWENTY-EIGHT

CASSIE

Regardless with what I told Jax, I am so fucking bored! There isn't anything on tv and the guys are busy in the gym sparring. Even watching them fight shirtless doesn't help! I must be losing it if that doesn't keep me occupied! It's only two in the afternoon and Jax's shift won't be done for another six hours. There is a commotion going on during the late morning, but nobody tells me what it's all about and I haven't had any contact with Jax since this morning. I try talking to him around noon time, but he says that he can't really talk at the moment and that he will contact me as soon as he can.

I grab hold of my stomach when I feel the familiar pain shoot through. I haven't fed since Jax left, so I head to the kitchen for a bag of blood, but when I open the fridge, there are no bags in there. What the fuck? I start searching the cabinets, but again, I find nothing. I'm starting to panic, only because the pains are so unbearable and the idea of dealing with them scares me.

I quickly make my way to the gym and enter as the guys are hanging their weapons up on the wall. They all look at me, but before I can say anything, another pain rips through me.

Max uses his vamp speed to get to me before I hit the floor, "What's wrong? Are you in labor?"

"I need to feed the baby!"

"There are blood bags in the fridge that Jax left you. Didn't he tell you before he left?"

"Yes, but there are no bags in the fridge, I just checked."

"That's funny, because I saw them in there when I put the left-over breakfast away this morning."

"I'll go double check." Kai says and then he is gone in a flash.

Another pain and Max picks me up and carries me to the rec room to lay me on the couch. Kai comes running in.

"Cassie is right, the bags are gone!"

"That bastard!" Kole roars, "It could only have been one person that could have done it!"

"Shit, what do we do Dane?" Dane is starting to freak out.

"The only thing we can do. Call Jax. He will have to fly back here, before the pains get too bad."

Just as Kole is about to call Jax, a Native American looking guy comes walking in, "What's all the commotion about?"

"Cassie needs to feed, and someone took the two bags of blood that Jax left for her." Kai sneers.

"Why would someone do that?" The new guy asks.

"I won't get into it right now; I need to call Jax and get him back here fast!" Again, Kole goes to call Jax.

"Just hold up, no need to call him and pull him from detail. I have his blood bags stocked up in the medical ward, I'll go grab a few."

"You, Raven, are a life saver!" Dane plants a quick hard kiss on the guy's forehead.

"You ever do that again, and I will gut you!" He is out the door with his last word and back again in less than thirty seconds.

"Damn you vamps are fast!" I say as I pull a painful face with another rip through my gut.

"Here, it won't be the same as drinking from the vein, but it will still have the same effect on the baby."

"Thank you, Raven. I'd kiss you, but I don't want to get gutted. Pretty sure I know what it would feel like!" I try to smile, but it hurts too much, so I start guzzling from the bag instead.

"Now you, I wouldn't gut, but Jax would probably gut me, so I'll pass anyway." He winks at me.

The gut pain starts to subside, but I still feel a slight pressure. Weird, it's never done this before. I drink down the second bag. I ask the guys to help me to my room so I could lay down for a bit. Kai literally shoves passed the others just so he can pick me up and carry me, but before we even make it to the room, I feel something weird and then a gushing from between my legs.

Kai stops short, "Cassie, please don't tell me that your daughter just made you pee on me!"

"Umm, I am pretty sure my water just broke."

"Oh my God, I think that may be worse than getting peed on!" He hands me over to Kole before taking off down the hall. I can't help but laugh.

"Great, don't say I have never done anything for you, Cassie!" Kole looks down at me and he looks like he is going to be sick.

"If it's that big of a deal, then just put me down, I can walk."

"No fucking way am I going to have the wrath of Jax come down on me if he finds out that we made you walk! I'll be fine." As he hurries down to my room.

Kole bursts though my door and quickly lays me on the bed, ripping his shirt off as soon as I am out of his arms. Man, these guys are comical! All big bad warriors but get a little amniotic fluid on them and they act like big babies! I shake my head.

"Should we go get the doctor.?" Max asks coming into the room.

"No, she said once my contractions are 5-7 minutes apart. I am thinking we should call Jax though."

"I'm on it!" His phone already to his ear.

Jax isn't answering his phone, though, and it is starting to worry me. I try contacting him myself. Finally, on the third try, he answers.

"Now is not a good time, babe."

"Okay, I just thought you would want to be here for the birth of your daughter. I will hold my contractions off until you get back later tonight, no biggie!" I break contact with him and won't answer him back.

Kole's phone starts ringing, he answers, and I can hear Jax yelling through the phone.

"I'd be pissed too if I were in labor, and the father was too busy to talk! You told us to call you, but you weren't answering!" He is fuming.

"Just tell him to take his time. I have four capable males here that can step in and help out!"

"Jax, you better get your mother fucking ass back here NOW!" The look of horror on Kole's face is priceless.

Another contraction starts, a little stronger this time around. I look at my watch so I can catch the next one. All of a sudden, I hear Jax in my head, "I am so sorry, Baby, I'm coming! I'll be there as quick as possible! Did you call Doc?"

"No, I am just starting to time them, but my water broke all over Kai." A giggle slips, "Just don't go too fast and be careful!"

"I will, I love you, Baby!"

"I love you too!"

JAX

My phone keeps buzzing in my pocket, but I have my head in the game, instructing the other five Elites on where I want them placed. Kole had called earlier with the information on the owner of the house. A Mr. Jason Kennedy, no coincidence there, even if I don't know Jason's last name. So, Duncan and I snuck up through the woods to get a closer look and sure enough, there is the son of a bitch, barking orders to the guys that are fixing the roof.

We go back to my pickup and devise a plan before calling in our back up. The last Elite showed up around a half hour ago and we start going over the plan that we came up with, asking for input from all, so there are no holes left uncovered. We aren't leaving here without Jill. Of course, we are outnumbered by at least two to one, but that has never stopped us before. We aren't called the Elite for nothing!

We are finishing up and about ready to go up the hill when Cassie comes through. Her water broke and she is now in labor! My little girl sure knows her timing, just like her mother. Except, her mother is always late, so maybe she takes after her aunt Jill.

"Jax, just go already! I can't have you miss your own daughter's birth! We will be fine, and I will bring Jill home tonight." This coming from Duncan.

"What if you are too outnumbered, I can't bare it if anything bad happens that could have been prevented if I stay."

"Jax, go be with your woman, that is an order!" Taven demands.

"Okay, but if anything happens, you call me!"

"That won't happen, so just go!" Duncan genuinely means for me to go, so I hop into my truck and take off.

I make it back to the Compound in thirty-five minutes. Dr. Howard is arriving with Kai and Dane as I pull into the driveway. At least I know that I'm not too late if Doc is just getting here. I was afraid to stay in contact while driving back in case something happened which would cause me to get into an accident. I most likely wouldn't die, but it would hold me up.

I am through the front door before Doc even makes it around the car. I tear through the door to our room, but it is empty. What the fuck? Where is she? I turn and run through the Compound until I find her in the medical ward, of course! Why didn't I think of that?

"I'm here, Baby, how are you doing?"

She grabs my hand and squeezes, apparently in the middle of a contraction. She eases up, "I'm good, but remember when I mentioned baby making? Yeah, there will be no more babies! At least not for another fifty years!"

"What do you need me to do?"

"Just stay with her and keep soothing her. Rub her lower back, give her ice chips, and let her squeeze your hand during her contractions." Doc advises me.

Cassie's labor goes on for about two hours. She can't have any pain meds because she is too far into the labor. Suddenly, she starts screaming that she needs to push, and Doc gives her the go ahead, but to do it slowly. After about three pushes, my daughter's head is out and on the next push, Doc is holding her in her arms, smiling.

"You did it, Baby, she's here!" I look down to see Cassie crying. I claim her lips with mine. I can't even describe the feelings that I have right now! This gorgeous woman came into my life, flipped it upside down, gave me love and now a beautiful child!

There is a loud wail and I look over to see our daughter kicking and flailing her arms furiously. Yep, her mother's child. I kiss Cassie's forehead and walk over to check her out. Doc hands me a pair of scissors and instructs me to cut the cord. I can't stop the tears that run down my cheeks as I snip the lifeline that my daughter used all these months.

Doc turns to me smiling, "Congratulations, you are now the father of a healthy eight-pound, six ounce, and twenty-one-inch-long baby girl! Why don't you take her over to see her mother?"

I carefully take her from the doctor and carry her over to Cassie, never taking my eyes off of her. I place her in her mother's arms and sit beside them on the bed.

She has such dark hair, almost black, and bright sapphire blue eyes. Apparently, vampire babies are different from regular babies when it comes to their sight. She can see clear as day and her eye color will forever be sapphire blue. She has her mother's nose and mouth, God help us if she has a mouth like a sailor, as her mother does!

"Does she have a name yet?" Dr. Howard inquires.

I look at Cassie and she nods her head yes. "Meet Jillian Marie Whitley!" she smiles.

I choke up, because she gave our daughter my mother's name, Marie. If only she could see her granddaughter! I press my lips to Cassie's temple and whisper softly, "Thank you, Baby. I love it!"

"Such a beautiful name for a beautiful little girl!" Doc says. "She will be wanting to be fed here in a bit. Since you just fed her about three hours ago, she will probably be fine for another two, but you will need to breastfeed her, she needs your milk too now. I have typed up some instructions to get you started, some of it from my own experiences, but do not hesitate to call me if you have any questions or concerns. I will stop by in a day or so, to check up on mommy and baby."

After cleaning up, Doc takes her leave, leaving the three of us alone. Cassie brings Jillian up to her breast and my little girl latches on with a vengeance, just like her daddy. It is a sight to behold. As she suckles from her mother's nipple, her tiny hand holds one of my fingers. Right then, my child steals my heart. Yep, I am her first victim, already whipped.

I move Cassie and Jillian over to our room after I send Kole to the store to buy a bassinet. We haven't had any time to buy baby stuff since our escape, but Cassie has a few items at her house, which I have Kole retrieve as well. It must be a funny sight to see, three grown ass men trying to assemble one little bassinet, but we get her done!

Jillian cries out once Cassie settles into bed with her in her arms, so she tries feeding her, but Jillian wants no part of it.

"Here, Babe, give her over. I think she may be needing her daddy right now." I slide in next to Cassie and carefully take Jillian from her arms. Cradling her with one arm, I bite into my wrist and place it at Jillian's mouth, where again, she latches on, acting as if she is starved. It is a weird feeling, unlike with Cassie where I get aroused, this is more like a swirling euphoria and I can actually feel the bond between us lock in place, in a manner of speaking.

Once Jillian has her fill, she pulls away and closes her eyes, falling fast asleep. I wipe her mouth and lay her down in the bassinet. Looking over at Cassie, she too is fast asleep. Keeping the door cracked open, in case the baby cries out, I make my way to the kitchen. Max, Kole, Kai, and Dane are gathered around the table with cigars and a bottle of Jack waiting in the center of the table. Raven had taken off to go replace me with the others as soon as I got home.

"Time to celebrate the new daddy!" Max slaps me on the shoulder, causing me to smile.

Dane pours the drinks while Kai hands out the cigars, "Thanks guys, but maybe we should wait until the others get here."

"Nah, we will just celebrate again once they get back. Hopefully, we will be celebrating two happy occasions." This coming from Kai.

I shrug my shoulders, "Sure, why not," and shoot down the Jack in my tumbler, the others follow suit. As I light my cigar, I look to the others, "Has anybody heard any news?"

"Raven text me just as he was arriving on scene and said it looked like a blood bath, but then nothing more." Kole looks gravely at his cigar.

I check my phone for messages, but there are none. I should have heard something by now, but maybe they figured I was too busy, so I send a quick text to Taven,

"Cassie had the baby, she's beautiful.
How are things going? Do you need
me? Cassie and baby are settled, so
I can come back if needed."

I wait, but got no response, causing me to worry even more. It's not like Taven not to answer me back, unless of course, he is in the middle of battle, but it shouldn't still be going on.

I am about to go check in on Cassie and the baby, then head back to help, when I hear a commotion outside. It sounds like a bunch of cars pulling in and screeching to a halt. I head toward the front door as it opens and all of the Elite start piling in. They are all covered in blood, Jayde holding up a wounded Kaid, Cooper is clutching his arm, trying to staunch blood flow from a wound, and Xavier is limping due to an arrow protruding out of his thigh. They are a sight, but at least they all came back and should be healed within the hour. I notice that Duncan isn't among the group.

"Where the hell is Duncan?" I panic, but just as I finish the question, here comes Duncan through the front door. An arrow lodged in his shoulder and one in his side, but that isn't what gets my attention. It is the woman he was carrying in his arms; It's Jill!

I can't help the smile that brightens my face as I look at my friend. What use to be despair in his eyes, is replaced with hope and happiness. I walk over to him and offer to take the now, sleeping Jill, so he can tend to his wounds, but he won't have it. Duncan takes Jill to his room with Raven following, medical supplies in hand.

Once the wounded are all tended to, we all meet in the rec room, and they recap what all had taken place in my absence. It sounds like I missed a damn good battle, but I wouldn't have traded seeing my child being born for all the battles in the world. I excuse myself as soon as I hear Jillian start to wake. I get to the room just before she really starts to fuss, Cassie is still sleeping soundly. Not wanting to wake her just yet, I pick Jillian up and take her out of the room.

As I walk back into the rec room, all goes quiet, and every eye is on me and the baby. All of a sudden, every Elite swarms to us, smiles on their faces. Jillian opens her eyes at the noise and all movement stops as they all stare at her bright blue sapphire eyes.

"Are her eyes supposed to look like that?" This coming from Xavier.

"Apparently so. She is also able to see everything and everyone clearly from the first day." I explain, "There is still so much we need to learn about our children, it's a lot to take in, but I am enjoying every bit of it!"

They are all in awe of my baby girl as am I. Cassie is right, Jillian is definitely going to have each one wrapped around her little finger!

CASSIE

I am nervous as Jax leads me down to Jill's room with Jillian in my arms. I cried when he told me that Jill was back and safe in the Compound. We take care of our daughter's needs before heading out to see my best friend.

Jax stops in front of a door and turns to me, "Are you ready for this?"

He had informed me that Jill hasn't said a word to anyone since her rescue and that she wouldn't even see Duncan. I hope she doesn't turn us away.

Jax knocks on the door, but there is no answer from the other side, so he knocks again, and I speak up, "Jill, it's me. Can I come in?" Still no answer, "I will break down this door if you do not open up right this instant, Earnhardt!"

There is a soft click as the door slowly opens, but then stops. I push it open the rest of the way and see Jill heading to her bed. I look at Jax and ask him to wait here as I go to enter. He smiles and nods.

I close the door behind me and walk over to the bed, where Jill is, completely covered under the comforter.

"Jill, you need to come out. There is someone here to see you."

Without saying a word, she peeks out from underneath and sees the bundle in my arms. She sits up quick and holds her arms out to the baby. I hand her over to Jill and smile. Finally, she speaks, "What's her name?"

"Jillian Marie Whitley. I named her after her aunt and Jax's mother."

"You named her after me?" Jill's eyes tear up.

"Of course! You are my best friend, my sister, the one who has always been there for me no matter what! I wouldn't give her any other name."

Jill goes quiet again for a moment and then speaks, "What took so long to come after me? I thought you guys had abandoned me and I was going to be stuck with Jason for the rest of my life."

My heart broke for her, "Jill, Jax and I were both held prisoner for two months in a warehouse and Duncan never once stopped looking for you, but all leads were dead ones." I spent the next hour explaining everything that had occurred since our abduction. She seems to understand, but it does nothing for her state of mind. I hope one day I will see my old fun-loving friend back, but I have a feeling that it will take time. Time is all we have right now, and I will be by her side all the way, fighting to bring her back. With the love of Jax, our daughter and all of the Elite, I will see to it that Jill gets her life back!

EPILOGUE

JAX

Six months after the birth of our daughter and Jill's return, life is going well. Jillian is growing like a weed and as of yesterday, no longer needs to have my blood. I am going to miss that, but it only means that she is right on track and is a healthy little girl. We are told that she will grow up just like any regular child, but will come in to her vampire senses and strength at the age of eighteen. The only difference is that she still needs to consume blood and she will heal faster, like all vamps.

Jill is still struggling every day to get her life back. This has put a hold on her and Duncan's life together, but he is so patient with her. It took about a week before she would speak to anyone except for Cassie and Jillian. Duncan's love for her and Cassie being by her side will see her through this.

Cassie's parents finally came by a few days after Jillian's birth and we sat them down and told them everything, not leaving anything out. Of course, Patricia was in shock, and it took a bit for her to get use to the idea of vampires in the world and her granddaughter being half vampire, but like everyone else, Jillian won over Patricia's heart. Gary, on the other hand, would not believe in such nonsense until I had to prove to him that vampires do exist. He jumped back when I extended my fangs, but then gave a hearty laugh, slapping his knee in the process. I had spent the next few hours answering all of his questions.

With Jill still not being herself, I decide that we will hold off on the wedding until Jill is ready. Cassie is a little heartbroken over it but understands why it needs to be done and she, too, wants Jill to be ready for when we tie the knot. We are shooting for having it on our one-year anniversary of meeting, but that is only two months away. I guess we will see.

Jill and the guys kidnap Jillian and hold her captive in the rec room, so Cassie and I can have some time to ourselves. I come out of our bathroom after my shower and there stands Cassie, leaning up against the foot of the bed, wearing a sexy red and black little leather number. Her legs are crossed, and the red stilettos stand out against the black thigh high panty hose that are attached by garters. In her hands swing a set of hand cuffs and just beyond her, laying on the bed, I see the spreader and leather whip.

My dick hardens immediately, and I stalk over to her slowly, "I see my sex kitten wants to play! Fuck, you are so damn hot in that outfit! Too bad it will be off within the next few minutes."

"Oh, you think you are using these on me?" She stands straight up and walks around the bed before I get to her, "Sorry, Baby. It's my turn to have a little fun with you, so get your fucking ass on the bed now!" She picks the whip up and lashes it down on the bed.

"I have just died and gone to heaven." I say as I crawl to the middle of the bed and lay down like a good boy.

She is fast as she restrains my wrists and attaches the spreader. She slides a blindfold around my eyes, and I swear I got even harder. Never once has anybody ever done this to me. I always like to be the one in control.

I feel her breath by my ear as she speaks, "Don't you dare fucking come." she then runs her tongue down my ear and gives a little suck to my lobe, "Oh, and if you make a sound, you may regret it." She graces me with her seductive laugh; this is going to be fun!

She moves her tongue down my body, nipping me every now and then with her fangs. I feel her hand wrap around my cock mere seconds before her mouth engulfs it in its wet warmth. Her fangs are scraping me as she swirls her tongue around my length. Taking me deep then sliding me out, just to suck on my tip. She continues to do this, and I feel my balls start to pull up.

She takes hold of my balls and massages them in one hand, letting a finger slip to rim my ass hole. I jerk, but then realize that it feels so fucking good. The assault on my cock, balls and ass continues until I don't think I can hold it anymore. My dick begins to swell and then all play stops. Talk about blue fucking balls!

I feel the whip come down on my abs and the desire comes back. A few more whips and then the game changes. All of a sudden, I am being muzzled by her pussy, "If you know what's good for you, you better start eating my pussy! I want to come all over your face!" She doesn't have to tell me again. I go to town, licking, sucking, and shoving my tongue into her hole. I go for her clit and suck hard, ripping the orgasm out of her. As I soak up her juices with my tongue, she takes possession of my cock, deep throating it until I am about to come, and then she stops. Fuck me! I need to explode soon!

She climbs off my face and slams her pussy down on my shaft in one hard stoke. The blindfold comes off and there she is, in all her glory riding my cock, her tits bouncing up and down. She throws her head back and moans as she plays with her clit. So, fucking gorgeous! She glances at me with hooded eyes, "Are you ready to fill me up Big Boy?" I nod my head yes.

"Speak up, tell me what you want."

"I want you to ride my dick so hard that you come all over. Once my dick is nice and slick, I want you to take it out of your pussy and stick it in your ass so I can fill it up with my explosion."

Cassie leans down and gives me her neck for me to bite. I oblige, bringing her to orgasm all over my cock. She then releases my wrists and impales her ass with my rock-hard member. I sit up and she yanks my head to the side piercing my neck with her fangs. It's all too much and I explode like a volcano into her ass, my cum shooting into her over and over. Another orgasm rips through her and we finish riding them out together.

Laying in each other's arm, spent. I brush aside a strand of her hair. I will never, for as long as I live, figure out what I did to deserve this woman. My life was non-existent before her and now it's so full of love and compassion, craziness, and laughter and above anything else, it is filled with a future. I will love this woman for eternity, my hell on wheels, my Hellion.

www.ingramcontent.com/pod-product-compliance
Lightning Source LLC
LaVergne TN
LVHW041659070526
838199LV00045B/1126